Beyond the Veil

The Crescent Witches return
for another fight against evil

Margaret McMahon

Crescent Witches 2 / Margaret McMahon – 1st edition

All rights reserved. No part of this publication may be reproduced, distributed or transmitted in any form or by any means, including photocopying, recording, or other electronic or mechanical methods, without the prior written permission of the author. Permission requests can be sent either directly to the author or to the publisher at the address below.

Copyright © 2023 Margaret McMahon
ISBN 978-1-910044-56-8

Shanway Press
15 Crumlin Road
Belfast
www.shanway.com

Illustrations: Janet Blades
Cover artwork: Margaret McMahon

This book is dedicated to my mother and father, Francis Joseph McMahon and Jean McMahon.

Chapter One

The parlour room is quiet. The only noise that can be heard is that of the giant clock tower chiming every hour, its loud echo being heard throughout the cold hollow halls of the tower, leaving in its wake an empty feeling of sadness filling every room. Every ticking moment, every passing hour, is just another dreaded reminder of the sorrow and sadness that now fills this once happy home.

It is a miserable day, the weather matching the atmosphere inside the tower itself. Outside seagulls can be heard circling overhead. It is almost 7 o'clock in the morning and there is an unusually cold chill in the air. Isadora, walking along Albert Bridge, can see her breath forming tiny puffs of smoke and dispersing into the morning air. A shiver runs down her spine and she can feel her toes beginning to numb inside her boots. She tugs the fur collar of her coat burying her face inside the soft fabric, wrapping the coat tightly around her, and hoping to fight off the cold winds. It is not a long walk from Albert Bridge to the Clock Tower, but in this weather, it feels more like a mountain hike.

Isadora takes a swift right and turns onto Queens Square. She is almost at the gates of the clock tower. The sky has turned a murky grey and she senses rain clouds rolling in. She is anxious to get to the clock tower and it isn't just the weather that has her feeling uneasy. She scans the area quickly, assessing any possible threats that could be lurking in the shadows. Then she quickens her pace along the old, cobbled streets.

Isadora arrives at the Belfast Albert Clock and gives three loud knocks on the entrance door.

"Who's there!" a voice shouts from the other side.

"Oh for goodness sake, darling! It's me! Open the door, Despina!" Isadora demands. "Let me in before I freeze to death."

At this point Isadora is convinced her toes have fallen off due to frostbite. Moments later the door slowly creaks open, and a familiar face cautiously pops her head around the side of the door.

"Oh Izzy! It is you. Sorry we can't be too careful." She opens the door and they both walk into the hallway.

"Yes, well considering recent events, I don't see how things could get much worse darling." Isadora enters the kitchen. She unbuttons her coat then quickly takes off her hat and gloves. She moves towards the fireplace rubbing her hands together and holding them outwards.

"Lasair," she whispers into the dying emblems. Magickal tiny flames spark and within seconds the fire is burning nicely, filling the room with warmth. Turning to Despina she whispers, "Is she still upstairs?"

Despina feeling deflated nods her head. "This can't go on like this. We need to get her out of that bedroom."

Chapter One

Despina looked at her with concern. "She still hasn't spoken a word. The poor girl is still in shock which, to be fair, is understandable."

Isadora nods in agreement. "I'm so worried about her. I can't get her to eat or drink. Can you possibly try Izzy? She listens to you."

Isadora smiles. "Yes of course," she answers. "I'll go up in a minute to check on her but first I'll need a cup of strong coffee."

Despina sets two cups and two saucers down on the table. She yawns. "I think I'll join you Izzy, the caffeine will do me good."

They both take their seats by the fire. The kitchen is so quiet, which is sad, because this little room in the clock tower is usually full of life and happiness. Both ladies sit in silence whilst they drink their coffee. A few minutes pass and Isadora looks at Despina.

Frustrated she shouts, "I wish she would just talk to us! Say something! Anything! It's been three days now, and not even my Cornelius can get her out of Amelia's bedroom. It's heartbreaking". Isadora shakes her head. "I'll pour her a cup of sweet tea and try again to get her to eat a little toast."

Despina agrees with a nod. "I'll go make some now."

Just as Despina stands up there is a knock on the front door.

"I'll get it, you sort the tea," Isadora says.

Minutes later Toby walks into the parlour room alongside Isadora, each looking as deflated as the other.

"It's raining cats and dogs out there," Toby exclaims taking off his paddy hat. He twists it tightly, squeezing out the lingering droplets of rain and allows them to fall to the floor, "

"Oops!" Toby says, looking down at the newly formed puddle he's just created at his feet. "I'll just dry that up."

Toby scans the room for a mop. Isadora rolls her eyes. "Oh, for heaven's sake darling! It's only a bit of water. Don't worry, I'll get it."

Toby smiles gratefully at Isadora, "Thank you Izzy."

Isadora looks at the puddle and says, "Evaporate." Within seconds the water droplets slowly rise from the floor as well as from Toby's clothes, forming magickal swirls of water, dancing around Toby until suddenly they're gone. Just a tiny puff of steam remains, slowly dispersing into the air, leaving the floor completely dry. And Toby too.

Toby grins and pats himself down. "Much better," he says.

"Would you like a cup of tea Toby? We were just about to make some for Georgette," Despina says.

A sadness creeps into Toby's eyes, a sadness Despina hasn't seen there in a long time. She feels an overwhelming urge to comfort him. Toby is a strong man, a protector. He loves the Crescent Family like his own Kin. She knew how hard the last few days have been for him.

Toby turns to both women and, in a concerned voice he asks, "Is she still not eating or talking to anyone?"

"No Toby, and she can't go on like this. She barely responds when we try to speak to her. I don't think the poor girl can even remember being taken home

Chapter One

from the field that day. She's devastated. I hate to see her in such pain. She hasn't left that bedroom since it happened."

Toby edges towards the door. "I'm going up now to check on her. Do you think I should try to get her out for a walk? The air might do her good."

Isadora puts her hand on his arm giving it a reassuring pat. "That would be lovely, Toby. But I doubt she will go darling. How about you take the tray up for me? Maybe we can persuade her to eat a little something. And please try and get the girl to talk to you. Heaven knows, we've all tried. Oh, and Toby," Isadora shouts to him just before he exits the room, "there's a plate of chicken for the shadows. Take that up as well please. That poor cat Bijou is distraught, he's lost without Mia. It's really taking its toll on him, the poor boy."

Toby takes the tray from Despina. He tries and fails to give them a reassuring smile. Both women can clearly see how upset he has been lately. His face is pale with red puffy eyes. He leaves the room in silence as he walks to the large spiral staircase, looking up he takes a long, apprehensive breath. He exhales and ascends, each step heavy on his heart.

Chapter Two

Toby reaches the top of the staircase. He gently knocks on the bedroom door. "Can I come in, young miss? It's only me, big Toby." Just as Toby expected there was no reply.

Looking down at the floor, his big grubby boots were frozen to the spot. He takes a big deep breath then tries again, knocking once more. "Please Georgie, let me come in? Talk to me. Let me try to help."

Toby puts his ear gently towards the bedroom door. He can hear Georgette sobbing. His voice filled with concern he announces, "I'm coming in young Miss." Opening the door slowly he pops his head around the corner. He takes a few apprehensive steps towards Georgette, sets the tray on the bedside cabinet. Then he takes a seat on the edge of the bed.

Very gently Toby takes her hand. Holding it, he gives it a little squeeze.

"Please Georgette. Talk to me."

But she doesn't answer. Toby frowns. "Then you must try to eat. Take this wee cup of tea for me and eat a small piece of toast. Or perhaps a walk if you like? We can take a short stroll around the docks to clear your head my dear."

Chapter Two

Georgette looks at Toby she tries to speak but no words come out. Her voice was low and hoarse. She has a terribly sore throat, a nasty aftereffect from her painful screams in the field that day, the day Mia was taken. It almost doesn't feel real. The memory comes flooding back to her. Her sister laying defenceless, unconscious on the ground. Those vile creatures taking Mia. The horrible sound of screams echoing throughout the Cavehill only to realise it was her own screaming that filled the air. Mia was gone. The Johnagock had taken her, and Georgette was filled with guilt in failing to protect another sister. She had failed again.

"Georgie?" Toby's caring voice brought her back to the present. Georgette tries to speak again. In a croaky voice she replies "I can't Toby. Please just leave me be. I want to be left alone. You don't understand. No one understands."

She takes a deep breath then presses her face deep into her pillow. Toby gently wipes the tears from her cheeks and moves her tear-soaked hair away from her face.

"Then talk to me Georgie. Help me understand."

But she gave no reply. The grief had taken over once more and all she could do was cry.

Toby stands up. He places a gentle kiss on her forehead. "When you are ready to talk, Georgie, I want you to know we are all here for you. We all love and care for you Georgette, so very much. You are stronger than this".

Toby strokes Bijou then Tailsa.

"I'll leave this wee plate of chicken for the cats on the floor young miss."

He closes the door quietly as he leaves.

Chapter Three

When Toby returns downstairs, he finds Isadora, Cornelius, and Despina in the kitchen. They are deep in conversation. When they see Toby approach, they all look to him with hopeful looks in their eyes. Toby shakes his head as he approaches.

"She's still not talking. All she said was she wants to be left alone. I left the tray on the bedside table, but I doubt she will even look at it".

Toby takes a seat at the table.

Cornelius gives him a pat on the back. "At least you tried big man. It's good to see you. I know you being here is helping Georgie too."

Despina hands Toby a large mug of tea. Toby looks at Cornelius properly for the first time since entering the room. He looks awful. With concern he asks, "have you still not slept my lad?"

Cornelius lifts his head. He looks at Toby.

"Don't worry about me big man, I'm Fine."

Toby looks at Cornelius with a mock expression.

"Aye lad you look positively peachy, especially with those bags under your eyes. Now all joking aside we already have one person we care about not speaking to us. Let's not make it two. Talk to us."

Cornelius knows there is no point in putting on a brave face. The people in this room are like family to him. He lets out a breath he hadn't even realised he was holding and blurts out, "I can't rest my mind at all. I keep going over the whole bloody thing in my head." He shouts, "I still can't believe Mia is stuck in that Hell hole. And with poor young Henry too. I hate seeing Georgette in so much pain. I would move Heaven and Earth for that woman, and I feel useless."

Toby gives a sympathetic smile. "I know how you feel Cornelius, those two girls are my family and I've let them down. I was supposed to protect them."

A tear begins to form in Toby's eye. He quickly wipes it away and clears his throat.

"Yes, well regardless how were feeling we need a plan of action, what can we do to move forward? How can we help Georgette?"

Isadora who has been particularly quiet, suddenly jumps from her seat startling Despina. Isadora exclaims, "I think we're going about this all wrong."

They all look at her with confused expressions.

"What do you Mean Izzy?" Toby asks.

"Oh, my darlings. We are all understandably devastated with recent events, but I have just had an epiphany," she beams.

"You might not necessarily like this. And you don't all have to agree with it, but just hear me out. I think this constantly tiptoeing around her isn't helping. I mean for goodness sake people, its Georgette Crescent! We all know she's a strong Witch. Her Magick is unparalleled. The Crescent family line is legendary.

Chapter Three

We just need to remind her of that. You've all heard of the old saying tough love. Well my friends I think it's time we take that advice ourselves. She needs to be motivated in some way, whether that be vengeful or angry. Anything is better than her current state. At least that will give her something to focus on and give us time to work on a plan!"

Toby, being protective in nature, especially when it comes to the Crescent sisters, and listening to Isadora can no longer contain his emotion. He raises his voice as he slams his mug down on the table.

"A plan!" he shouts. "A plan for what Izzy? Isadora explains. "A plan to open the Veil." The Veil is gone. Amelia and Henry are never coming back. Don't you think Georgette has been through enough? And now you want to give the girl false hope. I refuse to take any part in this. It's too cruel."

Despina interrupts trying to calm the situation. "Please Toby my dear friend. Try to control your temper. It's not like you to be this angry. We don't want Georgie to hear us."

She then asks Isadora in an exhausted voice, "Izzy, if you have any ideas, you can possibly think of to get us into that hell dimension, speak now. Tell us please because I have to agree with Toby. I can't go forward with this, giving false hope when there isn't any. I fear it will be too much for poor Georgette to bear."

Despina looks desperately for some spark of hope in Isadora's eyes.

She answers, "maybe it's a long shot. But as you already know Gregor is still in hiding, along with that wretched old crone Lady Celine. The authorities have rounded up most of the other participants, but they were unable to catch Gregor or Lady Celine. I have a suggestion you won't like but I'm putting it on the table anyway. What if we were to try and contact Gregor and ask for his help?"

A shocked expression crosses Toby's face. He interjects with a loud angry voice, "What? Why in the name of the stars would you say or want to do that? If I had that man in front of me now, I'd feed him to the dogs. In fact, no, I'd use him as fish bait."

Cornelius shouts approvingly, "Hear, Hear!"

Despina whispers loudly "The monster deserves no less, but can we all remain calm and quiet. I don't want to upset Georgette any further. She may very well hear you two bellowing. Let Isadora finish."

Isadora continues to speak "As I was saying, we need to be smart. Gregor is the only one that knows how to open that Veil single handily. He's been doing it for ten years now. Only he knows the Magick which was used and the very powerful potions that were brewed."

She ponders the thought. "No doubt black magick was afoot in all of this and even with his dark Magick it still took a very long time for him to make those potions, possibly years. We need to accept the fact that we need him. Otherwise we might never cross that veil to rescue Mia and Henry. Let's be honest about this situation. With all our powers combined, none of us would even come close to Gregor's magickal abilities. We all know it would take too long to brew that kind

Chapter Three

of Magick ourselves, and we don't even have the faintest idea where we would start. This is dark Magic. No respectable Witch or Wizard would want any association with it. Time is of the essence. Our only option is to swallow our pride and ask Gregor to help."

Despina nods as Isadora continues "If we get to him before anyone else, we could offer him some sort of a deal. We could perhaps suggest he blames all of his past indiscretions on Lady Celine. Gregor won't hesitate if he thought we would tell lies for him. Our inner circle are all well respected people. The Council will back us if we get our story right."

Toby shakes his head disapprovingly. "This is madness," he shouts.

Isadora shouts even louder. "To catch a fly, you need the honey. If we get Gregor to agree, then that will get some of us across the Veil. There's a chance of rescuing them, can't you see that, Toby?"

Suddenly Georgette appeared in the doorway. She looked very pale and tired. Her hair was tied up in a scraggly bun. She was still wearing the same dress from three days ago.

"I'm in" she croaks. "Let's do it."

There is a determination in her eyes. She addresses the room. "I don't care who joins me but I'm definitely crossing that Veil to get my sister back. Henry too. This is the first glimmer of hope I've had, and I am not letting it go! I don't care if I have to beg that snake Gregor to help me. We can deal with him after I get Mia back home."

Toby walks over to her. He hugs her tight and whispers, "then I'm coming with you. Where you go, I go too, young miss."

Cornelius was sitting very quietly at the far end of the table. He looks at Georgette. He was glad to see that familiar spark back in her eyes. He stands up and lifts a small cup to pour in some warm milk and then he adds a trickle of honey. "Here," he says, handing Georgette the cup. "Take this. It will help that sore throat until mother whips you up a tonic." He places the small China cup into her hands tenderly touching her fingers. Then he waits until she drinks the lot.

Georgette instinctively puts her hand onto her throat trying to ease her discomfort. Cornelius asks her, "did that help a little Georgie? Any better now?"

She smiles affectionately saying, "yes, actually it did thank you."

Cornelius could already see some colour coming back into her face. He touches her cheek, then tucks her hair behind her ear. He grins at her, happy to see her feeling a little better.

Despina and Isadora both look at Cornelius relieved. They were glad to see Georgette finally listening to someone. Isadora touches Georgette's arm, pulling her gaze away from Cornelius. "I'll get you that tonic made shortly darling. Shouldn't take long and I can guarantee it will clear that nasty sore throat right up."

Georgette gives her a grateful smile in return as she sets the little cup into the sink. She lifts the linen dish towel, grips it with both hands squeezing it tight. She turns around to face everyone. Addressing the room

Chapter Three

she says, "I'll get Gregor to agree one way or another trust me. This plan will work. And if at any point no one on the Council agrees, then they can keep their opinions to themselves. I'm quite determined to go ahead with this plan, and I promise you, nothing or no one will change my mind, or get in my way."

Isadora stands up. She looks at Georgette with pride. "I agree darling. You have my full support."

Despina adds, "count me in as well Georgette".

Cornelius walks over to Georgette not taking his eyes of her for a second. He takes her hand.

"I promise you I will do anything you ask of me. But first I need to tell you to control that temper of yours. You can't let your emotions get the better of you. Gregor will only see it as a weakness. And he will use it against you to wind you up like a play toy for his own amusement. We have only one shot at this, so get your emotions in check. We need to be smart Georgie."

Reassuringly squeezing Cornelius' hands Georgette draws a breath looking at everyone in the kitchen. She knew Cornelius was right. "Let's get my sister back," she says.

Isadora claps her hands together. "Perfect," she shouts. "We have a plan. Now we get everyone together from our inner circle and present it to the Council." Looking Georgette up and down she scurries her out the door saying, "You, young lady need a bath, Fix that hair, and change that dress. But, eat this sandwich first for goodness sake before you pass out."

Despina suggests, "Georgie, my dear, just before you go. I know you planned on taking your powers back with Amelia on the last full moon. But don't you perhaps think it might be best to do it sooner? We know of course you would have preferred to do this with your sister since it was what your father wanted. But things have now changed, I'm afraid. The next full moon is on Sunday. Will you consider this?"

Georgette nods. "I will restore my full powers on the next full moon. We will send the Cinder notes out immediately, informing everyone the meeting will be held in the Clock Tower tonight." She closes the door as she leaves.

Despina takes Isadora's hand in hers. "We have four days to find Gregor before the full Moon. Let's make this happen, agreed?" Despina then takes a seat at the kitchen table. Next to her was a large pile of parchment, stacked neatly, with a jar of ink and quills at the ready to send out cinder notes to the Council members.

Isadora speaks, "Well! Chop, chop everyone. You all heard the girl. Let's get a move on shall we. There is much to do before the council members arrive."

Chapter Four

In the Parlour room Isadora and Despina sit waiting for their fellow Witches and Wizards to arrive at the Clock Tower. Isadora is impatiently tapping her long red fingernails on the arm of the fireside chair she was sitting in. They had kept themselves busy all afternoon and could do nothing now other than wait for the others to arrive.

"Oh! I can't take this anymore. If I drink one more cup of tea I'll turn into a tea bag! There must be something we can do other than sit about. I want to do something useful."

Despina giggles, "Oh Izzy! Patience never was your strong suit. But you are right, all this waiting about is driving me insane too."

Isadora tilts her head and grins, clasping her hands. "I have an idea. Perhaps we should brew some potions together. It's been a while darling."

Despina was thrilled with this idea. "Oh yes, that's a fantastic idea Izzy." Excitedly they rush to the potion room, grabbing two white aprons from behind the door. Despina hands one too Isadora, then takes a small wooden crate from the side of the hearth. Tiny clinks and clangs sound as she lifts it onto the table. It was full of empty little glass bottles covered in dust.

Despina takes some potion bottles out of the box, blowing off the thick dust, and places them on the desk in preparation to be filled. Isadora ties her apron around her waist.

"It's been such a long time since I brewed a bubbling cauldron over an open fire," she grins. "I'm definitely going to enjoy this." She winks at her friend.

Despina smiles, saying, "You were always a gifted witch when it came to potions. Let's get this fire blazing and get to work."

Isadora pulls out a large cauldron. It was still hanging on its rusty hook by the hearth. She raises her hands and commands, "Solos!"

Green and orange flames rise in the grate, Isadora and Despina start to call out multiple magickal ingredients.

"Eucalyptus!" Isadora shouts.

"Geraniums!" Despina chants.

"Cedar wood," and "Jasmine."

Ingredients float overhead swirling around the kitchen and flying into the large cauldron. With every new ingredient a new spark of colour and sudden puff of glittering smoke shoot out from the fireplace, letting off the occasional crackle and pop sound, and filling the room with such amazing tranquil smells.

"Oh, I just love that scent. Don't you, Izzy?" Despina says giddily.

Isadora cackles, "Enjoy it while it lasts darling," knowing very well these beautiful scents would only last a little while. Isadora has known some potions to smell worse than frogs' breath! Giggling at the thought,

Chapter Four

a memory popped into her mind. She remembered working in the spell room as a young Witch with Sean and Mary Crescent. Still at school, they had exams coming up and tensions were high! Studying, they got so many things wrong that day. Poor Sean was the guinea pig. He had to drink their finished product. The poor boy ended up turning and nasty shade of green and, with a few additional boils popping up here and there, the two young Witches went into a fit of hysterics. Their laughter filled the Clock Tower that day. It took nearly three whole days for Sean's skin to return to its natural colour.

Isadora had so many wonderful memories of Mary and Sean she couldn't help letting another giggle escape her. Despina looked at her.

"Should I even ask?"

Isadora replied, "No darling, just reminiscing some lovely memories. That's all".

The large black pot starts to fill up fast. Loud bubbling pops and snaps begin to fill the room with sounds of delight. They cast their spell with chanting words on each turn of the large wooden paddle.

"Double Bubble Black and Trouble,
Stubble Black and Cry
Pop and Boil Mix and Toil Cook
Until Its Sly"

Toby enters the spell room waving his hand in front of his nose. "That smell is worse than a fisherman's foot!

What in the name of the stars are you Witches brewing in here!"

The fantastic smells from the start of the brew had now all but disappeared, leaving behind only a potent stench. This was fantastic news to Isadora as it meant the potions were now ready.

Isadora and Despina both grin wickedly at Toby's reaction.

"Hold your nose, Toby" Despina says, "we are going to be well prepared for anything thrown at us this time. We are leaving nothing to chance and there will be plenty of potions for everyone my good man. We won't be caught off guard again."

"Most definitely not," Isadora chirps in. "We have made some really strong potions. Powerful protection potions, sleeping and healing potions, too many to mention".

Despina interrupts. "Oh, and let's not be forgetting invisibility potions! Gregor's speciality. The rotten snake," she scowls.

Toby chuckles. "God help anyone getting in your way ladies, that's all I can say. Anyway, I'm away to sort some things out at the docks. I have an idea. I'll not explain until I know it's doable. What time will everyone arrive here for the meeting?"

Despina answers, "5 o'clock. It's the best they can all manage at such short notice. Georgette won't be happy, but it's understandable with it being last minute."

Toby replies, scrunching his nose. "I will be back by four thirty. Try to get this smell away by then. It's diabolical. Oh! I'm saving you two lovely ladies the

Chapter Four

bother of cooking this evening. I'm doing my famous champ with fish. And trust me there will be plenty for everyone! Could you make a wee loaf or two of fresh bread? That is if you have the time ladies." He grins from ear to ear rubbing his big belly.

Isadora bursts out laughing. "Well, we can hardly say no now can we! Just get you on about your business. We will make the time to bake you some fresh bread, but only because you asked so nicely."

Toby said his goodbyes and walked out of the potion room. Cornelius appeared from behind the main entrance door covering his nose with his hands.

"What is that smell? Toby it's worse than your big Tucker with a belly full of gruel."

Toby bellows. "That would be your mother with Despina. They're cooking up a pot of potions."

Cornelius scratches his head. "Well then, as my old granny always said, the stronger the whiff, the stronger the potion, the better the spell will be!"

Isadora's voice can be heard shouting down the hallway. "Is that my son I hear! Come in darling and help us brew a pot."

Cornelius rolls his eyes then shakes his head.

"Coming Mother dearest!"

Toby points at the potion room door, laughing quietly as he leaves.

Chapter Five

"Mother, that smell is diabolical. It's enough to knock out a horse," Cornelius complains.

Isadora places a kiss on his cheek. "Stop your moaning dear," she smiles rubbing both hands together as she places dozens and dozens of little potion bottles on the desk. They even had some placed on top of the fireplace mantel.

"Are you sure you've made enough mother?" Cornelius says in a sarcastic tone. "I can still see some space along the hearth," he jokes as he slumps into the fireside chair. He looks at his mother and Despina with a cheeky grin on his face.

"Oh hush," Isadora replies but can't help grinning in return. Her son's smile is infectious, and he knew it. Such powerful Witches Cornelius thought, letting himself feel an overwhelming sense of pride in the two women in front of him. He was happy to see their faces full of hope. They finally had a plan, and a good one at that. Yet he is so tired. Sinking deeper into his chair, he was finding it hard to keep his eyes open. He hadn't slept much since Amelia was taken and felt completely useless not knowing how to fix this nightmare, or how to comfort Georgie. But today was the first time he felt any relief. He watched as the dancing flames crackle around the cauldron with its red and orange glow, the snapping sounds of burning wood made a calming warm atmosphere. Cornelius, sinking further down into the depths of sleep, buried his head against the side of the chair. He stopped fighting, letting his exhaustion take over. Finally, he slept.

Isadora watching from the corner of her eye breathes a sigh of relief. "Finally," she says. Quietly lifting a blanket, she gently drapes it over his body taking a moment to look at her son with loving affection, She whispers to Despina, "I'll finish putting these lids on, then come and help you in the kitchen. Let's leave him here for an hour to sleep. Heaven knows the boy needs it."

The hour passes quickly. When Cornelius awakes, his mother is sitting at the roll top desk still pressing corks onto the tops of the potion bottles. He yawns, stretching his arms above his head. "How long was I out for?" he asked.

"Just an hour darling. You needed that little nap. It was long overdue."

"Where is Georgie mother?"

"She's in the kitchen, and I must say she's in better form, thank the stars."

Cornelius sits forward in his chair. "That's great. I hate to sound like doom and gloom but this plan we're going with isn't one hundred percent perfect, is it? I won't deny it sounds good in theory, but there's a big if in all of this and Georgie is pinning her hopes on it. We don't even know if we will manage to get hold of Gregor, let alone talking him into doing it."

Chapter Five

Isadora usually tries to see the positive in most things. She would consider herself a glass half full kind of person. "Shush! Cornelius," she whispers. "The last thing I need is Georgie hearing that. We've just got her out of that bedroom. She needs hope, and this is all we can offer her now, so don't let her hear you. There's still a chance this will work if we can get that snake Gregor to cooperate."

Cornelius frowns. "We have no idea where he is. How do we even begin to look for him? He's powerful enough to cloak himself with the best invisibility potions. I wonder if Lady Cracklin is helping him? Has anyone even searched her castle or its grounds? The Cracklin estate is closer to the Cave Hill entrance than any of the others."

This peaked Isadora's interest. "The Belfast Castle has many paths, all of which lead to the Cave Hill. They must have made their way back to the Cracklin estate, they are probably still hiding there under powerful spells no doubt."

Despina overheard the conversation as she entered the spell room. She hands Cornelius a large mug of coffee. "They searched the castle and the grounds Cornelius. I was there. I can tell you there was no stone left unturned. But yes, you do make a good point. They are powerful enough to hide and evade our search party."

Cornelius sips his coffee. "Then let's go back tonight. We can take a handful of these potions, cloak ourselves and have a proper look."

He looks at both women encouragingly. Isadora shakes her head in disapproval.

"I say we wait until after the meeting. There are powerful allies coming here later, stronger even than Gregor. You can't go looking for him yourself my darling. The man is much stronger than you. We all need to be smart about this."

Georgette entered the room holding her nose. "Is that Valerian root and Goosegab I smell?"

Despina answers, "Yes, it is indeed my dear."

Opening a window Georgette asks, "why didn't you wait for me? I could have helped. Then again, knowing you two, I'm sure the brew is powerful enough. It certainly smells strong enough." Georgette mocks, "but I'll be needing something a little stronger than sleeping potions and healing tonics if I'm to face the Johnagock."

The rest of the party were pattering about the room, getting ready for the other guests to arrive. Georgette walks to the far end of the room. There is a beautifully handcrafted potions cabinet, carved and engraved with swirls and ancient Celtic symbols along each side of the wood. Georgette places both hands on the cabinet doors. She hesitates, but only for a moment. "I need to do this" she tells herself." Taking a deep breath she quietly whispers,

"Crescent lock door and key open up just for me"

No sooner had she spoke the magickal words a face begins to form in the wooden frame, opening its mouth wide as if to mimic a yawn. The mouth then morphs into the shape of a keyhole. The cabinet is enchanted by woodland guardians, old fay magic, "long forgotten but very useful," Georgette thought to herself. The cabinet had been in the family for

Chapter Five

generations. Lifting her keychain, she finds the key she needs. It is a heavy, large key with dark swirling vines decorating its edges. Georgette knows very well if the wrong key is used, the enchanted guardian will spit various leaves and foliage through its large mouth and seal its doors shut. She doesn't have time to prepare a reopening spell. Carefully she pops the black key into the lock turning it three times. Hearing a loud click the door opens. Black salt falls from the old wooden shelf inside, spraying the floor below her feet.

This catches Isadora's attention. She looks at Despina and they share a look of concern. Black salt is used for protection. Someone must have placed it there for good reason, most likely Mary or Sean. Georgette slowly lifts out a small potion bottle. It was marked in green writing and labelled 'Aristotle', meaning 'life'. The second bottle was marked with black ink, the writing labelled 'Dispentorate', meaning 'death'.

Realising the severity of the situation, Isadora cautiously makes her away across the room with Despina walking quickly behind.

"Where did you get this?" Isadora asks unable to hide the shock from her face. "And please don't tell me you brewed that yourself. It is forbidden darling, you know this."

Unable to take her eyes off the two potions in both her hands, and in a trance like state Georgette whispers, "I didn't brew it. I know its forbidden."

Despina steps closer, urging Georgette to put the potions down. Georgette tightens her grip on the bottles. Her knuckles turning white.

"I need them. Don't you understand," she snaps. Looking at both women with a wildness in her eyes. "I'm taking them with me into the prison world. I will use this and stop anyone who gets in my way."

Isadora replies in a soothing voice, "it's alright Georgette, we understand. I just need you to hand me the potions."

Isadora grows increasingly concerned with every second that passes by that Georgette holds the potions. "This is dark magic," she tells herself. "Even the purest Witches soul can become corrupt meddling with death potions. She isn't thinking clearly."

Isadora takes a step closer making Georgette back further into the corner. "It was in my father's collection. I keep it hidden, cloaked under lock and key."

Despina looks concerned. "You know this potion kills, Georgie. It takes life. The other saves life. I've never known you to contemplate taking a life, even that of a Johnagock. If a witch takes a life, you know the outcome." A sad expression crosses her face.

"I know," Georgette shouts at Despina. "I know the outcome and I simply don't care. Do any of you really think for one second, I wouldn't trade my soul if it meant I got my sister back? I'll do everything in my power to make that happen. Johnagock are soulless creatures. Taking the life of a Johnagock isn't the same as taking the life of someone with a soul."

Isadora interrupts astonished. "It is the same. A life is a life. In the old witches Grimoire, you would lose the light from your own soul to go dark. And for what?

Chapter Five

The life of a wretched Johnagock? What is wrong with you girl?" she scolds.

Georgette retracts back as if burnt by Isadora's words, filling her with rage. "Georgette. you're not taking that potion with you. Give it to me now," Isadora demands. Holding out her hand she places a white handkerchief in her palm hoping to receive the bottle. "I'll get rid of it before the others arrive".

Despina pleadingly looks at both women. "Please. This is madness. Just hand Isadora the bottle, Georgie".

Suddenly Georgette lets out a loud piercing scream. Her eyes filling with streaks of black. Her skin snow white.

A coldness filled the room. She wails, "I told you no."

In an instant Tailsa appears in the doorway. She is fully formed, standing defensively by Georgette's side, her sharp claws digging into the floor, her eyes slowly losing their usual beautiful, blue colour, replaced with nothing but hollow, black emptiness. Snarling, baring her teeth aggressively.

Isadora and Despina cautiously take a few steps backwards in disbelief. Isadora shrieks, "Quickly, Cornelius do something."

Cornelius who had leapt from his seat, grabs one of the many recently crafted invisibility potions from the table and downs the liquid in one gulp. In an instant he's vanished. Quickly sneaking to the back of the room undetected, he snatches the death potion from Georgette's hand. Scrunching it shut in a thick piece of parchment he shoves it in his pocket. He then slowly and carefully pats Tailsa on the head saying softly, "it's okay my girl, stay calm, you're okay. She's safe now."

Isadora and Despina still shocked, look at Georgette confused. The potion was no longer in her hand, but the rage was still evident on her face. The darkness had already touched her.

Georgette genuinely felt fear shoot through her body. "I can't control this," she exclaims, a dark red mist now starting to form around her body, her eyes completely engulfed in a black vortex.

Cornelius runs to Georgette grabs her from behind, wrapping his strong arms around her small frame with both hands restraining her. He chants a powerful spell:

Undo the darkness.
Return to the light.
Reverse the potion but not the fight!
Its with love and magick ever so bright
For in the end
everything will be right.

Georgette struggles against Cornelius' grasp, trying to break free. He grips her tighter. She screams in agony as the darkness disperses from her body. Cornelius repeats the spell.

Isadora and Despina realising what he's doing they chant in unison, until they see the blue shards of colour slowly return to Georgette's eyes. The spell has worked. Exhausted Georgette collapses to the floor with Cornelius still cradling her. She bursts into tears.

Chapter Six

Cornelius wraps a shawl around Georgette's shoulders as they sit by the fireplace.

"What was that?" Georgette thinks aloud.

"Black magick darling," Isadora explains. "The death potion is dark to its core and even its essence, although contained in that bottle, still has the ability to corrupt even the purest soul".

Despina sits. "Probably why your father had it hidden in the cabinet. You know it's forbidden to us younger witches and wizards. We don't have the capability to control its influence. Only an elder can use this potion and only in defence. You already know this, Georgie. What were you thinking? You teach this to your first-year students in school. This kind of magick is dangerous."

Georgette hangs her head in shame. "I know. I'm sorry everyone. I wasn't thinking."

Cornelius holds her hand and gives her a reassuring squeeze. He stands up. "I'd like to get this potion back into the cabinet now if you don't mind, ladies. Georgie can I have your keys please? That is, if you feel safe with me putting it back?"

Georgette unfastens the keys from her belt. "Please put it back. I'm fine now, I promise. The sooner its locked away again, the better."

Cornelius takes the keychain from Georgette and walks to the cabinet. "Be sure to do a cleansing spell after you've put that safely away," Isadora tells him. Cornelius quickly does as he's asked.

Tailsa and Bijou both headbutt and rub their faces against Georgette. She strokes their coats reassuringly. "I'm fine my pets, no need to worry. I'll never do anything that silly again. I've never felt such rage." A shiver runs down her spine with the memory. She makes a mental note to destroy that potion the first chance she gets.

Cornelius looks at Georgette and chuckles. She looks at him bewildered. "What could you possibly have to laugh about after that whole ordeal?" she asks.

"Oh, nothing really, just that I've finally got something to hold over you,"

Georgette suspiciously raises one eyebrow. "And what would that be exactly?" she queries.

"I'm you're knight and shining armour," he winks.

"Oh for heaven's sake," she groans. "We will never hear the end of this, will we?"

Cornelius answers, "Nope. No, we won't." He grins proudly. The mood in the room lifted instantly.

Chapter Seven

Cornelius clears his throat and addresses the room. "The hero of the day would like to go for a stroll. Have we any takers?" he laughs as he gently nudges Georgette and whispers in her ear. "I'm taking you for a walk. Let's get you out of these walls. The fresh air is what you need. It will help calm you down before this meeting. We will have plenty of time as it's not happening now until 5 o'clock this evening."

Georgette snaps "What do you mean 5 o'clock? I said I wanted everyone here as soon as possible."

Cornelius burst out laughing. "Control your temper, woman. I received a cinder note and a few of our guests are running late. The world won't implode Georgie, if we have to wait a little longer. Now come on, get up before I carry you out myself."

Isadora and Despina both look the other way not wanting Georgette to see the amusement on their faces. Cornelius continues to playfully scold her. "I can't even blame this behaviour on that potion bottle because this Georgette Crescent is all you. Or is it? Let me have a look at those pretty eyes of yours," he jests. "Not a speck of black to be seen. It's okay everyone they're still blue."

Georgette playfully pushes him away, pulling her lips in tight to refrain from giving him the satisfaction of a smile. She knows he is right, and she knows that he knows it.

"Oh, shut up Cornelius."

He gives her a playful look. "That's decided then, I'm carrying you."

Georgette tries to get away stumbling backwards, but Cornelius catches her. He looks into her eyes. They really were beautiful, a shade of royal blue once more, his favourite colour. Placing his hands around her waist pulling her closer he holds her chin with his fingertips. Georgette half smiles. Surprising him, she hugs him. Resting her head on his chest.

"Okay, know it all. I'll go for that walk".

Isadora hands Cornelius a tonic. "Get her to drink this before you leave. It will clear up that sore throat, darling."

He smiled, taking the little bottle from his mother then walked into the hallway to meet Georgette.

"Here you go Georgie, get that down your neck as Toby likes to say."

She sniffs the elixir, wrinkling her nose.

"It smells disgusting," she remarks, "Which means it will taste just as bad."

Cornelius shrugs. "Only one way to find out."

She lets out a breath, then knocks it back in one go.

"Good grief that's so bad! Your mother could have added peppermint, or even lemon at least, to hide the taste."

Chapter Seven

Cornelius stifles a snigger. He thought it was so funny watching her gulp that nasty tonic. Georgette notices through the corner of her eye.

"Are you laughing at me?" she demands

"Of course not, Georgie. I would never. Now let's get going, or I'm telling my mother you'd like another one."

She throws her hands up in mock horror. "No thank you."

They both run out the door.

Chapter Eight

Meanwhile Toby was out at sea in a small rowing boat. The sun was coating the ocean surface with an array of delightful colours. Orange, red, purple, pink. The water was a bit choppy, rocking the small boat from side to side. He pulls the oars onto the boat and calls on his friend Cuttlefish. Moments later, a head pops up at the side of his boat.

"Hello my dear friend. What brings you out this far and at this time of day? Surely you're not fishing at this hour?"

Toby looks at Cuttlefish, dreading the conversation ahead. Cuttlefish was quite perceptive. He could tell something was bothering his friend. Pushing himself up into the boat, he steadied himself. He wasn't much good on dry land, a literal fish out of water as the human folk say. Holding onto either side of the boat, he got his bearings about him. His tail on the other hand was another story, flopping about and thrashing against the side of the boat.

"I swear this tail has a mind of its own," complained Cuttlefish.

Chapter Eight

This made Toby chuckle as it took several moments for Cuttlefish to stop his tail from flopping about, and his efforts always cheered Toby up.

"No, I'm not fishing. But I am here on a serious matter. I need to ask a favour Cuttle".

Cuttlefish looked at him questioningly.

"Of course, Toby. Anything my friend. What can I do? Just name it."

Toby takes off his paddy hat and runs his hands through his hair. Repositioning his hat, he exhales and begins telling Cuttlefish everything that has happened. Toby concludes his story.

"Can you possibly ask the Fisherweed council and the royal advisers if they can help? I wouldn't ask unless we were desperate. I need a binding Shamrock Contract."

Cuttlefish is shocked. "Can I ask who the contract is for?"

Toby explains, "I will tell you everything. But first we need to join forces. We need an audience, either in Salt Sea City, or waters near or as close to there as possible. Whatever suits your Council and your Queen. We are getting word out to all Seven Realms, and I thought it might be best to hold the meeting undersea. It's safer, away from any of Gregor's minions".

Cuttlefish looked worried. "Toby, do you think the Johnagock will come back my old friend? Is it possible they will return? It's frightening to think that could ever happen again. They were such dark days for my people. Everyone suffered at the hands of the Johnagock."

Cuttlefish lowers his head for a moment. "Word under the sea is spreading, the talk and whispers had many of our folk riled up. So much so, to be honest, that our soldiers have been patrolling our waters ever since Morning Star captured one of our pods. My people are a peaceful race as you already know, Toby. But they are preparing for the worst."

With a heavy heart Toby answers, "Yes, I hate to say this Cuttle, but there's a strong possibility they could return. They now have a Crescent sister and young Henry Hawthorn. I am sure knowing the Johnagock, they're doing all they can to try and drain what magick they can get from them, if any. Henry and Amelia are not babies, they're full-grown adults. Heaven help them. I can't allow myself to think on it too long. It drives me mad Cuttle. All I can do is concentrate on their rescue. I can't stress this enough my friend. We need a Shamrock Contract. And we can't get it without everyone's approval. The Royal seal would be the icing on the cake. We need this contract for Gregor."

Cuttlefish was shocked. "What? Why my friend? why him? I don't understand why help that monster?" he asks confused.

"We need to get Georgette and myself into that hell dimension, and that dirty rotten snake Gregor is the only person that can get us across the veil".

Toby can feel anger rising up inside him again. "Oh alright, now I understand. But I must say my old friend,

Chapter Eight

I really don't like this plan. And neither will the others. But I'm sure when they know it's the only option, then we might persuade them to agree."

Toby pats Cuttlefish on the shoulder. "Let's hope so Cuttle."

The sun had finally set.

"I'd best be getting back now Cuttle".

Cuttlefish agrees. "I'll inform my Queen and the Salt Sea council right away. I'll do my best to make them understand."

Toby shakes Cuttle's hand. "I'll call back later tonight. Find out what news you have for me. Say 8 o'clock at the end of the dock wall?"

Cuttle then slips his body off the side of the boat and disappears under the water.

An hour later Toby finally reached Belfast dock and his beloved station house where big Tucker was howling and barking with excitement when he hears Toby's footsteps approach. Toby opens the door to a loving welcome. Tucker standing up with his big paws resting on Toby's shoulders, licking his face. He laughs telling him to get down. Toby gives him one last pat on the head before he lays down on his rug in front of the fire. Toby's starts to work on making his champ and fish. Enough to feed an army.

"Better to have too much than too little I suppose," he beams to himself.

After sorting the food, he starts sending out cinder notes. He wants everyone to know about his idea in regard to the Shamrock Contract.

He pours himself a large Irish coffee with plenty of whisky, taking off his heavy boots. He slips his feet into his favourite slippers, sits down and rests his feet on the stool by the fire,. He feels a slight breeze, only to notice a hole in his slipper.

"Tucker!" he shouts. "What have I told you about using my slippers as chew toys!"

Tucker guiltily grunts in response burying his head in his large paws. Lifting his pipe Toby settles into his fireside chair waiting on his cinder note replies.

The afternoon went in quickly for Toby. Looking at his pocket watch he exclaims, "good grief, look at the time! I must get a move on." He pops linen cloths over the enormous pots then puts the lids on. Setting a large bowl of food down beside Tucker.

"Now get that down ye, before we leave and make it quick or I'm gonna be late."

Tucker barks in approval, then gets stuck into his dish of food.

Toby gathers everything he needs. He ponders, "It's a bit nippy out there today, even though the sun was out. I think I'll put the heavy coat on."

After a few moments fastening his last brass button he announces, "Ready to go big lad?"

Tucker stands at the door with Toby's cap gently held between his teeth. "Thank you, my boy." He pops his hat on his head. Tucker barks, then opens the door with his big paws.

"After you, my boy."

Chapter Eight

Once outside he sets the big large pot with the tray of fish on his door step, then taking his key out, he locks the door. "Okay, that's us all sorted. Let's get a move on Tucker."

As they walk towards the Albert bridge, he starts to sing an old song called 'Go Lassie Go' to pass the time, an old fisherman's favourite.

Chapter Nine

It doesn't take Toby long to reach the clock tower. He looks up at its perfect, white face giving off a soft glow in the distance. It's just turned 4.30pm.

"Yes," he said, "I'm just on time. The champ is still nice and hot."

Knocking on the door he waits for an answer. There are lots of voices coming from inside. He knocks again. There is a loud clink as the door unlocks from the other side. As it opens, he is greeted with a welcoming smile. It was Lord Riverdale.

"Aww look who it is, now. How are you, big man? It's been too long, Toby. Let me help you with these pots. Is that champ I smell?"

Happy with the offer to help, Toby hands over a large pot. "It is indeed sir. And fresh haddock too."

Lord Riverdale was a longtime family friend, and fond of his food too, not unlike Toby himself.

"I'm looking forward to this. It's been a while since I've had dockers grub".

He sniffs the pots enthusiastically. They walk to the hallway and set the food on the console table to their left. Toby puts both arms out, exchanging manly hugs. Then they proceed through the corridor.

Chapter Nine

"Come into the parlour Toby. There's more of us arrived early. There is one person especially eager to see you again," Lord Riverdale chuckles.

"Who could it be," Toby ponders to himself.

Entering the room Toby couldn't believe his eyes. Standing by the fireplace was Cuttlefish. And, to Toby's amazement, with a set of legs! His deep booming laugh reverberated around the room, catching the attention of the other guests.

"Oh, my stars. Look at you lad. You finally had enough of that pesky tail of yours, eh?" Toby jokes, giving him a gentle pat on the back. "How on earth did you get things sorted so quickly? I met with you only this morning. What did your kin think of my idea?"

Cuttlefish finding his balance moves towards Toby and gestures for him to lean down, Toby is a big man after all. He whispers, "I'll explain everything, once the meeting starts."

Toby nods. "As you wish Cuttle, but I must ask...," he chuckles. "how're the legs feeling?"

Cuttlefish grins sheepishly. "It has taken me a little while getting adjusted, I won't lie. Also might have fell over once or twice, but I got used to them eventually. Between you and me, it's not the legs that's the problem, it's the toes. Why does there have to be so many of them? I can't seem to wrap my head around it. Give me fins any day."

Toby laughs saying, "well I think you look fantastic. They suit you well my friend".

Hickory addresses the room, "Dear friends, can I have everyone's attention please. Master Cuttlefish has an announcement to make. Please tell us what news you bring from Salt Sea City my friend."

Cuttlefish looks around the room, politely acknowledging his friends. I was sent directly by Her Majesty Queen Opala. I met with Toby this morning to discuss recent events you are all aware of. As soon as I delivered Toby's message to her, she has requested that you all attend an emergency meeting at Salt Sea City tonight. Word has been sent to all seven realms to attend by Royal invitation only. So, I'm letting you all know, you're not alone. Salt Sea City stands with you."

The room erupts into cheer. Respectfully Cuttlefish nods. "I've been advised to arrange the numbers attending tonight's event and dish out these potions. They will help you 'landgoers' breathe underwater. Can't accidentally have you all drowning on me now can I," he mocks. "They sent me with ten bottles, enough for each magickal person. Three witches, one fairy, three wizards, one elf and two protectors."

Toby looks confused. "Ah, you messed that up Cuttle. There's only one Protector here and that's me, big Toby." He pounds his fists to his chest.

Lord Riverdale interrupts. "I think you got it wrong Toby," he smiles. "There are two protectors going. You and the other is in the kitchen with the ladies."

Taken a little surprised, Toby shouts, "What? Who? Its news to me. Do I know him? What's his name?" Eagerly he claps both hands rubbing them together. "Have I got a bit of competition?"

A voice from the doorway grasps his attention.

"Yes, you do indeed."

Chapter Nine

Toby, caught off guard, turns to see a somewhat curvy lady with roaring red shoulder length, curly hair, the most beautiful green eyes and rosy cheeks. She stands almost as tall as Toby, with a belly near as big as his. Toby thought she was the prettiest lady he'd ever seen. The woman approaches.

"Hello Toby! My name is Flanna. How are you big man?" she asks in a heavy scouse accent.

Toby's face feels hot. He can tell his cheeks are turning bright red. Tongue-tied he stutters, trying to get words to leave his lips, but nothing comes out.

"Am I dreaming? Nope, I feel fine. Say something Toby. Anything ya big eejit," he silently pleads with himself. Taking a slow breath, pulling himself together, he finally responds saying

"Hi." Doe eyed he smiles.

"Hi back," Flanna grins. "I believe you made some food, yes?"

He nods "I did, aye, yes," he mumbles. "It's in the hall. I'll go fetch it."

They both walk to exit the room. Trying to squeeze past her in the doorway, there wasn't enough space, and making the situation even more humiliating for himself, he accidentally stands on Flanna's foot. She lets out a yelp.

"Sorry!" Toby shouts. Feeling flustered they both simultaneously bend down to check her foot is alright and accidentally bump heads, to Toby's utter embarrassment. Toby's face is now bright purple. Cuttlefish seeing the encounter can't help appreciating the humour in it.

Georgette, Isadora and Despina walk into the hallway hearing so much commotion. "What's going on?" Isadora asks.

Toby looks at her. "Nothing, nothing at all! I've made 'famp and cish'. It's still hot, I'm just going to grab it."

Georgette tried not to laugh. "Do you mean champ and fish Toby?"

Composing himself he answers, "Yes, why? What did I say? Ah never mind, I'll go grab the grub".

Gathering the food from the hallway he walks into the kitchen. Once he is safely inside the kitchen, he lets out a sigh of relief. He looks to the left of the kitchen, thinking he was seeing double. Rubbing his eyes, he looks again. It was another big, grey haired Irish wolfhound sitting beside Tucker. The only difference was Tucker was slightly taller with brown eyes. The other dog had green eyes.

Suddenly a tap on his shoulder made him jump! It was Flanna. "That's my girl. Isn't she a beauty? Her name is Nora."

Toby happily smiles. He absolutely loves animals, especially Irish wolfhounds. They're a rare breed indeed.

"She certainly is a beauty. My Tucker seems to have taken to her; he pats both dogs on their heads."

Flanna says, "I've made a great big pot of 'scouse' are you hungry?"

He looks at her and asks, "What's scouse?"

Her eyes widen with excitement. "Oh, you're in for a treat. It's called stew here but we both make it the same way."

Chapter Nine

He thought to himself, "if this stew is as good as mine then she's some woman. I'll take a wee drop after the meeting." Aloud he says, "It smells good."

Flanna slaps his shoulder enthusiastically, "Yes, and it tastes just as good too, I'll have you know."

Toby then tries to make small talk, with his face still blushing bright red. "So, Flanna. That's some accent you have there. What part of England are you from?" he asks curiously.

She replies, "I'm from just across the pond, Toby. Liverpool born and bred. To be honest, its very like Belfast you know."

Surprised he says, "Oh, is that right, I've never been to Liverpool before. What's it like?"

Flanna loved talking about her hometown. "Well you are more than welcome to come and see for yourself once all this madness is sorted, big man. Just say the word and I'll fix you right up," she winks.

Chapter Ten

Isadora looks about the overcrowded room. There are so many people in here. "Do you all mind waiting in the hallway for a moment please. Just until we cast a spell to widen the room."

The guests all spill out into the main hall while Isadora, Georgette and Despina chant:

Small to big within this space
Wide to worn
This time and place

Within seconds the floors and walls begin to stretch making the room twice as big as its original state. Isadora then tells everyone to come back inside.

In attendance were Lord Anthony with Flanna, Lord Riverdale with Fin Frazzle, Isadora with Cornelius, Despina then Hickory, Georgette with Toby and Cuttlefish.

Toby addresses the room.

"First of all can I just say thank you to everyone. I know it was at short notice asking you all here, but I thought it best to get things started as soon as possible. You are all aware I've requested a Shamrock Contract

Chapter Ten

be drawn up to entice Gregor into helping us open the veil to the Johnagock dimension."

Astounded by this news, Georgette interrupts. "What are you talking about? No one told me about a Shamrock Contract. Why am I only hearing about this now, Toby? You can't be serious. After everything Gregor has done. If he gets his hands on that contract, he gets off scot-free." She clenches her fists in anger.

Toby gives her a sympathetic look. "Don't go losing your temper just yet, young miss. Just listen. Give me a moment and I will explain."

Georgette reluctantly nods her head and waits for Toby to continue.

"If we offer this to the dirty dog in exchange for passage across the veil, he won't turn it down. I believe he will jump at the offer. It's too perfect for him to turn it down, think about it, Georgette."

Georgette sat in silence. Thinking over what Toby had said.

Lord Anthony interjected, "I like this plan, but I don't think there is any justice if Gregor isn't held accountable for his actions."

Hickory agrees. "Yes, you're right. But let's sort that out once we convince him to open the veil. Promise the fiend the moon and the stars for all I care, but give him nothing in the end. It would be unjust for the punishment to not fit the crime, don't you all agree?"

Lord Riverdale nods. "Listen, the wizard is over 300 years old. He is not stupid. He will see right through this. We need a better plan."

The room erupts into argumentative chaos. Toby throws his hands up in defeat. Raising his voice demanding everyone calm down.

"I've had enough of this bickering! We need to work together, each of us take a turn with suggestions. And be warned the first person to speak out of turn, I'll have my Tucker lick the face of ye. And he's had more than his fill of fish gruel today, so I wouldn't recommend it."

A look of horror passes over each of their faces at the thought.

"Now please, if you wouldn't mind, can you start first Izzy? Then we will make our way around the table, agreed?"

The room falls silent as they all look to Isadora.

"Yes, well thank you Toby. Okay, first we need to determine who will be crossing the Veil with Georgette. We can't all cross at once. Gregor is only powerful enough to get two through at a time. Georgette needs someone powerful to cross with her."

To everyone's surprise Flanna is the first to speak. "I would like to give my opinion please, I think miss Georgette needs a protector going in with her, not a witch or wizard. Once Georgette takes her powers on the next full moon, she will be more than capable of looking after herself. We don't know how long she will be in this hellish dimension. It will be unfamiliar to her. I vote Toby goes in with her. He's the best choice if you ask me. He's the Crescent family protector. No one will take better care of her than him."

Toby smiles with gratitude. "Thank you Flanna, those were very kind words. You all know Mia and

Chapter Ten

Georgie are family to me. The decisions been made. I will be crossing the veil with Georgette. Does anyone have a problem with that?"

He eyes the room daring someone to object.

"No issue? Brilliant. That's that sorted then. Next order of business."

Lord Riverdale takes an opportunity to speak.

"Alright that's the first part of the plan sorted. Now moving on. We need to find Lady Celine and Gregor. The Council and guards have combed every part of Ireland."

Lord Anthony asks, "so if we manage to make contact with them, then what?"

Georgette answers. "I offer him the contract and he accepts. I then cross the veil with Toby and get everyone back."

Lord Anthony considers this. "But surely, we are not really letting this man go free. After everything he has done?"

Hickory agrees. "This concerns me also. A binding Shamrock Contract is unbreakable. Gregor knows this. If Gregor thinks he's been offered this, he knows by the law of the land and all its realms above the sea and below it can't be undone."

Despina paces the room frustrated. "But Toby, this means the man would be free. He would keep his wealth, his estate, his money. My god, he can even keep his position in the Causeway Army! We can't agree to this dear. Surely not."

Toby says with a sly grin, "I say we offer this contract to him. Yes, it will be real not false. I've known Gregor long enough to know he would smell a rat if he thought its parchment was fake. So here's what I suggest. We get him the real deal. Queen Opala will hopefully give it a royal stamp, magically binding it. And yes, this means Gregor will be untouchable while he's under the protection of the Shamrock Contract. But here's where it gets tricky. We tell him the parchment must be cut in half. I will take one half with me into the hell dimension and Gregor can hold on to the other half until we have all returned safely."

Cornelius grins, liking where this plan is headed. "Okay, say this plan works. Then what about lady Celine and the others?"

Toby answers, "Ah I'm glad you asked." He chuckles, "The little cherry on top of the cake. We tell Gregor to pin everything on her."

Upon hearing this, Cornelius laughs wickedly. "Toby you're a genius." Everyone in the room applauds.

Hickory pats Toby on the back. "Fantastic plan, my good man. I do have one suggestion though. Once we get everyone back over the Veil, We could use a bit of muscle to push Gregor across the Veil, just before it closes. Leave him in there where he belongs with all his Johnagock friends. He deserves no less. I am sure the Fae folk can cook up a binding spell to temporarily strip him of his powers keeping him stuck in there. At least until we can figure out a permanent solution. What say you Fin Frazzle?"

Fin smiled with pride. "Why yes, I can say with hand on heart my people would be honoured to help."

Chapter Ten

Toby looks at Cornelius. "I propose master Cornelius to do the job. I'm sure this big lad is more than capable."

Cornelius beams in approval. "Yes! Finally, I get to help. I'll get him thrown back into that veil with one swift kick of my boot, don't you worry."

A little worried with hearing this, Isadora voices her concerns. "As lovely as that visual image is darling, we have a snag ladies and gentlemen. How in the name of the stars do we get the seven realms to agree on a binding Shamrock Contract?"

Cuttlefish raises his hand requesting permission to speak. "I say we meet tonight in salt sea city with all seven realms. We tell them our plan and hopefully they agree. But may I add, my Queen is in favour of Toby's plan. So perhaps this may help sway them."

Georgette stands up. She takes a steadying breath. "Thank you everyone, I think it's the best option we have, and I appreciate your kindness and everything you're doing. I love this idea. Toby, well done. Let's all hope tonight is agreed on, and we go forth with hope."

Exhausted, Isadora addresses the room, "Are we all forgetting one small thing here. We still don't know Gregor's whereabouts."

"She's right," Toby said aloud. The room went silent.

Georgette jumps to her feet startling everyone. "Oh my goodness, I completely forgot. I know how to contact him. The Celtic table. How could I forget, it's my direct link to him. My father enchanted it for Mia and myself years ago."

Lord Anthony speaks, "I didn't know there were even any left in existence, they're so rare".

Georgette answers, "Well there's one here, in our potion room and I'm pretty sure if I call upon Gregor he definitely will answer."

Hickory interrupts, "Let's not do anything in haste. Let's hold off until tomorrow. It's best put off until the seven realms agree on the contract and then we can try to contact him through the table. Is everyone in agreement? Let's vote," he suggests.

"YES," they say one by one.

Happy with their progress, Toby invites everyone into the kitchen. "Well now that this meeting is finished, and we're all agreed, let's eat. All this talking has worked up an appetite and I'm starving."

Flanna shouts, "Finally a man after my own heart! Yes, let's get everyone a big bowl of scouse and a plate of Toby's champ and fish."

She leads everyone into the kitchen.

Chapter Eleven

After finishing their meal everyone gathers in the main entrance. Big Toby stands at the front door with Cuttlefish by his side.

"Now everyone, we just want to assure you all that Queen Opala has had these underwater potions made personally by only the best potion brewer's this side of Ireland. No connection whatsoever to the old sea hag's work on the lough shore. So please don't worry about our journey. Cuttlefish will take the best of care with us. Now wrap up well, it's a bit nippy that far out to sea. Oh, and Flanna and I have made snacks for everyone, well, those who don't get seasick," he chuckled.

Suddenly cinder notes appear, one in everyone's hands simultaneously. Immediately they all look at each other, confused. This is very unusual. Hickory spotted the green mark on his parchment first, instantly causing alarm. He raises his voice and shouts to the others, "Don't open anything. Stay perfectly still."

Fin Frazzle is confused and asks, "Why? what's wrong. I don't understand, they're only cinder notes my friend. I feel a little left out," he jests.

Hickory gives him a stern stare, silencing him immediately. "Consider yourself lucky you didn't receive one Fin. Listen to me carefully, all of you. These notes are cursed. Do not open them."

Standing perfectly still, everyone does exactly as they are told. Hickory specialized in dark magic, says "Quickly Fin, go into the parlour room get the cauldron at once."

Fin, still shocked, did as he was told. He returned in moments. Hovering with his wings fluttering, he waits for further instruction.

"Fin, you need to hold the pot still while I cast this spell."

Cover case this time and place
Protect, prevent!
these notes now sent

Immediately the cinder notes began to float from everyone's hands and lift into the air. Poor Fin was trying his best to flutter as still as possible. A thin trickle of green and black swirling smoke followed each cinder note as they rose upwards. Then slowly swaying side to side and falling gently downwards, resting in the black cauldron. When Hickory has seen the last note enter the pot, he finishes his spell:

Flames of light destroy, ignite
Return these notes to their original flight

White plumes of smoke swirl out of the cauldron, evaporating into tiny puffs. Hickory asks Fin to place the pot on the griddle. He then commands, "Solos!"

Chapter Eleven

Flames of yellow, green, and red swallow the pot whole, leaving behind a flash of green light and a disgusting stench seeping from the grate. Georgette storms toward the fireplace and shouts, "What the hell was that Hickory!"

Hickory looks at everyone horrified. "Death Notes!" he mutters. Despina gasps in horror, with the others putting their hands to their mouths in complete shock. Walking to Hickory she wraps her arms around him tightly, pulling him into an embrace. Relieved everyone is okay she breathes a sigh of relief. "You just saved the lives of everyone in this room. I am so proud of you."

A confused Fin asks, "Can someone please explain to me what a death note is?"

"Black magic," Hickory replies. "I'm glad you were here Fin. Thank you for your help."

An upset Isadora shouts, "This kind of black magick hasn't been used since the Great War! Gregor must be behind this. Is there no end to his madness?"

Toby was livid. To think how much danger his friends were in just moments ago made his blood boil. "That dirty, no good scummy, evil snake tried to kill us!"

Lord Riverdale walks over to Hickory and pats his shoulder. "We owe you a great debt my friend. Well spotted Hickory. But it is with great regret. I'm afraid we will need to put our journey to Salt Sea City on hold this evening. Lord Anthony and I need to return to Causeway City immediately. We need to report what's happened here. I'm sorry but under the circumstances we have no choice. Can you possibly inform Queen

Opala for us? Send her our deepest apologies and request that the meeting be postponed until tomorrow."

Cuttlefish is happy to oblige. "Yes of course I can, I completely understand. I shall return home within the hour to inform my Queen and shall call back tomorrow morning to advise you of the new arrangements".

Georgette takes everyone upstairs to let them pass through the Clock Tower. Lord Anthony was the last one to enter the passer's door. He takes Georgette's hand in his. He furrows his brow. "Georgette you must cast a protection spell inside and outside this Clock Tower. Use only the very best of your herbs, plenty of mug wart and sage, as I am sure you already know my dear. Sweep this hallway out with your best broom as soon as we've all left. Please stay safe. I'll send you a cinder note later in regards to our travel arrangements for the morning. However, in the meantime keep Toby close by your side. Gregor somehow knew we were all gathered here and that's worrying me. He could have someone in the docks watching the Tower."

Georgette was fond of Lord Anthony. He was a kind man who knew her father well. She had the upmost respect for him. She never considered there could be a possible spy in their midst.

"But who? I can't think of anyone from the docks that would side with him, or want to hurt us."

Lord Anthony slowly closes the passers door. "Heaven only knows who it could be young lady. Just be careful who you talk to."

Lifting her key chain to lock the door she bids Lord Anthony farewell.

Chapter Twelve

Cornelius, Toby, and Isadora remain in the parlour room. Georgette could hear Cornelius raising his voice as she entered the room.

"I swear by the stars, I'll throttle that man. He tried to kill us. Actually tried to kill us." His strong arms were tense, his fists clenched. Aggression was coming off him in waves.

Georgette was usually the one with a temper, not Cornelius. She knew she needed to help calm him down. Walking to him she gently places both hands on either side of his face.

"Please sit, Cornelius. It's not like you to get so angry. Were safe now." His expression softens at her touch.

"Angry Georgie? This has gotten out of hand. The man tried to kill us. This can't go on anymore. He needs to be stopped."

Toby listening in says, "Cornelius is right Georgette, Gregor fears no one. We need this Shamrock Contract done and dusted. It's the only way to draw that evil lowlife out of hiding. Before someone gets hurt."

Georgette takes his big hand in hers. "I agree Toby. I have every faith that your plan will work. I promise he will get what's coming to him. Mark my words."

Isadora pours everyone a large glass of brandy. "Cornelius, we need to cross the veil we need to check on your father and put a protection spell around the house. Gregor has been in our home. We need to make sure everyone is safe."

Cornelius looks at her. He can't believe that with everything that's happened today, he didn't think to put an enchantment around his own home.

"Good god mother you're right. We will leave right away. Toby can stay with Georgie until we return this evening. Is that okay, Georgie?"

"Yes, my goodness, go. And please make sure Francis is okay. Send me a cinder note once you get everything sorted."

Cornelius hugs her tight then puts his coat on. Isadora takes both Georgette's hands in hers.

"I'll keep him calm darling. Just stay on your guard. Don't be leaving the tower alone. We will be back soon."

Toby sees them out and locks the gates and door behind them.

Only Georgette and Toby remain. She tells him about Lord Anthony's advice, and about his thoughts on one of the dockers that were perhaps helping Gregor.

Toby shakes his head. "If it's one of our own, then God help the witch or wizard, because they will be dealt with. But let's not think about that just now. We need to get this clock tower sealed."

Georgette then set to work on her protection spell with Toby staying close by her side.

Chapter Thirteen

Early Next morning Georgette was first to wake up. It was still dark outside. She made a large pot of strong coffee, cutting thick slices of bread to prepare for toast. She knew Toby would expect it, and Cornelius too.

She herself couldn't bear the thought of eating yet. Her stomach was in knots. Her mind was elsewhere, thinking about Amelia. Wondering if she was awake. Was she able to eat? Has anyone harmed her? Horrible thoughts, playing repeatedly in her mind, on a never-ending loop. She also thought of Gregor and the events that took place yesterday. How close she and her friends had come to death.

A light knock on the kitchen door pulled her back to reality.

Cornelius pops his head through the doorway, yawning. "Good morning, Georgie. Is that coffee I smell?"

Georgette looks at him amused; his hair still ruffled, messy from sleep. "Yes, it is. It's good and strong too. I'm making some toast. Are you hungry?"

He gives her a sleepy grin. "I'm always hungry woman, you know this," he replies. "Need any help?" he asks. Georgette tells him to cut some ham for Toby.

She knew he would like a bit on his toast when he returns. Cornelius slicing the ham notices Georgette lost in thought. He sets the food aside on the kitchen table, bending down he places a gentle kiss on her cheek. This is a welcome surprise. Georgette turns to look at him, blushing. Placing her delicate hands on his broad chest. He responds by holding them there. Resting her head against his muscular frame, listening to his heartbeat, she relaxes. Cornelius can feel Georgette's fingertips slowly tracing along the front of his half-opened shirt. He lets her fingers slide further, accidentally unfastening another button. She can feel his warm skin through the soft fabric. She inhales his scent, a mixture of sandalwood and jasmine. It was somehow calming yet stimulating at the same time. He smelt how a man should smell. Cornelius moves his large hands around her tiny waist pulling her in tighter. It was moments like this he never wanted to let her go. There was undeniably an intimate spark between them, a passionate flame that could never die. Nervous, Cornelius allows himself to trace his hand down the middle of Georgettes back. She leans in closer encouraging him to go further. She felt a tingling sensation run through her entire body as his hands move lower. Georgette allows herself to carefully place her hands onto his bare chest, slowly moving upwards she caresses his hard shoulders, pushing herself closer to him. Their eyes meet. There was an intensity, a passion she has never felt before. In that moment nothing else mattered. Georgette's heart was racing as Cornelius slowly moves closer toward

Chapter Thirteen

her, softly touching her chin he tilts her face toward his. Gently rubbing his thumb across her cheek, he moves closer again, His lips inches from hers, so close she could feel his breath. Georgette standing on her tiptoes slowly closes her eyes in anticipation. Finally, just as their lips are about to meet, Isadora enters the room.

Embarrassment causes them both to jump two feet apart. She shouts, "Oh my goodness. The smell of that coffee got me out of bed young lady. It smells divine."

Georgette grabs a mug and fills it with coffee for Isadora. Praying to the stars she didn't see anything before she entered.

Isadora looks at them both. "Are you alright, Cornelius? You look a little flustered darling. Are you feeling alright?"

A little embarrassed he clears his throat. "Sorry Mother, I'm fine. More than fine. You're right, the coffee does smell good. But will it taste good. After all, it's Georgie that has made it. She's not the best cook in the house," he teases.

Georgette swipes him with the dish cloth saying, "Make your own coffee next time."

A loud knock on the front door shakes the walls of the Clock Tower. Georgette laughs into her coffee cup. "I'll give you one guess who that will be."

Isadora rolls her eyes with a half-smile. "Good grief. That man isn't gentle is he?"

Cornelius stifles a chuckle. "I'll let him in. He gives Georgette a sneaky wink and puckers his lips as he walks past causing her to choke on her coffee.

"Are you okay, darling," Isadora asks.

"Yes, I'm fine thank you. Just went down the wrong way, that's all," she replies continuing to sip her coffee.

Toby enters the kitchen with big Tucker and Cuttlefish trailing not too far behind, "Mmmm, that smells good." Rubbing his belly he asks, "What are we having for breakfast ladies?"

Georgette answers, "Thick toast with ham and honey. I've a pot of coffee made. Help yourself."

Cuttlefish looks at Toby. He shrugs, "I'll give it a go."

Toby gives him an encouraging pat on the back, almost knocking Cuttlefish's coffee cup out of his hands. "Oops! Sorry about that. Don't know my own strength at times."

Steadying himself Cuttle reassures Toby he is okay. Toby nods, "You'll like the food, Cuttle. Trust me. It's good. I would know".

Isadora takes a seat at the table quietly sipping her coffee. She doesn't like dark early mornings. Toby takes a seat beside her. "It's a bit nippy out there today, so wrap up well ladies."

The clock strikes 6 o'clock. Georgette stands. "I'd better go up and let our guests in. They will be arriving soon." She leaves the room and makes her way upstairs to the passage door.

Isadora takes the opportunity to look at Cornelius with a knowing smile. She teases him. "I should have taken an extra ten minutes in bed this morning, shouldn't I?"

Chapter Thirteen

Toby not knowing the morning's events agrees. "Oh, an extra ten minutes in bed on a cold dark morning makes all the difference."

Cornelius rolls his eyes. "Be quiet woman."

Isadora smirks, "Did I happen to walk in at the wrong time my darling?" she asks eagerly.

Toby looks at Isadora rubbing his chin. "What do you mean, Izzy. Why do I feel like I'm missing something?"

Cornelius tuts in disapproval. "Mother hold your tongue," he warns.

She laughs excitedly. "I'll tell you later Toby."

Toby catching onto the situation grins, ecstatic. "I'll try not to pry too much." He then winks at Isadora.

The sound of many footsteps can now be heard coming down the spiral staircase. "That would be my cue to fetch my hat and cloak," says Isadora.

Everyone greeted each other in the hallway. Lord Anthony makes an announcement. "Can I just give everyone an update on what the Council have said?" The hall goes silent, everyone giving him their undivided attention.

"Okay everyone the Council have agreed with Toby's plan, but only on one condition. They say it's an absolute must that Gregor be trapped in the hell dimension, with his powers stripped forever. Now I know the fairies will do a grand job on creating a powder. But this will only last a few hours at most. So, we need to come up with something else that will make the effects of the stripping powder permanent."

Lord Riverdale suggests, "We need every High Elder from each realm to cast the stripping spell in unison. Seven Elders need to join together and sacrifice a small piece of their own magickal powers to combine them as one. We will need a Witch, Wizard, Fairy, Fisherweed, an Elf, a Leprechaun and a Giant. This is the only way Gregor can be stripped of his powers for good. In theory it could practically make him human."

Isadora gasps. "Who would possibly even consider giving such a sacrifice? To lose ones magic, even a small portion of it is a lot to ask of anyone."

Lord Anthony and Lord Riverdale look at Hickory. They both knew he would be the one to volunteer.

Hickory stands. "That would be myself, Isadora," Hickory smiles. "I would like to volunteer myself, on behalf of my fellow wizards."

Despina taking his hand in hers says, "Then I, too, will volunteer myself on behalf of the Witches."

Georgette interrupts sharply. "No Despina, no. This is too much. I can't ask this of my friends."

"It's already been decided," Hickory says with a kind expression. Looking at Despina he pats her hand. "But not you my dear. We hadn't discussed you giving up part of your powers."

Despina looks around the room at each of her friends. "I'm not as young as I'd like to be. I'm almost as old as Hickory. Two hundred years give or take a decade or two. But who's counting," she mocks. "I don't need my full powers anymore, certainly not as much as a young Witch would. And besides, Georgette is basically running the school already. She will take over as headmistress soon. I'm almost ready to hang up my broom. So, I feel it's only right you all give me

Chapter Thirteen

this opportunity to do my bit to help. I've made up my mind and as most of you already know once that's done, there's no changing it."

Georgette wraps her arms around Despina. Filled with emotion she whispers, "I'll never be able to thank you enough for this. Thank you to you both".

Chapter Fourteen

Once outside the Clock Tower Cuttlefish hands out the small bottles of underwater potion. "Just a quick reminder everyone, please don't take your potion until I tell you to. We will take Toby's fishing boat out to sea. Once we've passed Wickery Wreath, you may take them there. The royal Salt Sea guards will meet us at this point. They will bring under water transport to speed up our journey."

Fin Frazzle, looking a little concerned, eyes Cuttlefish suspiciously. "What do you mean exactly? What kind of transport?" he asks. "I prefer flying. I'm a little nervous to be honest. I don't know how to swim," he admits a little embarrassed.

Cuttlefish puts his hand on Fins shoulder. "Please try not to worry. I'll stay by your side the whole time my friend. The transport they're sending are beautiful creatures called Dolfino. They're very friendly. You just mount them like you would horses on dry land."

Fin looks at him, still concerned, but agrees to proceed. "I trust you, but I'm still not looking forward to this."

Georgette turns the key locking the Clock Tower door. Everyone moves off. Tailsa and Bijou, both fully sized, with big Tucker and Nora, walk side by side.

Chapter Fourteen

Toby had suggested last night that the Shadows stay in the station house. He was going to have some dockers call in and keep an eye on them. "They'll be very comfortable with their food bowls full, laying by the fireplace."

Dawn was just starting to break, splashes of orange and pink peering through the clouds, decorating the sky above and reflecting sparkles on the jumping waves. Toby gets the Shadows inside and settled. Georgette speaks to Tailsa and Bijou.

"I promise you I won't be long. We are going to get help to bring Mia back. Please be good and don't misbehave for Toby's friend Harlow." She hugs them both and kisses them goodbye.

Toby closes the door behind him he walks to the end of the sea wall where everyone was waiting. His little fishing boat was tied up, bobbing from side to side on the choppy waves.

"Come on now, ladies first. In you go."

Cornelius helps the women on board, then everyone else joins them. It was a tight squeeze, but they just about managed to fit in. Cuttlefish was the last person standing on shore. He sits down on the dock wall, taking a quick look around then drops into the water. Moments later his head appears at the back of the boat. His clothes floating away on top of the oncoming tide. Cornelius takes up the oars with his strong arms and begins to row. Cuttlefish helps by pushing them forward, swimming from the rear. The sea is quiet and the salty air cold. No one spoke as they set out to sea. Their thoughts all very apparent on their worried faces.

Seagulls followed overhead, swooping low. One landed on Toby's head. It lightened the mood, amusing everyone on board. Toby shouts, "Get off me, you stupid bird," He begins flapping his arms about to scare the bird, causing the boat to rock to and frow. This upset poor Fin Frazzle more than the bird itself. The seagull took flight, leaving Toby a nasty gift on top of his favourite hat.

Flanna tells him, "Give it here Toby." Toby obliges. Handing her his hat, she pulls out her handkerchief and dips it in the Ocean, cleaning the mess the bird left. "There now. All better. Pop that back on big man."

Toby gives her a bashful smile, tilting his head downward trying to hide his flushed cheeks under his hat. "Thank you, Flanna," he murmurs. Cuttlefish shouts from the back of the boat "We're coming up to Wickery Wreath soon. Please remove your coats, cloaks and hats and place them into the baskets below your feet. Any other belongings you won't want to get wet too. I've left some bags on the floor, and cotton towels for your journey home. The boat will remain here in this exact the same spot for your return."

The sound of a seashell horn can be heard coming from the distance. Everyone turns to look in its direction. As they draw closer, they can see a figure bobbing just above the water. Ten Salt Sea City guards appear, one by one, with silver spears cutting into the dancing waves. Their heads and shoulders are barely breaking the ocean top. Lining up, side by side, they each slowly rise from the water's surface. Each of them is holding a set of reigns. Once their torsos are

Chapter Fourteen

fully out of the water, giant creature's heads begin to appear from underneath the water's surface. Amazing, mystical sea creatures. Their heads look somewhat like a land horse and their body like that of a dolphin. It was the Dolfino. Magnificent animals, they each had their own unique colour. Not one was the same, each stunning in every way. Rising further up from the water, their tails were covered in an array of beautiful scales that sparkled almost like diamonds. Everyone on board were mesmerised by the creatures. They were a rare breed even amongst magickal folk.

The guards were large, looming over the small boat. They were adorned with white shell-shaped armour.

Cuttlefish smiled with pride. "It's time. Can you each take your potion on the count of three please. It's important you all drink them at the same time." Everyone was ready to do as instructed but Fin was still nervous. Cuttlefish looks at Fin. He could see by his little face he wasn't happy. "Fin," he says giving a reassuring smile. "We won't go until you're ready. I promise you there is nothing to fear. Once you're under water, the potion will make everyone the same size, reason being you all need to accommodate your Dolfino. Even the giant folk in attendance today will shrink in size."

Fin feels a little shaky. "I'll be the first fairy to do this you know. We Fey don't do water, not on top of it or most definitely not underneath it. Will the potion definitely work? I won't get carried away by the tide. If you haven't noticed I'm not exactly the biggest of the group."

Cuttlefish takes his hand. "I give you my word, the potion will work. Trust me. I promise I won't leave your side."

Fin nods. "Okay, just you say the word and I'll take the plunge."

Cuttlefish shouts, "Let's do this. On the count of three! A haon, a dò, a tri!"

Each of them drinks their potion, within moments their feet and hands begin to transform, their fingers and toes mould together, creating a type of shiny webbed foot effect, almost resembling duck's feet. Their necks change, with gills appearing on either side. One by one they jump overboard into the sea. Fin Frazzle hits the water and immediately begins to panic. He feels a hand take his. He turns to see Cuttlefish smiling at him with caring eyes.

"See, I told you not to worry," he grins. "Stay still, try not to move. I'll let you steady yourself first before we swim."

Fin felt comfort knowing Cuttlefish was looking after him.

After a few minutes in the water everyone was now ready to continue their journey. The guards swam toward them, presenting each of them with a Dolfino. Cuttlefish tells everyone "Just mount them as you would a land horse. It's pretty much the same thing. The Dolfino have a lovely temperament, and they are very friendly."

Each of the party take their Dolfino. Fin holds on to his mount and looks to Cuttlefish who gives him a wink. "I told you all would be okay. Now let's go

Chapter Fourteen

everyone. Salt Sea City is an hour from here and we have no time to waste."

The Dolfino rise above the sea surface. With everyone mounted, they were ready to go. Taking off with great speed, racing over high waves and strong winds, ducking and diving above and below the ocean, everyone holding on tight.

Eventually they reach Salt Sea City. Just as the sun was reaching the sky, a rainbow of colours could be seen spread across the seabed, with a white mist forming on top. Cuttlefish announces, "We are here everyone. We will now descend to our city below. Please dismount your beasts and follow me."

Once under water Cuttlefish leads the way with Fin close by his side. Using their newly formed hands and feet the group could easily manoeuvre their way through the water. Lights could be seen deep beneath the sea below.

Seawater flowed with every passing ripple. A variety of fish and sea creatures could be seen swimming around getting caught up in the underwater current. The further they descend, the brighter the lights become. A large wall made of various seashells surrounds the city, with guards posted along the outskirts. Enormous cream pearl gates stand in the centre of the entrance. Alongside it are two gigantic pillars, standing by each side. Sparkling lanterns sit on posts filled with flashing magickal sea mist, Each one pouring an abundance of amazing, bright, colourful lights.

As the group swim towards the gates, they begin to open slowly, allowing them to enter.

Cornelius, Georgette, Flanna and Fin have never travelled to the underwater city before. They were amazed by its astonishing beauty. The others in their party have visited the city in the past. Isadora had been only once, as a child with her parents. It is every bit as breathtaking now as it was back then. Once inside the gates of the city, Isadora takes the time to gaze at all it's beauty. Remembering the thrills she had the first time she had seen it. There were hundreds of seashell houses, lined with pretty pebble seabed pathways. Enormous columns made of coquina stood tall in front of large stately buildings. Gorgeous, green foliage with gold and copper coral lined the Fisherweed houses, with swaying seaweed in an abundance of many colours. So many shades of the ocean filling the streets with light.

Swimming through the City was a delight for the entire group. There was so much to see. They arrive at the city hall entrance.

"This is where I leave you friends. Lord Sharkconly will bring you in," Cuttlefish says.

Fin looks disappointed. "Wait, why?" he asks.

Cuttlefish replies "I've to run and errand to the royal jewellers. Not sure why. But I only do as I am asked. Lord Sharkconly will accompany you all".

Fin asks, "Will you be here after the meeting Cuttle?"

Cuttle nods, "Yes, I'll be here Fin. I'll be taking you back to the boat later. And I'll be staying with Toby when we return. He's going to put up with me for one more night".

Chapter Fourteen

Toby smiles. "Yes I am indeed. But you're doing the cooking this time. And don't forget to bring more of that fisherweed coil rum," he winks.

A voice speaks from across the street. "Ah there you all are." It is Lord Sharkconly, an older Fisherweed male. His long white flowing hair sweeping and swirling in formation behind him as he swims toward them. His upper body is strong with large shoulders and muscular arms. His tail is grey and smooth. It had a pattern of scattered white specks spread throughout. His fins were sharp like that of a whale shark and his torso was covered in body armour. It was pearlized white and it shone bright with glimpses of opal and moon stone. In his hand he held a long black triton.

"Welcome my friends! Welcome to Salt Sea City." He swims directly over to Lord Anthony and Lord Riverdale, hugging them each in turn. "Please introduce me to everyone."

Lord Anthony is happy to do so. "It's so good to see you again Sharky. It's been too long my friend. I just wish it was under better circumstances."

Lord Riverdale makes the introductions, then Lord Sharkconly welcomes each of them in turn. He tells the party to follow him, their destination being just around the next corner.

Georgette was astonished to see a magnificent, large building, even taller than the Belfast Albert Clock. Its columns were made of coral and calcite. It had enormous statues of Fisherweed warriors, men and women carved in white aragonite, holding spears with silver arrow tips. Its pathways were lined with white and silver pebbles and small peridotite stones, lights bouncing from every direction, filling the space with an abundance of brightness. Two silver decadent gates opened as they reached the end of the path. Inside the walls the area resembled a large stadium, with columns circling themselves around the building. In the centre of the circle sat a giant table made from coquina, and in its centre a carved embellishment of queen Shelleala with her baby.

Stools surrounded the table. Each seat was taken but ten seats remained empty. Every realm had sent advisers to attend the meeting. A Fisherweed guard sounded a large shell horn. A voice then commands, "Please take your seats."

The meeting begins.

Lord Sharkconly is the first to speak. He thanks everyone for attending. Then everyone takes turns to speak about what has taken place. Each person from each realm agreeing and disagreeing on many suggestions, plans of action and ideas. The arguments seem to go on forever.

Georgette could feel her frustration growing. This pointless quarrelling was wasting time. Rising up she commands, "Solos!" Her palms spark with flames. Isadora and Despina smile with pride. Not every witch or wizard could pull this off, lighting flames under water was a difficult task even for an elder. But Georgette Crescent was no ordinary witch. Her emotions have heightened her powers.

This took everyone by surprise. "Good. Now that I have your attention, I'd like to speak. You all know

Chapter Fourteen

why I am here. I'll get straight to the point. We need a Shamrock Contract as well as a Ripping spell."

Council members begin to shout. Lord Sharkconly raising his voice bellows, "Be quiet!

Let the witch speak."

Georgette nods to say thank you, then continues. "First of all, you know why we need the Shamrock Contract. It's the only thing we can use to lure Gregor out of hiding and to get him to agree on our plan. Second, we need a Ripping spell to strip Gregor of his power. I know it's asking a lot, but we need five more brave souls to sacrifice a piece of their power to make the spell work. Once we trap Gregor inside the hell dimension and strip him of his powers, he and the Johnagock will never return. The fair folk have offered a binding powder, but it won't be strong enough to strip his powers for long. We ourselves have two amazing, brave thoughtful people that have already offered to help with the ripping spell. Both are here today." She smiles in the direction of Hickory and Despina. "The first to offer his help was Hickory on behalf of the Wizards and then Despina on behalf of the Witches. We need five more volunteers, one from each realm to complete the spell. I know it's a lot to ask. Giving away a piece of your magic. It's a hard decision for anyone. But I must remind you, it's for the greater good. I am going into the Johnagock domain. I don't want to disrespect anyone here, but I need you all to agree. You all remember what it was like when the Johnagock were here in our world. Do you really want that to happen again." She eyes the room. "I promise, once I get back with Mia and Henry, we will lock this hell dimension forever. Gregor will be trapped and the Johnagock will never return to any of our realms ever again."

A few moments pass with quiet voices heard muttering and whispering around the table. Suddenly Seamus McDonough, an elder from the Leprechaun folk, stands up. He taps his shillelagh on the table. He is a small man with a strong Irish accent.

"I want to offer myself on behalf of the Irish Leprechauns. I'm almost five hundred years old. I'll be honoured to part with a little of my old magick for the greater good."

Lord Sharkconly stood up next. "I offer a piece of my magick on behalf of the Fisherweed people. I, too, am almost four hundred years old. I will be proud to help."

Cornelius nudges Georgette and whispers, "It's working Georgie."

A Giant seated next to Toby, raises his hand to his chest. "I, Harry Mulcahy, accept my part on behalf of the Giants."

Lord Riverdale stands. "Oh well, I might as well join in," he laughs. "Why not! But I must say I'm not as old as you lot, I am only three hundred years old, still in my prime."

This made everyone chuckle. He looks to Georgette. "I'll do what's right on behalf of the elves my dear."

Georgette speaks, "Thank you all so much, that just leaves us needing one more."

Chapter Fourteen

Poor Fin was the only fairy there. "I'll put myself forward on behalf of my people."

Georgette smiles. "Fin that's so noble of you and brave but I'm afraid you're not old enough. You're only fifty plus years old. It must be a fairy elder, but perhaps you can relay the request on to your elders when we return to dry land."

A soft gentle voice interrupts them. A beautiful woman rises from her seat. Her hair was long, coloured with a shade of silverish white. She has dark hazel green eyes and a perfect pink smile, with small, pointed ears.

"I volunteer on behalf of the forest folk." It was a pixie. Her name was Donna Velosa Evergreen. "A lady never reveals her age but let's just say I wish I was four hundred years old again," she giggles. "I can volunteer on behalf of not just my kind but my cousins too, the Fairies. So, young Fin Frazzle, you won't need to ask your elders to assist. But may I say thank you on their behalf, because that was very loyal and brave of you to offer your power, Fin."

Fin can feel his eyes begin to burn, feeling overwhelmed with pride hearing this.

A hooded figure at the far end of the table stands. Wearing a long silver cloak, its hood covering her eyes. Sliding the hood down slowly, to everyone's astonishment they couldn't believe their eyes. It was Queen Opala, great granddaughter of Queen Shelleala.

Her hair was snow white it fell gracefully in waves below her waist. She wore a gold crown. It was embellished with aquamarine gemstones, pearls and opals. Her eyes were ebony black with lips as red as blood dark roses.

"I'm sorry I had to remain in silence. I didn't want my presence to sway any decision made. But I feel there has been enough words spoken." She motions to Georgette. "Please come here, my dear. Let me introduce myself to you properly."

Georgette slowly makes her way towards the Queen. She bows to her. "Forgive me your, Majesty. I wasn't aware you would be here."

Queen Opala gracefully bows her head. "Shush now. No one knew I would be here, not even my own Council. I must tell you, I thought it was excellent how you got everyone's attention. I was very impressed with that underwater flame you conjured up young lady. Very impressed indeed. Not an easy task to do at such depths under the sea. You're quite a powerful intelligent young witch, I must say. But I need to move things along to a more serious matter. Let's talk about this binding Shamrock Contract. Tell me, Miss Crescent, do you really think Gregor will agree to your terms?"

Georgette truly felt this plan would work. With hope in her eyes she replies, "Yes, your Majesty I do."

Queen Opala takes a seat inviting Georgette to join her. She addresses the table "I have heard everyone's opinion's this morning. I feel that the Young Miss Crescents plan seems to be the only one I believe will work. I would also like to give thanks to all of you that have offered to partake in this Ripping spell. I do however have a request of my own. I believe each

Chapter Fourteen

realm should further help by giving Miss Crescent a gift of some sorts, to help her with her quest as she crosses the veil." Queen Opala takes Georgettes hands. She places a glowing clam in her open palm. Georgette places her finger on the clam and watches as it opens at her touch. Inside was a ring with a black ebony stone. "This was my great grandmother's. It is a protection stone. Within it, it holds the power of strength. It does only as its owner commands. The magick within it is very powerful and it will only work when needed to do good. I had it placed into a piece of jewellery this very day. Wear it my dear when you cross that veil. On behalf of the Fisherweed Kingdom and myself, I wish you well on this difficult journey ahead. I also give to you the Shamrock Contract."

Rolling out the contract Queen Opala presses her royal seal of approval upon it and places it in the middle of the table.

Each representative from each realm stood up. They offer their gifts. The Fey folk offer Fairy dust. A powerful broomstick is offered from the Witches. A black candle from the Wizards. A gold coin from the Leprechauns. A ball of twine from the forest folk. And finally, a small white flower from the Giants. Each places their gift in the centre of the table.

Queen Opala then asks if everyone agrees, and if so to raise their hand. Happy with the outcome Queen Opala nods and as each hand rises in approval their signature magically appears on the Shamrock Contract.

"Then its settled. Take these gifts, Miss Crescent, and use them when needed. You are a brave young lady and a very gifted Witch. I hope next time we meet it will be on a happier occasion my dear."

Georgette smiles, then thanks Queen Opala. The Queen addresses the table. "I'd like to thank all of you for attending this morning. I wish you all the very best of blessings. Please take a little time to enjoy my beautiful city while you are here. The potions you have taken will be in effect for another few hours. My guards will see you back to your boat when you are ready. Good day everyone."

Lord Sharkconly suggests, "For those of you that have never been here before may I suggest you take the remaining time to enjoy and appreciate this beautiful city. Unfortunately, we only have an hour to explore before we have to make the trip back to the boat. May I quickly say thank you and farewell to all in attendance here today. Let us hope the next time we meet the veil to the hell dimension is locked and sealed forever and the Johnagock will never return. I pray to the stars the Crescent family are reunited and Gregor gets the punishment he deserves. As for the Ripping spell, I say we do it the day before Georgette crosses the veil."

After a few moments Despina says, "I have an idea. Why not come to the school Carrickfergus Castle. I'd be more than happy to accommodate everyone. And the school will have all the ingredients needed to perform the spell."

An excited Hickory agrees, "Excellent idea."

As they start to leave each of the gifts is put into a bag for Georgette. The bag is only the size of her hand. It was, of course, enchanted. Small but powerful

Chapter Fourteen

enough to hold everything and more for her crossing. Georgette thanks each person as they pass her. Taking the clam out of the bag, opening it, she examines the ring gifted by Queen Opala. Cornelius snatches it from her hand and grins. "Hold out your finger," he tells her. "Pick whichever hand you prefer," he laughs. Georgette looks at both her hands, then looks at Cornelius.

Raising one eyebrow suspiciously she replies, "Just give me it. I'll do it myself." Holding out her right hand she puts the ring on her index finger.

Cornelius winks at her in approval. I knew you'd pick that hand and that finger. You're so fond of pointing it in my direction all the time, especially when you're scolding me," he mocks.

Georgette looks at him for a brief moment. "Shut up."

Cornelius mimics her voice, "Shut up, Cornelius. Yes, yes, I know," he laughs. "Let's go, the others are waiting."

Chapter Fifteen

Waiting outside with a great big smile was Cuttlefish, happy to see everyone again.

"Well tell me," he asks hopefully. "Did they agree to the plan?"

Fin who is much more relaxed now answers him with a smile. "Yes, they all agreed. We have the seal of approval from the Queen herself. We have an hour to explore the city. Can I possibly ask you to show me around Cuttle? I would love to know more about your home. It's such a beautiful place."

Cuttlefish, blushing, agrees. "Fin I would be honoured to show you. Just follow me. I've so much to squeeze into less than an hour." Cuttlefish swims past in a hurry and grabs Fin by the hand as they head off, happy in each other's company.

Everyone else partnered up. Toby and Flanna, Hickory and Despina, Cornelius with Georgette. Looking around, Lord Anthony announces, "That just leaves us Isadora. Would you like to join myself and Lord Riverdale? We are going to the library. It's got the most amazing collection of history books. We are hoping to borrow a few."

Isadora answers, "Why yes, of course. I would be delighted."

Chapter Fifteen

Cornelius holds out his hand to take Georgettes. She places her hand in his. He grins, "Well now, where too first Miss Crescent."

Georgette frowns. "We only have an hour, where do you suggest?"

Cornelius answers, "I think it might be a good idea to see the salt sea coral caves. They're made from emerald rock crystals. And that's not all. The royal musicians apparently practice there. I'd love to hear them play. My mother told me she never forgot how amazing they were when she saw them as a child. What do you think?"

Georgette looks at Cornelius. She could see he really wanted to go so she agreed. She was eager to get home to Belfast and put their plans into motion. Honestly, she was in no mood for sightseeing. But she knew she had to pass an hour and she didn't want to disappoint Cornelius. Putting on her happy face she agrees to accompany him.

The cave was covered in emeralds, green sparkling light filling it as far as the eye could see. Once inside there were lots of little caverns splitting off into different paths. Every type of green gemstone filled its walls, jade, amazonite, tourmaline, and alexandrite. Too many gems to mention. As they swam deeper into the cave, the soft, sweet sound of singing could be heard echoing throughout the walls, with tingling tones of chimes starting to play deep within the cave. The music was so tranquil.

"Which path should we take?" Georgette asks Cornelius.

"Let's just follow the sound of this heavenly music," he answers.

They swim down the narrow middle corridor, white thick sand beneath them with walls sparkling on each side. The music getting louder as they reached the end of the narrow path. An enormous open cavern appears with an array of stones in a circle. It was huge, big enough to hold at least five thousand souls. Aquamarine blue waves of light slid back and forth, shimmering in motion above their heads as they draw closer to the beautiful sounds. Georgette was stunned by its size and beauty. The musicians were sat in the middle of the cavern, neatly in three rows with a conductor placed in front. The choir of Fisherweed singing under water was so blissful and relaxing with musical instruments harmonizing perfectly alongside their voices. It gave Georgette goosebumps. She and Cornelius stay hidden at the back of the cave. They take a seat next to each other. Georgette rests her head on his shoulder. He takes her hand.

"I know you didn't want to go sightseeing," he says.

Surprised she asks him, "How did you know?"

He shrugs, "I know what you're like. You probably wanted to return home as soon as possible. So I thought this would be perfect. I know we can't leave without everyone else so this was the best thing I could think of to help the time pass faster for you. I was hoping it would help you relax. Plus, you know my ideas are always the best," he gloats.

Chapter Fifteen

Georgette rolls her eyes then smiles. Telling him to be quiet she suggests, "Let's just listen to the music, no talking smarty pants."

Cornelius wraps his big arm around her, pulling her close to him. "Okay, I'll shut up. But only because you asked so nicely. And also because I want to listen as well."

Georgette closes her eyes, enjoying the sweet sounds of the choir and the orchestra.

Chapter Sixteen

The hour passed quickly. They all returned to meet up again. The ten Salt Sea guards were waiting with their Dolfinos. They all mount the sea creatures and set off leaving this beautiful city behind them. The guards take them as far as the Fisherweed borders. They are told to continue their journey with Cuttlefish leading the way.

The sun is high in the sky, beams of sunlight sparkling through the surface, waves crashing with each ripple, creating dazzling bubbles. The group break through the water's surface, cold air immediately hitting their faces with the cooling sea breeze. They can feel the warmth of the sun drying their skin. As each person breaks through the water they take a deep breath, filling their lungs with fresh sea air.

Toby shouts, "Oh, it's so good to be home. Above the Irish waves, on top of Ireland's waters."

Cuttlefish shouts, "Who's up for a race? Let us see who's got the fastest Dolfino," he grins.

Cornelius grabs hold of his reigns first. "I'm in," he shouts. He was always very competitive.

Toby yells, "Me to."

Fin laughs, "Let's make a wager. Ten coins to the winner. Whoever reaches Toby's boat first."

Chapter Sixteen

Excited, Flanna wants to take part. "Hey now, wait just a minute lads. No one asked us ladies if we wanted to join in. And what about the older folks."

Isadora grunts, "Excuse me. Less of the old, please."

Cornelius laughs. "Okay, Flanna. You're in. What about you Georgie?"

She shouts, "Oh go on then, I might as well."

Isadora tells them, "Line up and I'll start you off. No cheating. On your marks, Get ready, Go"

Off they go in a flash, each one rushing through the giant waves, riding the current with the Dolfino occasionally diving under the waves then springing up high above the ocean, leaping out of the water.

Cornelius looks at Georgette. She was right behind him, her hair drying in the wind and her cheeks glowing. He loved watching her enjoy herself.

Taking the lead was Cuttlefish. Toby yells, "I see my boat. Look, she's dead ahead lads. Come on ladies."

They push on at speed, each one hoping to win. But it is Cuttlefish in front. He gets there first, followed by Cornelius and Georgette, then Toby, Flanna and Fin. They all enjoyed the race. It lifted everyone's spirits. Cuttlefish screams with excitement. "I won! I can't believe, I won!" He does a little victory dance in the water. This makes Fin giggle.

"That was great fun wasn't it? Better than any land horse, that's for sure. Pay up land lovers," he shouts with pride.

Toby huffs, "Next time we can even the playing field. It will be on dry land and with horses. I'll win my coin back, you can be sure on that my friend."

Cuttlefish laughs harder. "I'll hold you to it Toby. Now let's get you all onboard. There are soft towels in bags, and I left a flask of rum to warm you all up."

Once on board and everyone dried off, Cornelius takes the oars.

Isadora asks, "So what's happening once we dock?"

Georgette replies, "We all stay together. Come to the clock tower. We will eat, rest and discuss our next move."

Toby adds, "We contact Brigadier 'Slopfish Face'. We catch him and get this plan in motion."

Isadora goes into hysterics laughing "Slopfish? Really Toby?" she giggles.

Toby grunts, "I've worse names for that man. I'm just being polite in front of you ladies."

Cornelius climbs out of the boat first. He helps the women onto the dock. Gathering outside Toby's house, loud barks and howling could be heard coming from inside. Big Tuckers face can be seen peering through the window, snot dripping from his snout, smearing the glass panes. Toby looks at him. "Look at the big eejitt. The mess he's made of my windows."

Toby opens the front door. Tailsa runs out first to greet Georgette, followed by Nora then Tucker. Georgette walks into the house to find poor Bijou curled up on the same spot near the fireplace. He looks so sad and distant. Georgette walks over to him lifting him up into her arms. She kisses his head and whispers, "Please don't give up hope Bijou. I promise I'll get Mia back soon." Hugging him tight, she sets him on the floor. "Let's get you home."

Chapter Sixteen

The walk back to Albert Clock was pleasantly distracting. Everyone joining in on each other's conversation. The mood had certainly lifted from this morning. Georgette unlocks the door. She enters the hallway first and commands, "Solos." The room lights up. "Come in everyone. Make yourselves comfortable in the parlour please. Izzy can you and Despina cast a spell to widen the space. I'll put some tea on."

Once everyone was settled and seated, Isadora lights the fire and prepares the table for a spot of food. Georgette was in the kitchen with Tailsa, Bijou, Tucker and Nora. They were all curled up on the rug, snuggling together. Kneeling down Georgette looks at Bijou. She feels so sorry for him. She knows he is missing Amelia just as much as she is. Although Georgette took comfort in knowing as long as Bijou was still alive, it meant Amelia was alive too. A Shadow cats life essence is connected to that of their Witch or Wizard. They only live as long as their soul mates. Forever bonded in life and the afterlife as well.

Georgette takes a steadying breath. "Amelia is still alive, so there is hope," she whispers to herself.

Cornelius enters the kitchen. "Who you talking to, Georgie?"

Startled she answers, "No one Cornelius, just checking on the Shadows."

Cornelius pets Bijou. "How's he doing?"

Georgette looks at Cornelius, managing to hold back her tears. Smiling she says, "He's sad, Cornelius we all are. I feel his sorrow. Its heavy but I promised him, I'll get Mia back. I'm feeling hopeful now, more than ever."

Cornelius holds out his hand to help her up. Giving Bijou one last kiss on his head, she takes Cornelius' hand as he helps her rise from the floor. "Let's get this tea into the parlour. There are some biscuits on the table that need brought in as well. She smiles as she lifts a tray of scones.

Cornelius takes the tea tray and nods. He jokes in a sarcastic tone, "Come on then, let's give everyone a nice cup of your hot delicious tea! We can compare it to your wonderful coffee."

Georgette raises one eyebrow. "Oh, so you don't like my coffee now."

Cornelius laughs raising his eyebrow to mimic her. "I've never enjoyed your coffee woman. It's so strong you could practically stand on it," he smirks bumping her with his hip.

Georgette can't shout at him or keep a straight face. He looks so goofy standing there in the doorway, holding the tray, being his usual daft, silly self. "Shut up Cornelius, or ill serve you salt water next. See what tastes better then?" She bumps him back with her hip, gesturing him to move out of her way. As she walks past, Cornelius takes a moment to watch her walk away. She turns around. "Hey Cornelius, what are you looking at?" she asks.

Grinning and winking he says, "Just admiring the view woman."

"Oh, for goodness sake! Get in there." She pushes him into the parlour room.

Chapter Sixteen

Georgette sets down her teacup. "All right now. Can I first say thank you to all of you for everything you've done to help my family and me. I'd like to move on with this plan to entice Gregor. I would like to propose we try and contact him through the Celtic table. The day before the full moon. We offer the Shamrock Contract to reel him in first, and convince him to blame everything on Lady Celine. It will give him time to think things over. He won't agree to anything right away, so let's tease him with the contract first. I think it's been a long day for everyone, let's all take tomorrow to rest up and gather our strength. We don't know what will come at us once this veil is open".

Isadora says, "Let's get you all home. I'm sure you're tired and need your own beds." She asks Georgette to take everyone up and send them through the passers door. "I'll wash up the dishes. Cornelius, you can help me." They move into the kitchen.

Toby was sitting by the fireplace in the large white rocking chair. He lights his tobacco pipe and settles back in his seat taking a moment to enjoy the quiet. Closing his eyes, he listens to the sound of the firewood crackling on the hearth. He feels a wetness brush his hand, it is big Tucker. Toby smiles, "Hello my big lad, did those stinky cats kick you out of the kitchen? Never you mind them," he comforts Tucker, petting his head. "Just you lay yourself down next to me by the fire".

Meanwhile Isadora is in the kitchen with Cornelius. She tells him to take a seat at the table. Cornelius concerned asks, "What's wrong, mother? You look so serious."

Isadora takes his hand. "I am so worried my son. I wish it was me going with Georgette. She's been through so much ever since we lost Mary and Sean. It's not fair to have lost so much for someone so young. She's a beautiful girl, inside and out."

Cornelius can't help but smile. "Mother, Georgette is the strongest woman I've ever known. She will get through this. I just know she will. And yes, very easy on the eye, but don't tell her I said that," he chuckles.

Isadora pats his hand. "You love her, don't you?"

Cornelius looks at his mother with a seriousness to his face. "I've loved that woman since the first day I saw her. And more and more every day since."

Isadora fills with emotion. "Then what's taking you so long to wed the girl? She's clearly smitten with you too darling."

Cornelius gives a half-hearted smile. "Is she though, sometimes I think she is, then other times I feel her holding back. Maybe she only wants our close friendship." He runs his hands through his hair. "I don't know. I think part of me is frightened. I don't want to ruin the relationship we have."

Isadora places her hand on his cheek. "You'll never know, unless you try."

Chapter Seventeen

Georgette had made her way back downstairs. She smiles, seeing Toby dozing in his rocking chair. "He must be worn out," she thinks to herself. She lifts a blanket and drapes it over him, then quietly makes her way into the kitchen.

"Well, what's going on here then? You both look so serious." Looking from Cornelius to Isadora she continues, "Are you both okay?"

Isadora stands up and walks towards her. She gives her a tight hug. Georgette embraces the hug and looks toward Cornelius for an explanation. She silently mouths to him, "What's wrong with your mother?"

Cornelius shrugs saying under his breath, "How should I know?"

Isadora releases Georgette then asks, "Are you hungry? There's some leftover stew, or should I say there's mountains of left over stew. Flanna is worse than Toby, they cook like they're feeding an army."

Cornelius, amused, answers, "That's not a bad thing."

Georgette tells them Toby and Tucker are out for the count in the parlour room. "Let the big man sleep, it will do him good."

Cornelius says, "Mother, you look tired too. Why don't you get an hour's rest? I can wake you for supper if you like."

Isadora answers, "Yes, I think I will darling. What about you, Georgie? Are you not tired my dear?"

Georgette shakes her head. "No, Izzy. I'm grand thank you. I think I need a walk. It will help me sleep tonight. I'll take Bijou and Tailsa for a stroll around the docks. Would you like to join me, Cornelius?"

Cornelius' eyes light up at the invite. "Yes, I will join you. But let me send a quick cinder note to granny. She's minding our shadows. She thinks we're all on a trip to New York," he laughs. "We didn't want to worry her with the truth."

Isadora dramatically rolls her eyes. "Keep it short. You know what's she's like for gossip."

Cornelius jokingly stands to attention and salutes, "Yes ma'am." Then he marches out of the room.

Georgette covers her mouth to contain her laughter. "There isn't a serious bone in that man's body, is there?" Isadora asks.

Georgette replies, "No ma'am"

"Oh, for heaven's sake he's rubbing off on you now too," Georgette helps Isadora up, "Go get some rest, we will wake you when we return." She smiles as Isadora leaves the room and heads upstairs.

Georgette walks to the potion room. Cornelius had just sent his cinder note. Standing up he helps Georgette put on her cloak, draping it over her shoulders. Georgette lifts her wide brim witches' hat. Placing it on top of her head and tilting it to one side.

Chapter Seventeen

She turns around and looks at Cornelius, placing her hands on both hips, striking a pose.

"Well, will I do, Mr Delaney?" she asks.

He smiles that cheeky smile that he only gives Georgette, saying, "Yes Miss Crescent. You'll do just fine."

Gathering their Shadows from the kitchen, Cornelius opens the door, and they quietly leave the clock tower.

Once outside Cornelius takes Georgette's hand and places it on his arm. "Are you warm enough?" he asks. "It is a little nippy," he continues.

There was a slight chill to the air, but Georgette found it quite nice. "I'm fine, thank you," she replies.

As they approach the docks, the street lanterns are being lit for the night ahead. Soft glows of orange and yellow come from each glass case at the top of the lampposts. Horses trailing carriages and fancy shiny cars travelling along old, cobbled streets can be seen across the veil. Ladies with enormous hats and strange moving objects called penny farthing bicycles wobbled past as they crossed the road.

"I'll never understand why Mia finds the veil people so fascinating," Georgette states. "She just loves the style and these strange vehicles they invent. Give me a broomstick any day."

Georgette thinks aloud, "Cornelius, do you miss living here on this side of the veil? I watch the veil people at times, I see them even now, as they pass through us, blissfully unaware of the magickal veil separating us from their world. They're always in such a hurry. Their lives are so short and yet they live each day, the same as the day before."

Cornelius thinks about this before he answers her. "I know they can't see us, and we pass through them like a cloud of smoke, but somehow my mother and father found each other and fell completely in love with one another."

Georgette interrupts, "Oh my goodness. I didn't mean to sound so judgemental. I know your father is a veil man. An amazing man of medicine. He is a brilliant doctor. So caring and full of life. It's easy to see how much they both love each other, but doesn't it frighten you to know his life will be short lived compared to that of your mother?"

Cornelius shakes his head. "It doesn't, it really doesn't, Georgie. Across the veil in the human realm, we live life day by day, but on this side of the veil people don't appreciate everyday life. They constantly worry about the future. Life is for living Georgie. Enjoy every day, that's what my father always tells me."

Georgette curiously asks. "Will you remain across the veil when this is all over? Do you think you'll ever live here again?"

Cornelius ponders this. "I'm not sure. It all depends."

Georgette raises one eyebrow. "Depends on what Cornelius?"

Grinning he says, "That's a conversation for better times. Let's head back home. I am getting hungry. Which means big Toby will be awake soon, and no doubt looking his grub."

Chapter Seventeen

Toby awakens to the sound of the front door opening. Georgette and Cornelius enter the room.

"Hello, you two," Toby stretches his arms above his head. "Where did you young ones get to?"

Cornelius answers, "Just a wee walk into town. It's a bit nippy out there. I'll get more logs on the fire. It's starting to die down. Is my mother still resting?"

Georgette takes off her hat and cloak. "I'll go up and wake her. If I don't, she won't sleep tonight."

Toby stands up and stretches once more. "I'll go fix us some grub. Are you all hungry?"

Cornelius rubs his belly. "Why even ask? I'm always hungry."

Toby chuckles. "I'll go see what's in the kitchen, maybe heat that stew up."

A short time later, Isadora comes downstairs with Georgette. Isadora asks Cornelius, "What's that lovely smell?"

Cornelius smacks his lips. "That would be Toby in the kitchen. He's heating left overs and heaven knows what else. I am so hungry, I'll take whatever is given to me."

A while later that evening, everyone's bellies were full. Toby had made a small feast. No food went to waste. They all sat in the parlour relaxed, enjoying each other's company. Toby sang a few old Irish songs and Cornelius played along with a bodhran drum that he found in the bedroom he was staying in. Georgette laughed when he first brought it downstairs.

"Oh my goodness, that was my fathers. My mother disliked it very much, very much indeed," she laughs at the fond memory.

Isadora giggles, "I remember it well. Bless him, he was an amazing man and gifted wizard. But he wasn't gifted in music or at playing any musical instruments for that matter. He did it anyway and it drove poor Mary up the clock walls every time he took it out."

Georgette is overjoyed. "I am just so pleased its finally getting a chance to be played again, and played well too might I add," she smiles at Cornelius.

The clock strikes ten o'clock and everyone is looking forward to their beds. Toby stands up. "I'll be doing my rounds shortly," he announces. He calls big Tucker. "Come on boy, lets be going now. Thank you, my lovely friends, for quite an enjoyable evening. Get yourself to bed and gather all your strength for the days ahead. I'll call back tomorrow afternoon around two o'clock. Goodnight, ladies and young sir." He tips his hat as he exits into the hallway.

Cornelius follows shortly behind to lock the door, then locks the gates, securing the tower for the night. Everyone is exhausted after too much food and Salt Sea rum. They are all ready to retire for the night. Making their way upstairs, as the last candle is blown out, the clock tower is silent.

Chapter Eighteen

The next morning Georgette was the first to rise. She was always the first up in the morning. She makes a large pot of coffee and set to work making fresh scones and soda bread. Everyone's favourite!

Reminiscing, she remembers the last morning she was baking in the kitchen. Amelia was there, teasing her about Cornelius coming to visit. She giggled out loud thinking about the flowery mess she'd made, and how funny her sister thought it was. She remembers Amelia's laughter and how she lit up every room. It was a bittersweet memory.

Loud footsteps were heard coming down the stairwell. "That will be Cornelius," she thought.

Cornelius greets her as he enters the kitchen. "Soda bread and scones Miss Crescent. You spoil me!"

"They're not all for you," she shouts, swatting his hand away as he tries to lift a scone. "They're still cooling. You'll turn your tongue to sandpaper if you eat one now," she warns.

Cornelius pouts. Ignoring him she says, "I made your favourite coffee, it's in the kettle. I was sure to add extra saltwater, just how you like it," she grins slyly.

Amused Cornelius grabs a cup. "You've been busy. What time did you rise?" he asks.

"Oh, around six this morning. Is your mother awake yet?" Georgette wonders.

"Good grief no!" says Cornelius. "She hates early mornings. I'd say give her at least another hour. How are you coping with all this, Georgie? Are you okay?"

Turning to him she says, "I'm okay, Cornelius. I do really hope we are right about Gregor though. As long as he opens that veil, nothing else matters."

Cornelius gives her a reassuring look. "Georgie, I can't see him turning down this offer. He's not a daft man. He will take the deal, trust me. Now, let's get that dusty old Celtic table out and placed in the room. In the meantime, try not to worry until there's something to worry about." Taking her hands in his he whispers, "I just wish it was me going into that hell dimension with you. I won't rest until I know you're back safe in my arms."

Georgette gives him a gentle hug. "I know Cornelius, I feel the same way, the quicker we get in the closer we will be to having Amelia and Henry home."

A loud rumble is heard coming from Cornelius stomach. "In the meantime, woman, get those delicious scones over here. I'm wasting away," he jokes.

Georgette hands him a tray of food. Stuffing the remainder of the scone into his mouth he says, "Toby will be overjoyed to know you're baking again. He will probably smell it from the docks," he laughs as he devours another piece of soda bread.

Chapter Eighteen

The day ahead dragged on. Georgette kept looking at the clock. She cleaned the clock tower from top to bottom, trying to keep busy. Cornelius did offer several times to take her for a long walk, but she didn't accept.

Isadora asked if she would like to cross the veil with her, she had to pop back home and see Francis.

Georgette replied, "No thank you. I'd rather be on this side of the veil just in case anything should happen."

Cornelius had a thought. "Let me take you for a walk into town. You have been up since the crack of dawn, Georgie, and you need out of these walls for a while. Oh, and here's a thought. Why don't you pick up a few things for Mia's return, little gifts perhaps?"

Georgette beams from ear to ear. "Yes!" she gasps. "That's a fantastic idea. Why didn't I think of that sooner. I remember Mia wanting one of the fairies' oil paintings, from the Mystique Enchantments shop. I wasn't paying much attention to her the last time we were in there. Hopefully they still have them. I'll go get my hat and cloak."

Isadora' nods, smiling at Cornelius. "Well-done darling."

Cornelius and Georgette leave together arm and arm. "Where would you like to go first Georgie?" He asks.

"I've two shops in mind, Cornelius. Annie Reilly's, then Mystique Enchantments of course. I need new duck feather pillows for Amelias bedroom. I'll get them from old Annie's shop, then spend a little more time next door in Mystique Enchantments."

"Okay then, let's go Miss Crescent."

The sun was still shining. It was a lovely day. A short time later they arrive in town. The two magick shops were next door to each other.

Walking side by side, Georgette and Cornelius head into Annie's shop first. Annie the owner was standing at the counter. She was an older elf with grey hair, bright blue eyes, pointed ears, and she wore a smart green dress with a white apron. Smiling as Georgette enters, she says, "Hello you two. How can I help you?"

Georgette waves, "Hello Annie. I need new pillows and a soft throw. And some yarn please."

Annie walks to gather the items. "Coming right up my dear." Annie wraps everything in brown paper and neatly ties the packages with string.

Georgette lifts her little purse from her cloak pocket. "How much do I owe you, Annie?"

Annie pats Georgette's hand. "Not a penny young lady, take these bits and pieces as a gift."

Taken aback, Georgette says, "No, no, no! I couldn't possibly! Please let me pay."

Old Annie just shakes her head. "Don't be silly dear." Annie pushes the packages towards Cornelius. "Now master Cornelius. Please take these. Please! you carry them for Miss Crescent." Walking to the other side of the counter Annie looks directly at Georgette. "I miss young Mia too. I can't even contemplate how you feel my dear Georgette. Mia was in my shop at least once a week. We all know what you're trying to do, and the entire magickal community of Belfast are backing you. I think you're so brave. I can't do anything to help

Chapter Eighteen

so please let an old elf feel good today and take these gifts. The new pillows and blankets will help comfort your sister when you get her home."

Georgette bends down and places a gentle kiss on her cheek. "Thank you, Annie. That's very thoughtful."

As they leave the shop, Cornelius winks at Annie, mouthing, "Thank you," as he closes the shop door behind them.

They make their way next door to Mystique Enchantments. This was one of Amelia's favourite shops in Belfast. Janet the shop owner opened the door for them. She could sense them coming. Janet knew of their situation, as did all the magick folk in Belfast. She puts her arms out to hug Georgette as soon as she walks through the door. Janet has known the Crescent Sisters since they were little girls. Their mother Mary would always treat them to something in the shop when they would visit. Janet was about the same age as Isadora. Her hair was jet black, long, and shiny, like strands of silk. Her eyes were dark green. She always wore a long black dress with Celtic embroidery along the neckline. Her Tara brooch was gold with a beautiful green serpentine stone.

Georgette breathes in her sent as she hugs her. It reminds her of her own mother. "Come in miss Georgette. I'm so pleased to see you." Janet calls her daughter Becky telling her to go into the storeroom and get the Crescent Witches order.

Georgette has a puzzled expression on her face. Confused she tells Janet, "I don't remember placing an order, Janet."

Becky gives a sympathetic smile. "It was Amelia's order." Janet sighs, "Forgive me. Yes, of course it is. I thought you knew Georgette," Janet smiles. "Come with me and I'll show you." Becky opens a black door at the far end of the shop. Mystique Enchantments had just about everything a Witch or Wizard could ever need. It was a small shop but every single part of it was filled with amazing merchandise. Heading towards the door, Janet leads Georgette and Cornelius through.

The room was breathtaking. Once they crossed over the doorway, on the other side was a small, enchanted forest, with grey stone walls covered in ivy and various wildflowers. An illusion spell had been cast over the room, turning the ceiling into a glorious midnight blue sky, twinkling with a soft glow of a thousand stars and illuminating the forest around them. Its floor was cobbled with moss growing in between each brick. An old, round, wooden table sat in the centre of the room, its roots buried deep beneath the ground below their feet. There was a single, large, purple candle placed in the middle of the table. In the far corner of the forest sat a black raven, perched on top of the branches of an old willow tree. Below the tree lay two black shadow cats. Becky raises both hands and commands, "Solos!". The room blazes to life, with light coming from tiny fireflies surrounding the forest, and the candle in the centre of the room ignites. The raven squawks loudly, then spreads its wings, taking flight it rises high, into the twinkling sky above.

Becky places both her hands on the wall and chants:

Chapter Eighteen

As above so below
open door lock and key
present this parcel
for all to see

The wall behind Becky suddenly splits, causing a large crack in the stone. The wall begins to separate, creating an opening. A white mist begins to fall around the wall, swirling around the forest floor and unveiling a brown parcel. Slowly the mist surrounds the parcel, levitating it towards Becky. Gently taking hold of the parcel she hands it to her mother. Cornelius takes Georgette's hand as Janet carefully sets the package on the table.

"Would you like to open it? she asks Georgette. Walking to the table, Georgette traces her hands along the parcel loosening the string. Unfolding the wrappings, Georgette smooth's out the brown paper and smiles happily. She looks from the opened parcel to Becky and then to Janet. A little white box with a small bag of scented candles sits on the table.

Becky explains, "That's a little bird house trinket box. You can use them for jewellery or spells or keys. They can be used for lots of things, but Amelia told me she wanted to surprise you."

Emotional, Georgette opens the little white box. It was so delicate. Kissing it, she whispers under her breath, "I love it, Mia. Thank you, sister."

Cornelius puts his arm around her waist, giving her a gentle squeeze.

Janet smiles. "Now, let's get these wrapped up again and popped into a basket. I need to show you something else."

They leave the room and enter the shop again. "Look at these," she says, pointing to the shop window. There lay little oil paintings, the size of your hand, on tiny easels. Beautiful artwork, handcrafted by Frazzle Fairies.

Janet takes three paintings out of the window display and hands them to Georgette telling her, "The last day Amelia was here, she told me she adored these. So I would like to give you three, as a gift from me and Becky."

Georgette giggles, "Yes, I remember. She told me about these, and I was hoping they were still in stock. Thank you, Janet. You're very thoughtful." She then hands Cornelius the basket and hugs Janet, then Becky. "They really are beautiful. I'll be sure to put one into my sister's bedroom. Can I ask why you gifted me three paintings Janet? Not that I'm complaining," Georgette asks curiously.

Janet just gives a warm smile. "I'm not exactly sure. I just feel like three is the right number. Three is a lucky number after all, don't you agree?"

Janet then slips a tiny glass vile of black salt into Georgette's hand. She then gently squeezes her palm. "Stay safe. I pray to the moon and stars you find Mia."

Cornelius opens the door as they say their goodbyes.

Chapter Nineteen

It wasn't long before they arrived back at Albert Clock. Georgette went straight up to Amelia's bedroom and carefully placed the little Frazzle Fairy oil paintings and trinket box on her bedside table. She then puts the new pillow and soft blanket on her bed. She spent a lot of time in Amelia's bedroom, most of the morning. She wanted it clean and tidy for Amelias return.

Cornelius was by her side all day. Mostly getting in her way, but Georgette didn't really mind. She kept finding chores for him as well. Truthfully, she was glad of his company.

Finally, the clock struck two o'clock. "Thank goodness," she thought as she plates the pastries and prepares everything for her guests. Tidying her hair up in a neat bun, she dusts down her dress and lifts her keys.

"I'll go up now and let the first lot of our guests pass. Cornelius, you listen for the front door please. Your mother and Toby should arrive soon." She then climbs the spiral staircase.

A loud knock on the door. Cornelius didn't need to guess who that could be. "It will be big Toby. He thought that man's fists are like big old shovels. He nearly takes the door off its hinges every time he knocks on the wood."

Cornelius opens the door. His mother greets him with a gentle hug. "Hello my darling, give your mother a kiss." He bends down, "Hello mother." He pecks her on the cheek, asking how his father is doing. "He's fine, dear. I've had the cats sent back home to keep your father company and to be honest I feel better knowing they're with him, it's probably safer."

Cornelius agrees. "Very good mother, now move on in woman. Let's not take all day." Placing his hands on either side of her waist he lifts her high up in the air, setting her over the threshold. "There now mother, in you go." She shoves him as she passes him telling him to behave.

Big Toby was next to enter the house, then Cuttlefish following behind him. Toby sticks his nose up in the air sniffing excitedly. "Oh, is that fresh baked goodies I smell?"

Cornelius laughs. "Yes, it is. But don't even think of touching any or Georgette will have my head. You will have to wait like everyone else big man."

Toby grunts, walking past him.

Cornelius looking down greets Cuttlefish. "Hello Cuttle, And how are you?"

Cuttle looks up. "I am great young sir. Nervous about the outcome today, but ready all the same."

He walks into the hallway. Cornelius locks the door.

Isadora had already cast the spell to widen the parlour room. Georgette was now coming down the

Chapter Nineteen

stairs. Lord Anthony enters with Flanna and Lord Riverdale closely behind her.

Flanna glances at Toby and he smiles at her with a great big grin. Georgette shouts to Isadora, "Can you please bring the trays in from the kitchen with tea and coffee. Cornelius, go and help your mother."

Cornelius rolls his eyes saying, "She's bossing me about something shocking all day, Toby" Cuttlefish burst out laughing. Georgette lets the last of their guests pass through. It was, Hickory, Fin, and Despina.

Despina stops Georgette before entering the parlour room. "I know you're a very smart woman, and a very gifted witch. Remember Gregor can be cunning. I want you to be prepared before you make contact. Just because he's older, doesn't mean he's smarter. Stand your ground and get him to give you what you want. You are in control not him."

Georgette hugs Despina. "You always know the right things to say. Let's go in and get this started."

The Celtic table is placed in the centre of the room. Georgette unties the ribbon around her neck. Removing her Tara brooch, she places it in the centre of the table.

In times of fear
take us here
present your brooch
call the host

The room stays silent. She calls again. Toby on his guard, cautiously scans the room.

Suddenly a cold breeze enters the room. Then an old, husky voice echoes throughout the walls. "Hello Georgette." It is Gregor!!!

"Clever girl. I was wondering how long it would take you to remember the Celtic table is the only way to contact me."

Georgette clenches her fists. "Gregor, I'll get straight to the point. I have a deal to offer you."

His voice was condescending. This made Georgettes temper flare.

"A deal? I don't need any deal girl. No one can find me. My magick is powerful enough to conceal me. What could you possibly have to offer me?"

Georgette sharply interrupts. "I'm offering you a binding Shamrock Contract."

The room was so quiet you could hear a pin drop. "Don't lie to me girl." His tone had changed. Georgette knew she had him.

"I'm not lying, Gregor". A moment of silence passes. "I know someone of your stature couldn't get a Shamrock Contract without help. Only someone in a position of power could retrieve such a thing. So out with it, Miss Crescent, explain yourself. Give me the details and be quick about it," he demands.

"I have Lord Riverdale and Lord Anthony with me. The Shamrock Contract comes with certain conditions," she explains.

"What conditions?" he asks frustrated.

"I want my sister back. And Henry. I want you to open the veil and let me and Toby pass. We alone will go in together to rescue them. We also want any remaining potions you have left to ensure we all make it back safely."

Gregor laughs wickedly. "Is that all you ask? Tell me, how will I know if the contract is real?"

Georgette answers, "I personally went to Salt Sea City. Queen Opala stamped it with her own royal seal. All seven realms signed it. This is my proposal. I meet with you tonight. I bring Toby for protection. Toby will show you the scroll in person. You will know looking at it, that its authentic. You're a smart man. You will know immediately it's not a fake."

There was silence again for several moments while Gregor considers the proposal. "So let me get this straight. If this is real, I'm a free man. I am cleared of any wrongdoing. I keep my good name, my wealth, my position in the Causeway army?"

Georgette getting impatient snaps, "Yes all of it!"

Gregor interrupts. "But what about Lady Celine and the others. They will go against me."

Georgette's anger has reached its limit. "We've already thought about this. We propose you blame everything on Lady Celine. We will back your story up. I'm sure you'll think of something convincing. We will leave that part up to you. It's only a story to convince the public you're innocent. The higher powers and people that count already know you're a lying snake. I take my full powers back tomorrow on the harvest moon. I want to cross the veil afterwards. For our own protection, the contract will be torn in two halves by your own hand. Toby will take one half and you hold on to the other. You will get the other half back upon our return. You're more than capable of mending the scroll afterward. This is your last chance, Gregor. I won't offer you this deal again."

Gregor answers through gritted teeth. "Lord Anthony what will happen to Lady Celine if I follow this through? Who will get her Castle and her estate?"

Lord Anthony answers, "She will be sent to Portmarnock Jail. She will never see the light of day again. We have caught most of the others involved. It's only a matter of time until the rest are found. They will be dealt with accordingly. With regards to Lady Celine's estate, it will go to Lord Henry of course."

Gregor grunts, "Hmmm, I forgot about him. That is if he returns. And should he not return, then I want the castle, the entire estate. These are my counter proposals."

Georgette was furious. "I can't answer that now. But Lord Anthony and Lord Riverdale will ask the council about the estate. Now what time are we to meet tonight?" she demands.

Gregor answers with a patronizing tone, "I'll meet you both at the Belfast Castle, let's say nine o'clock. And I want to know by then if I get the Cracklin estate. Oh, and Georgette dear, you are not to bring any Shadow cats. Strictly just you and Toby. Remember I have eyes everywhere. I will know if you try to deceive me. Is that understood?"

Georgette grits her teeth, "Understood. Goodbye Gregor."

Georgette lifts her Tara brooch from the centre of the table. The room is silent. Everyone around the

Chapter Nineteen

room filled with mixed emotions. Happy Gregor took the bait, yet angry at how arrogant and selfish the man was. Toby eyes the room suspiciously, narrowing his eyes as he looks at every corner of the room. He whispers, "Is he gone Georgette? Can he no longer hear us?"

She grins saying, "No, he can't hear us, Toby. The connection was broken as soon as I lifted my Tara brooch."

Toby then stands up and shouts, "Good! He's nothing but a no good, sneaky lying gombeen!" Red faced, he continues to rant, "I despise that man, and his self-righteousness, still thinking he's above everyone else. After all the evil deeds he's done, he makes my blood boil! Oh, but you've done amazing Georgie! You handled him very well! But he's still an old gombeen!"

Toby's face furrows. Georgette agrees, "We all feel the same way, Toby. You're not alone in your thoughts," she reassures him.

A wickedly delightful grin crosses Cornelius' face. "Let's see how arrogant and self-righteous he will be when I give him a swift kick across that veil tomorrow night."

Lord Anthony chuckles. "I agree, Cornelius. Well said young man. But let's work out a plan for this evening. I think you and Toby should go in my carriage as far as the castle gates."

Georgette disagrees. "No Lord Anthony, sorry but we are going by broom."

Toby's mouth drops open. "Did you say broom, Georgie?"

She nods her head. "Yes Toby, we will be using the broom gifted to me by the witches during our meeting at Salt Sea City. It's a powerful broom and I fully intend to use it. Besides I'd rather our feet didn't walk on any of the castle grounds. Heaven only knows what traps Gregor has laid out for us in that forest."

Toby twiddles his thumbs anxiously. "I understand, Georgie. It's just I'm a big man and that's just one tiny wee broom. And also I have a wee confession to make. I am not the best at flying."

Georgette gives Toby a reassuring pat on the back. "You'll be fine, Toby. I'll protect you."

Toby's eyebrows shoot up. "But that's my job. I'm your protector," he exclaims.

Georgette laughs. "Then we will protect each other. I promise you, I won't let you fall off the broom."

Toby nods. Despina tells Georgette, "Remember to put one of each potion we made into that adorable little bag Queen Opala gave you."

Flanna adds, "and make sure you wear the ring she gave you as well."

Isadora feeling concerned says, "Just promise me you'll both be careful. I don't trust that man or that old crone, Cracklin, I feel like we are sending you both into the lion's den."

Holding a tray with eight glasses on top Isadora asks everyone to take a glass of Toby's finest rum and join her in a toast. Filling their glasses, holding them in the air they toast to their friends. "Slainte!"

Chapter Twenty

Standing at the top of the Clock tower surrounded by her friends, Georgette reaches her hand into her little magickal bag, pulling out her broomstick. Despina is taken aback. "My goodness! It's quite a broomstick, isn't it?"

Isadora laughs, "Well at least there's plenty of room on it!"

Georgette giggles. "Really! Look at it. Its enormous! Twice the size of a normal broom. I wonder why?"

Hickory answers, "I know why. I've only seen this broom once before. It gets even bigger on command you know."

Lord Anthony snaps his fingers! "I get why they gave you it! This broom can hold multiple people. Think about it. If you're taking it into the hell dimension, this broom can fly everyone out at the same time. How clever."

Georgette touches the broom. "Yes, I agree. But let's just hope I can navigate it. Come on Toby, no time like the present."

Toby swallows with a loud gulp. "Really! I mean wouldn't you rather try a wee test run first?"

Everyone was trying hard to hide their amusement. Everyone apart from Flanna that is. Flanna bust into giggles. "You're a big scaredy cat, Toby."

Horrified he shouts, "I am not! It's just I don't really like flying and well this broom is new. And she isn't even sure if she knows how well she can fly the damn thing yet. What if we try taking off from a few floors down?" Toby asks hopeful.

Flanna smiles. "I'm just teasing you. Go get on the silly stick. I'm sure miss Georgette won't try and kill you."

Georgette pops her hat on tilting it to one side. Tying her cloak on tight she fastens the small magickal bag to her belt. She steps onto the ledge of the clocktower. "Come on Toby, lets be going. Just don't look down."

They all stand back. Cornelius, hiding his anxiety, gives Georgette a little wink. She grins as she mounts the broom. Toby takes his time, trying to be gentle he sits on the back of the broom. He asks, "Are you sure it will take my weight? I'm a big man, you know."

Georgette giggles. "We will soon find out, won't we?" And with that they fly straight ahead. Taking off at such a speed they leave a trail of green magickal smoke behind them.

Cornelius jumps back. "Wow! That woman can put her mind to anything she wants. Isn't she fantastic?" he shouts.

Everyone looks at him amused. Embarrassed by his sudden outburst of affection for Georgette, he feels his face redden. "Oh, like you all aren't thinking the same thing," he defends himself. The group chuckle.

Chapter Twenty

Isadora, rescuing her son before he dies of embarrassment says, "Well, now that we know she can fly without killing Toby, shall we all wait inside where its warm?" They all agree and head back inside.

Georgette was soaring high above the clouds. She wasn't nervous flying at all. She felt exhilarated. "This broom is wonderful," she thinks aloud. "How are you doing back there, Toby?"

Poor Toby was holding on for dear life. He had his eyes shut tight. He was petrified. "I'm grand young miss, just grand," he lied. He wasn't grand at all. He imagines his face has turned green at this point, he was certainly beginning to feel a bit nauseous.

"Deep breaths, in through the nose, out through the mouth," he tells himself. Toby couldn't wait to get his feet on hard ground again.

Georgette had taken the long way up to Cave Hill. She knew their meeting wasn't until nine o'clock, and she wanted to scout the area first for any potential threats. Also, she was enjoying herself a little. But she didn't want to tell Toby that.

They land outside the castle gates. Two large pillars stand at each side off the ornamental railings. On top of each pillar sits a carved dog, holding a shield carved in stone. The gates are closed. They stand waiting for permission to enter. Looking at Toby for the first time since landing, Georgette notices his complexion. "Are you alright, Toby? You look a little pale." She sounds concerned.

"Yes, young miss. I am just glad to be on the ground again."

She asks, "Are you ready for this?"

A look of determination crosses his face. "Yes," he answers, patting his coat pocket. "I have the scroll right here."

Georgette pops back on the broom. "Let's stay calm and remember to hold our tempers."

The gates begin to open slowly. A low grey fog begins swirling around the gates, settling on top of the pathway. Georgette was flying only a few feet from the ground. They carefully hover just above the thick plumes of fog, along a winding muddy road, covered in fallen rustic foliage. Small gusts of wind blow dried shrubbery across the ground, creating a swirling, cascading dance of leaves around their feet.

Tall, ancient trees lined each side of the pathway. It was dark with only the sound of a cold, whistling, lonely wind blowing through the surrounding forest. The sensation of strangers' eyes watching them from deep within the forest was felt with every passing bend.

Toby on high alert, whispers, "I don't like this Georgie. Not one bit."

A few more minutes pass before they turn the last corner. The castle sits nestled on top of a hill, overlooking Belfast. It could be seen from the city below and beyond its many sister mountains, even far out to sea. Its lights, when lit were always a beacon of home to many incoming ships. Moonlight was peering through the clouds, illuminating the castle. A midnight blue sky was bedded behind its bricks. Beams of white light shone over its walls and beautiful gardens. Its

Chapter Twenty

many windows were dark with no light or life within them. Just one large window on the middle floor was illuminating an orange glow. From a distance it looked like the fireplace was lit, with just one chimney pot, streaming a thin trickle of smoke from the top of its spout. As they drew nearer the castle, suddenly a small blue flame appeared just at the entrance door. Swaying back and forth willing them to follow.

Georgette and Toby dismount the broom. Standing up, she wills the broom to shrink in size, watching it, as it transfigures into a miniature version of what it previously was. Sitting in the palm of her hand, she picks up the broom and slips it into her bag. Clutching two potions from the bag, she slips one into Toby's hand.

"What's this?" Toby asks under his breath. He wasn't sure if Gregor could be listening in.

"They're invisibility potions," Georgette explains. "I don't know what that blue flame is exactly, but I have a feeling its connected to Gregor. I want us to have potions at the ready, just in case we need to make a quick escape."

Toby nods, agreeing with her. They both cautiously follow the small blue flame. It disappears through the large oak, entrance door. Toby pushes the door open. They both walk into the hallway. A huge mahogany staircase stands in front of them. Dominating the space, a wide thick handrail cascades to the top floor, folding its way round a decadent balcony surrounding a large wide proportioned landing. The scent of old wood and turf could be smelt throughout the castle.

The entire place was in darkness. The only light was that of the small blue flame leading the way up the stairs. They follow with apprehension. Georgette commands, "Solos," but not a single light appears. Her brow furrows. Turning to Toby she whispers, "Gregor has enchanted the castle. He must have put a magick barrier up. My powers won't work here. Be on your guard Toby."

They continue to follow the blue flame, hovering a few feet in front of them, lighting their way. Toby instinctively moves closer to Georgette. "I don't like this Georgie."

Georgette stays close to Toby's side. "It's okay, Toby. Just hold your potion tight."

The blue flame abruptly stops at the top of the stairs. There is a sudden eerie atmosphere. Toby protectively stands in front of Georgette, gently moving her behind him. Gregor's voice is suddenly heard, the sound filling the entire castle. They couldn't pinpoint his location. It echo's deeply throughout the halls giving Toby uncomfortable chills.

Gregor laughs, "Clever little witch. Yes, I did enchant the castle. I can't have you playing any tricks now, can I?"

Georgette answers him with a sharp tone. "Show yourself! You know we're alone. We kept our word. Now stop with the dramatic displays of nonsense."

Gregor slowly appears from the darkness at the top of the stairs, with his shadow cat, fully formed by his side. "Please, come join me in the Ben Madigan room."

Toby shouts, "Turn the damn lights on, Gregor."

Chapter Twenty

Gregor mocks him. "You're not afraid of the dark are you, Toby?"

Toby has a sudden burst of confidence in his voice. "Not at all, Gregor. I would just prefer to see your face when I knock that smug look off it," Toby grins in anticipation.

Georgette touches Toby's shoulder and mouths for him to calm down.

Gregor, sounding more serious, with not a hint of mockery in his voice announces, "I think it best the lights stay as they are."

Georgette interrupts, "Oh for goodness sake. Just lead the way and let's get this finished."

They both walk further along to landing. Toby stops abruptly in front of the door to the Ben Madigan room, causing Georgette to bump into him. Looking directly at Gregor, he demands, "You go first."

Gregor looks at Toby with anger in his eyes, aggravated that he dares speak to him in such a disrespectful manner. Biting his tongue, he walks into the room. Toby follows, with Georgette close beside him.

The room is long in length with a very high ceiling. Its windows were tall and wide. They were draped in red velvet curtains. Each window had breathtaking views of every angle of Belfast. Thousands of warm lights twinkling across the city from magick folk's homes. Street lanterns as far as the eye could see, stretching their beauty across the city, then gradually fading their glow as they scattered further out to the distant mountains.

In the centre of the room between the windows stood a single door. It led to a concrete spiral staircase. The steps lead to many paths. Each path joined with another, all of them rotating their way back to the perfect landscaped gardens. The spiral steps were carved from thick, grey stone, its bollards winding with display of opulence. Every twist and turn, was built to perfection. Its design made to captivate. A cream marble fireplace was lit at the bottom end of the room. It was burning low on its grid, casting shadows on the walls, adding to the uneasy atmosphere.

Dark mahogany furniture was placed throughout the room, with two green velvet sofas facing each other at the fireplace. Portraits hung on the walls, but strangely they were covered up with large white sheets.

Georgette noticed some grains of white rice on the hearth. She wondered why they were there, rice is normally used in trapping spells. This made her even more vigilant. Gregor stood in front of the fireplace. He commanded, "Solos!" The ceiling candelabras flickered with flames, filling the room with a softer light.

Toby rolls his eyes saying, "About time too."

Gregor ignores him. "Show me the Shamrock Contract."

Toby looks at Georgette for approval. "Go ahead, Toby, show it to him."

Toby reaches into his breast pocket. He cautiously retrieves the scroll and speaks, "The deal is, you rip it. I take one half, you take the other. Or I throw the whole thing into the fire." He holds the scroll tightly, in front of Gregor.

Chapter Twenty

Gregor takes the long kestrel feather from his tam cap and quickly slices the scroll in half, just missing Toby's fingers. Toby's nostrils flare, his patience has just about run out. If it wasn't for his quick reflexes, Gregor would have cut him. Gold sparkling dust falls to the floor as the parchment slices into two pieces. Toby quickly puts his half back in his pocket. Gregor examines his half with excitement, knowing immediately, the contract was real. He smiles, delighted in his victory.

"Where is Lady Celine? What lies have you concocted to have her caught?"

Gregor casually waves his hand in the air. "She is of no further use to me. She is currently in hiding, being kept under my protection. However, now that I have my Shamrock Contract, and I am a free man, I'll have her come here and you can inform the authorities. I shall send for her within the hour. It's probably best you let Lord Anthony and Lord Riverdale know. Inform them I wish to report a crime," he says in an insincere tone.

Toby asks, "What crime would that be?"

Gregor gives a sly smirk, "Why the murder of Lady Hawthorn. Master Henry's mother."

Toby and Georgette are shocked. They were sickened by Gregor's unconscious lack of remorse. Toby trying hard to control his temper asks, "Are you telling us, Lady Celine is responsible for the death of Lady Hawthorn?"

Gregor snaps, "That's what I said! Well, her and Lord Hawthorn as well. It was done to unite two powerful families the Cracklin's and Hawthorn's. It was quite genius really, a story was made up by myself.

I suggested they say she fell overboard on Morning Star, far out to sea during a storm. Everyone believed it. Why wouldn't they? I am after all a Brigadier in the Causeway Army. Because of my position I made sure there were no questions asked. Even when the Fisherweed found her body and came to me to report it, I took care of that as well."

Horrified Georgette asks, "How did she really die?"

"Lady Celine put a knife into her heart. I made sure her body would never be found," Gregor says proudly.

Georgette walks over to Gregor, Toby right by her side. She looks him straight in the eye and speaks through gritted teeth, "You think you're so smart, don't you? But you're just a pathetic, evil, nasty old man. There are no words strong enough to say how I feel about you. Good people have died because of you and your sick twisted friends. You disgust me, old man. I am glad the Johnagock left nothing but your grandson's bones for you to mourn. I am glad that child never got the chance to know you as a grandfather. You are corrupt. You deserve no love or compassion. You took Henry's mother from him. You took my parents away from me," she screams. "It's your fault my sisters are gone. You destroyed Lord Swift's family. Seamus and Molly never recovered from losing those twin boys." Georgette angrily points in Gregor's face. "You will get what's coming to you some day, mark my words. And I hope I am there when it happens."

Gregor notices the magick ring on Georgette's finger. Shocked, he grabs her hand. "Where did you get this ring?"

Chapter Twenty

She snaps her hand away from him. Toby moves protectively in front of her. Georgette answers with a smile on her face. "Queen Opala."

Gregor looks irate. "How is it you were bestowed such a gift?"

Ignoring him, Georgette walks away. "I am leaving now. I can't stand being in this room with you any longer." She looks to Toby. "Take me home, please."

Gregor snarls, "You clearly don't know of the powers it possesses, girl. But no matter. Off you both go then. Remember to have Lord Anthony send his guards here tonight for Lady Celine. I will speak to him directly in regard to opening the veil tomorrow night.

As Georgette and Toby leave, suddenly the white linen sheet covering the portrait above the fireplace falls to the floor. It didn't just drop. It slowly floats, as if it were being carried by a soft breeze. Georgette was stunned to see the portrait. It was Henry Hawthorn's mother. A beautiful woman, wearing a long royal blue, off the shoulder gown. She had long, black, curly hair that draped around her shoulders. Her lips were pink, the colour of polyantha roses.

Georgette quickly looks at the portrait. She could have sworn it just moved. But Gregor swiftly casts a spell, chanting:

hide and seek
don't speak
cover canvas wood and glass
see no more of this past

The sheet was off the floor within seconds, covering the portrait once more. Georgette felt a cold chill run through her. She looks at Toby. He takes her arm, saying, "We're leaving," slamming the door behind him as they leave.

Making their way down the stairs, Georgette whispers, "Did you see that, Toby? The picture. It moved." Toby nods. "Yes, but don't speak, say nothing," he whispers. "Wait until we're out of here."

Once outside, the fresh air felt good. Georgette takes her broom out of her bag, and they quickly mount it, taking off immediately. They shoot up into the night sky. She tells Toby as she holds her broom tightly, "I am not going through those forest grounds again. I don't trust Gregor. Let's get home. It will be faster if I fly straight ahead Toby, so hold on tight."

Chapter Twenty-One

Back at Albert Clock everyone sits patiently waiting on Georgette and Toby's return. Isadora is getting impatient. "They should have been back by now, what's taking them so long?" she asks.

Cornelius takes his mother's hand, hoping to calm her. Tailsa runs out to the hall, with Bijou following right behind her.

Despina lets out a sigh of relief. "Oh, thank goodness, that will be them now."

Sure enough, the front door opens. Toby walks in first. "There's so much we need to tell you. But first of all I need Lord Anthony and Lord Riverdale to send for guards."

Isadora asks, "Why, what's happened?"

Toby continues to tell them about everything that had just taken place at Belfast Castle. Lord Anthony asks Georgette, "Do you mind if I use your spell room, I need to send some cinder notes immediately."

Georgette agrees, "Please go right ahead. I need to ask you all a question. When we were at the Castle, I noticed a portrait of a woman. I thought I saw the picture move. I know it wasn't my imagination because Toby saw it too."

Toby looks sad. "It was the late Lady Hawthorn, young Henry's mother. I knew that lovely woman. I know in my heart Gregor has trapped her soul in that painting, after she was murdered."

Georgette remembers then that she saw grains of white rice along the hearth in the castle. She explains to the others what she saw. They all agreed that a soul has been trapped. "Can we help her, Hickory?" Georgette asks. "You're the most educated in dark magic, can you free her?"

Hickory thinks for a moment. "Yes, if her soul was trapped by Gregor's hand, I think I can release her. However, I can only undo his spell when he is no longer in our realm. I will need to do this when he is in the hell dimension. I'll need a black candle to cast the spell though, they can be hard to come by."

Georgette remembers something. "I have such a thing as a black candle. It was a gift from the wizards during our meeting at Salt Sea City. I will happily give it to you when you cast the spell."

Hickory gives a grateful smile. "I promise you when this is all over, I will make it my priority to release Lady Hawthorns soul. However, time is of the essence, and we need to get Lady Cracklin under lock and key tonight. No doubt she will sing like a canary, telling us whatever she can to get leniency. With any luck she will tell us where the remainder of the other criminals are. Let her keep talking I say. Get the lot of them put in Portmarnock jail before the nights through."

Georgette can't seem to settle. Maybe it was her argument with Gregor, or maybe she is just nervous

Chapter Twenty-One

about crossing the veil tomorrow. But she needed to burn off some energy. "I think I'd like to go out. Perhaps go for a ride on my broom."

Cornelius eyes light up. "Yes, can I come too? Don't even bothering answering that, I am coming anyway, Georgie," he grins.

Georgette laughs. "It's not me you want to keep company is it? It's my new broomstick you're after."

He shrugs, "A bit of both. Now shut up woman let's go. I am dying to see how fast it can really fly."

Isadora's anxiety shoots through the roof. "Oh please be careful, you two. And don't stay out too late."

Cornelius rolls his eyes. Georgette says, "We won't Izzy. I'll have him back in less than an hour."

Georgette looks around the room as she was leaving. Everyone was busy discussing tonight's events and the plan for tomorrow. She was glad to get away from it all for a while.

Isadora walks them both to the gate. "It's probably better you stay out for just a little while. Let these big men think there taking care of things. But you and I both know that it's us ladies that get the jobs done," she winks.

"Hey mother, that's not nice," Cornelius huffs.

"Oh shush, Cornelius," she smiles. "Can I just tell you miss Georgette how proud your parents would be. You have done so well with all of this. Tomorrow will be a good day. Now go get your head cleared for a while and take this big lump with you," she points to Cornelius. "And try not to drop him from a height, his father would never forgive you," she jokes.

Georgette hugs Isadora. "I'll get him back to you in one piece. I promise."

Georgette holds out her broomstick. "Well hop on then. Where to Cornelius?"

He thinks about it for a moment. "I think I'd like you to take me to the very top of the Cave Hill. Let's just sit on top of the cliffside and watch as old Lady Cracklin gets dragged away in chains. The guards should be arriving soon, and we will have a good view." Happy with his idea, he jumps on the broom. Georgette looks over her shoulder at him, raising her eyebrow and saying sarcastically, "Really Cornelius!"

He looks at her with a cheeky grin. "What? That's a good idea, what's not to like? Oh come on, Georgie, you know you'd like that too."

She can't help but take some guilty pleasure at the thought of that vile woman getting dragged away by the guards. "Oh, okay then, you twisted my arm."

With that said they shoot off fast. Thick white fluffy clouds surround them, sending chills of excitement through their bodies. It was exhilarating. Cornelius looks below, taking in the view, it was just amazing. They glide across the sky, watching the lights from the city below fading in and out of view as they disappeared between the clouds. Cornelius wrapped his big arms around Georgette's waist, holding on tight until they reach the top of the Cavehill Mountain.

As they land, Cornelius takes off his coat and places it on the ground. They both sit and wait patiently. He jokes saying, "I really didn't think this through, did I? I should have brought some food, hot coffee, maybe a

Chapter Twenty-One

warm blanket. It would have been some nice to have a little food before tonight's show."

Georgette scoffs, "What are you like, always thinking about your belly? You're getting as bad as Toby."

Untying the ribbon around her neck, opening her cloak, she wraps it around Cornelius shoulders, giving him a playful look. "Here," she says. "I can see you're chilly and you are being a gentleman as usual, putting your coat on the ground. Now you've left yourself cold. Just share my cloak if it keeps you warm and shuts you up."

The heavy, black velvet cloak covers them both. Georgette rests her head on his muscular shoulder. He wraps his arm around her, holding her close by his side. Enjoying the time alone with her.

"Look Cornelius, look!" All of the castle lights were lit. Outside and in. Street lanterns along the pathway leading up through the forest now dimly glowing as well. "I can see the old crone, Lady Celine. Can you see her?" Georgette asks. "Yes look! They have her in chains. And oh my stars she looks mad. Furious even."

Cornelius almost falls over laughing. "Look who's with her. It's that nasty old crone from the towpath. You know the one that takes coins for potions."

Georgette giggles, "Yes, I remember her. It makes sense for someone as nasty as her to be involved. I knew there was something I didn't like about that woman."

A familiar man's voice can be heard from below, echoing throughout the hills, "You snake Gregor. You set me up. He's involved in this too, arrest him as well. Put him in chains. He's the main man in all of this."

Georgette is shocked. "Oh my goodness! Is that Harlow? From Morning Star?"

Cornelius stands up to get a closer look. "Oh no, Toby is not going to be happy about this."

Georgette put her hands out and Cornelius helps her up off the ground. She dusts off her dress. "Yes, well at least Toby will now know who Gregor's informant was. We did suspect it was someone from the docks."

Cornelius put his hand out taking Georgette's hand in his. "Right, you. Let's be going. I think you've seen enough of Gregor for one day." They both take one last look at the castle below, the grounds now full of soldiers. Gregor was standing like an oversized peacock enjoying his freedom and newly restored authority. Lady Celine on the other hand was still screaming on the top of her lungs as they shuffled her in chains into the prison wagon. Cornelius, points, and in a fit of laughter says, "Oh Georgie, I'm so glad we came here, honestly you couldn't pay for entertainment like this." He lifts his coat from the grass. "Let's go home, we've had one good victory tonight. Tomorrow, we'll get another."

Georgette kisses his cheek before they mount the broom and begin their journey back home.

Chapter Twenty-Two

Soaring above Belfast, Georgette asks Cornelius if he would like to see the view from the top of the clock tower. "It's a lovely night, and to be honest I don't really want to mingle downstairs with everyone just yet. There's only so much coffee and small talk I can do in one day."

Cornelius chuckles, "I've been waiting on your breaking point all day. I knew everyone was driving you nuts. The usual peace and harmony of your beloved clock tower has been too noisy and very much disturbed."

Georgette dips her broom, coming in fast towards Belfast docks. They could see the clock tower glowing in the distance. "It's not that I'm not grateful, of course I am. It's just I miss the normality, I miss Mia."

Cornelius wraps his arms tighter around her waist. "I know Georgie, I understand."

She slows down coming to a stop. Hovering just in front of the clock face. "Look how beautiful it is. I just take my home for granted. I sometimes forget how amazing the tower looks. Especially at night."

Manoeuvring the broom, they land in the bell room at the very top of the tower. The room was bare, with only a large gold bell hanging in its centre. Georgette leans her broom against the wall, then takes the small black velvet bag from her waist. The broom shrinks, and she pops it back into the bag. She removes her hat, allowing her thick white hair to fall around her waist, and allowing the night breeze to flow through its silky strands. She rests her elbows on the stone ledge of the window arches.

Gazing out to sea from the open arched walls, Georgette smiles. Inhaling, she takes in the smell of the night air. Looking down at the quiet, Belfast streets below. This was her favourite time of day. Moonlight creating glossy, silver streaks on top of a black ocean, its bright, white beams reflecting on the sails of every vessel docked in the harbour. Blue light peering through the clear glass windows of the tiny houses below. It was beautiful. Georgette could smell fresh air mixed with a hint of smoke flowing from tall chimney pots. The cobbled roads beneath them were empty and still. The wind has picked up and there was a slight howling noise flowing through the tower. From this height, you could see Belfast from every angle. On a clear day you could even see as far as the Mourn Mountains, but the Cavehill and Black Mountain were very clearly seen.

"Mia loved it here, and I loved coming up here with our father. It was his favourite place in the tower. He would tell us such amazing stories and teach us clever little enchantments. Mother would be baking downstairs, of course. She was such an amazing cook. There was always a sweet aroma throughout the tower. It always made us hungry," she smiles fondly. "I have such happy memories here, Cornelius. I miss my

Chapter Twenty-Two

parents so much. There's not a day that passes that I don't think of them."

Cornelius moves closer. Georgette lays her head on his firm shoulder. Both just taking a moment, looking out to sea. Only the sound of distant buoys bells was heard clanging low in the distance, warning incoming ships and seamen of fog.

Looking around, Cornelius is enjoying the time alone with Georgette. With everything going on this past week, it was difficult for them to be truly alone at all. He thinks back to the morning when they were in the kitchen together, before his mother interrupted. The memory makes him blush. Turning around, he faces away from the dim lights of the city below and leans his back against the clock tower wall. Focusing on the giant golden bell in front of him. It really was magnificent. He could see a glimmer, and, squinting his eyes he focuses, taking a closer look. He moves toward the bell. He notices tiny Celtic engravements, imbedded along the bells base. Placing his hands along the engravements, he wipes away thick layers of black dust, revealing words underneath. The Celtic swirls were not just a simple design, they had meaning. The words begin to glow at his touch. As he looks closer, he can make out the writings. "Mary, Sean, Georgette, Amelia, Christine. We, the Crescents, are the keepers of this Clock."

"Georgie! Come quick look at this."

Georgette takes her attention away from the Belfast view and turns to Cornelius. "What is it?" she asks, walking towards him. Cornelius points to the engraved names.

"Did you know about this? Examining the writing Georgette places her hands along the inscription. She starts to cry. Cornelius panics, "Oh no, Georgie. I'm sorry, don't cry. I'm an idiot, I never meant for this to upset you."

Georgette laughs through a tiny sob. "No Cornelius, I'm okay," she insists.

Giving her a sympathetic smile, he asks, "Then why are you crying?"

She wipes her tearstained face. "These are happy tears," she explains. "My Father must have written this for us when Christine was born. He never had the chance to show us. It's beautiful. Thank you."

Cornelius wraps her tightly in his arms, hugging her. Another sob escapes her. "Sorry," she apologises. "I promise, I'm not upset."

Cornelius kisses the top of her head. "Just let it out Georgie, you don't have to be strong all the time. Not with me. So, stop saying sorry."

She rests her head on his chest. "You're right. Sorry."

Cornelius chuckles. "What did I just say, woman?"

This makes Georgette giggle. She squeezes him tighter. "Fine, I'm not sorry then."

After some time, Cornelius steps back. "Shall we go downstairs now? I'll let you make me a cup of coffee and I'll even pretend to like it," he grins.

Georgette playfully pushes him off. "Fine, we can go downstairs, and you can make me the coffee."

Chapter Twenty-Two

Cornelius holds his hands up in defeat. "Okay fine. But I'm thinking we should swap coffee for maybe some camomile tea. We've had enough excitement for one day don't you think?"

Georgette taking notice of his hands says, "You're not making me anything until you wash those hands. They're filthy!" she laughs. "What were you doing?"

Cornelius, looking down at his hands, notices they're black with dirt. "Ah, that would be the dust from the bell, I think. "Besides you're one to talk Miss Crescent," he grins.

"What are you referring to? My hands are fine," Georgette states. "Yes, your hands are mighty fine. But your face, on the other hand, is not."

Confused Georgette touches her face. "What's wrong with it?" she asks.

"As beautiful as your face is, at this moment you somewhat resemble a Panda." Unbeknown to Georgette, she had earlier wiped the tears from her face and in their place left large black smudges.

"Oh no, I must look a mess," she exclaims.

Cornelius has a mischievous look on his face. "Oh, I don't know. You could look worse." He slowly raises both his hands, wiggling his filthy fingers covered in dust and dirt towards Georgette's face.

She feigns shock. "You wouldn't dare!" she shouts. But to Georgettes disbelief he pounces towards her. Letting out a squeal, she attempts to dodge him, but it's too late. Georgette tries to run as Cornelius wraps her in an embrace, sneakily lifting his arms, he wipes both his hands down her cheeks leaving great big dirty streaks. She looks at him trying but failing to keep a straight face. "I can't believe you actually did that." They both burst into laughter.

Cornelius then continues trying to lift the end of her cloak to dust off his hands. She grabs his hands, laughing and saying, "Oh no you don't! You already messed my face. You're not messing my cloak as well."

Cornelius looks at her with his boyish charm. Moonlight shining on her, enhancing her beauty with a radiant glow. Realizing she is still holding his hands, he clutches them a little tighter, not wanting to let her go. She looks at Cornelius through her thick lashes, gazing into her gorgeous royal blue eyes. He knew this was the moment he longed for. His stomach is doing tiny flips with anticipation. Georgette arches her back further into his body. Gently caressing her face, he bends down closer. Georgette, feeling a sudden rush of emotion is overwhelmed with burning intensity. A soft breeze blows a few strands of her hair across her face. Cornelius carefully drapes her hair over her shoulder, brushing her neck as he does so. The movement sends a flutter of chills down her spine. Their eyes meet. He can feel the heat coming from her body. Cornelius' pulse is racing. Georgette presses her tiny hands hard against his back. Closing the distance between them. Their lips inches apart. Georgette lets out a small sigh, whispering, "Kiss me, Cornelius.". And he does.

All doubt and any uncertainty Cornelius felt before was gone. Georgette wanted him and he finally knew it. Their lips meet. Georgette can feel the heat of his mouth. He tasted even better than she had imagined.

Chapter Twenty-Two

The kiss was soft at first, gentle. Georgettes hands move up his neck, running her fingers up through his hair, the kiss intensifies. She kisses him with more urgency. It was everything she ever wanted it to be, and Cornelius felt the same. They were lost in the taste of one another. Georgette's head was spinning in the most amazing way. Cornelius parts his lips from hers slowly, taking a breath, inhaling her delicious scent, his hand gently caressing her jaw. There was a want in their eyes.

A voice from the stairwell shouts, startling them both. "Get back down here you silly cat. I'll turn you into a dog I swear, if you don't pay heed to me, Tailsa!"

Georgette and Cornelius break free from their embrace. The door bursts opens and Tailsa dashes through jumping up into Georgette's arms. Isadora stands in the doorway, holding onto the frame panting for breath.

"Oh, there you both are," she beams. "That misbehaving shadow of yours. I tell you, she's been a nightmare all evening. She won't do a thing she's been told. At least now I know why she wanted up here. When did you get back?" Isadora asks still trying to catch her breath. She commands, "Solos". Two little lanterns at each side of the doorway in the hall luminate, slowly beginning to spill their light into the room. Isadora suspiciously looks at Cornelius, then at Georgette. Putting her hands to her mouth, she stifles a giggle.

Cornelius asks, "What? What is it mother?"

Isadora can't hold it any longer. She explodes with laughter. Georgette then asks, "Oh come on, what's so funny?"

Georgette turns to look at Cornelius. To her mortification, she can now see his lips and chin are covered in black dust. "You should see your face," she exclaims.

Cornelius chuckles. "Well, if you think this is bad, pointing to his face circulating his index finger, you should see the mess your face is in."

Georgette commands, "Almeria!" Suddenly a small, mirrored silver cloud appears floating in front of her. Looking at her refection, Georgette had black dusty smudges all over her lips, cheeks, neck and shoulders! "Oh, my goodness, look at me." She can feel her cheeks burning bright red. Cornelius grabs her turning her in the opposite direction from his mother, attempting to hide her face.

Realising what had just happened, Isadora excitedly begins jumping up and down on the spot, trying to contain her joy. "Well, let's just say it's about time." Isadora smiles, "I think you two need a quick wash before coming downstairs. Then we can have a chat and catch up."

Cornelius asks his mother if she would like a bit of gossip, knowing very well she would.

Isadora looking over her shoulder at her son says, "Always."

Cornelius grins. "Knew you would. We saw Lady Celine getting arrested tonight. Up at the castle, and you'll never guess who they took with her."

Chapter Twenty-Two

Isadora asks with anticipation, "Who, tell me quick?"

"The old crone that took your coin for potions at Loughshore. And Harlow from Morning Star. They were both shackled away in chains"

Isadora gasps, "Oh my stars, Toby won't be happy about that. But he will be relieved to finally know who Gregor had spying for him. That's certainly made my day. Well, that amongst other things," she winks at the two of them. "Now off you chop. Get washed up and meet me downstairs for some food. I think we all need an early night".

Chapter Twenty-Three

Isadora had a roaring fire lit in the parlour. The room was cosy and comfortable. Cornelius cannot take his eyes away from Georgette. The amber glow from the flames were enhancing her beauty. Her blue eyes sparkle like sapphires. She catches his gaze and smiles shyly.

They were both thinking the same thing, remembering their kiss, wanting it to happen again.

Isadora stretches, tiredness taking over her body after a long day. "Shall we all get to bed? We all need our rest for tomorrow."

Cornelius breaks his gaze from Georgette. "Hmmm? Did you say something mother?" he asks a little dazed.

"Oh, for heaven's sake, get to bed," she rolls her eyes. "Young love," she mutters as they all walk out the door and upstairs to retire for the night.

Chapter Twenty-Four

Next morning Cornelius woke up early, actually he had barely slept a wink. He spent all night tossing and turning, thinking of Georgette, their kiss and her going into the Johnagock realm today. He wanted to try and make breakfast for Georgette and his mother. Making his way downstairs, standing in the middle of the kitchen confused, he scratches his head looking round the room.

"Where do I start?" he thinks aloud. "Coffee? Yip, I can make that. Okay, toast? Yes, I can definitely do toast. Try not to burn it," he chuckles. "I wonder if there's any ham left over from yesterday. Georgie and Toby like a bit of ham and honey," he thinks to himself. He starts to look around the kitchen again, moving some pots and pans around. Lifting a jam jar, he spots in the corner of the counter, he takes a spoonful and pops the spoon in his mouth. "Think now. Where would Georgie put the ham?"

Just then there is a knock on the door. Cornelius walks to the hallway. He was expecting Toby, and sure enough it was him. "Good morning, young sir. What a beautiful morning it is too. I've brought breakfast, I hope you're hungry."

Chapter Twenty-Four

Cornelius' face lights up with delight. "Good morning to you as well sir. Now what's on the menu? I was just about to make coffee."

Toby's face twists in a grimace of disgust. "Yuck!" he sticks his tongue out. "No thank you. I'd rather drink from the trough outside than sample your coffee."

Cornelius, puts his hand to his heart, saying sarcastically, "That hurts, Toby. Maybe you'll prefer tea over trough water?" he smirks.

Toby bends down picking up a large teapot at his side. "Well ahead of you. Look I came prepared. I brought my own," he beams. "Are the ladies awake yet?" he asks.

"No, they're still sleeping. I thought they would enjoy a wee lie in. I was just about to cook breakfast when you came knocking, saving me the bother," he smiles.

Toby scoffs walking into the kitchen. "Ha! You cook? Now that I'd love to see," he jokes.

Toby and Cornelius get to work dishing out the food, the smell, making its way upstairs.

Isadora shouts to Georgette, "Are you awake darling?"

Georgette sits up in bed. "Yes," she shouts back.

Isadora asks, "Am I dreaming or is that breakfast I smell downstairs?"

Georgette jumps out of bed, putting her dressing gown on, and walks into the next bedroom to meet Isadora, who has now sat up in bed. "I smell it as well. It can't be Cornelius making breakfast. He can't cook."

Isadora furrows, "Oh, I know my dear. He can't even make a pot of coffee. He's useless in a kitchen. Let's go check on him before he burns the tower down." They both giggled.

"Actually, no need to panic. That smells like Toby's full Irish breakfast. Now there's a man who can cook. Maybe he will teach my Cornelius a thing or two." They both laugh as they make their way downstairs.

Everything was set out on the kitchen table. Food plated, coffee poured and hot toast ready to butter. Cornelius smiles ear to ear upon seeing Georgette enter the room. "I've just prepared breakfast, ladies," he says confidently.

Isadora slaps his shoulder saying, "You're a big fat liar."

Georgette shakes her head, laughing, ignoring him. She walks to Toby. "I'm sorry about Harlow, Toby. I know he was your friend," she gives him a sympathetic smile.

Toby shrugs. "Foolish lad. He chose the wrong side."

They all take a seat at the kitchen table. The food tasted even better than it looked. Everyone cleared their plates.

Later that evening when the moon was full in the sky, it was now time for Georgette to reclaim her powers. Carefully holding the ship in the bottle in one hand, she takes Cornelius' hand with the other. They both ascend the spiral staircase to the top of the clock tower.

Stepping into the bell tower room, tiny raindrops begin to fall, gradually getting heavier and creating

Chapter Twenty-Four

tiny puddles beneath their feet. Releasing her hand, Cornelius steps back, giving her space. Georgette gently places the ship in the bottle at her feet, its reflection mirrored in the puddles around the floor. She looks over her shoulder and says, "I'm glad it's you here with me, Cornelius."

Georgette chants softly:

> *Moon beams white*
> *moon beams light*
> *restore my powers within this night*
> *for which was mine*
> *shall be once more*
> *fully restored for evermore*

Suddenly the moon grows bigger and brighter, filling the room with shards of colour. Blue, green, white and silver. Cornelius stands watching in amazement as Georgettes body begins to illuminate, covering her skin in a shower of diamonds. Georgette can feel the power wash over her body, touching every nerve ending, flowing through her very soul. The feeling was euphoric. Such power and strength. She welcomes it fully, surrendering her body to it completely. She consumes it whole.

Cornelius quietly asks, "Well? How do you feel Georgie? Are you okay?"

Turning to face him, Georgette replies confidently, "I feel amazing. I feel strong. I am ready to go get my sister."

Chapter Twenty-Five

Georgette is flying into the sky. Heading at high speed towards the Cavehill Mountains. Cornelius is flying close by her side. As they approach the large field, just below the caves, they cannot believe the number of people who have gathered below. Gregor was seen standing with a dozen Causeway guards outside the largest cave entrance. They land on the grass, side by side, greeted by Toby, Isadora, Despina and Hickory, who were patiently waiting on their arrival.

Gregor strides towards her. Toby steps in front of him, blocking his path. "Stop right there," Toby snaps at him. "That's far enough."

Hickory asks in a stern voice, "Where are the extra potions?"

Gregor smirks, in a condescending tone he asks, "Where are the deeds to the castle?"

Hickory furrows his brow. "You jump too quickly, Gregor. You assume young Henry is lost forever and not coming back. You get the deeds only if he doesn't return. But we get the potions from you now. That was the arrangement. Hand them over and don't hold any back," he warns.

Chapter Twenty-Five

Gregor hands Hickory a small brown woollen bag. Hickory opens it. Counting ten small vials of elixir. He then hands the bag to Georgette. Gregor noticing a change in Georgette's appearance eyes her curiously. "I see by your appearance, Miss Crescent, you finally took your powers back."

Georgette gives him a scornful look. "Shut up," she snaps, "Don't speak to me. Just open the veil and tell me the spell I need to use to get us back," she demands.

Dismissing her, Gregor walks over to the centre of the cave entrance, holding both his hands in the air he chants:

open this world far from here
drop its veil for me to steer
its fabric veil torn in two
permit me now the passage through

Gregor, addressing Georgette and Toby says, "Well drink up then, take the potion and do it quickly." A zigzagging split slowly appears in front of them, tearing itself in two. Cracking the veil, creating an opening. Black and red flashes begin to appear on its outer sides, the split getting a little wider as Toby and Georgette draw closer. Everyone could now see through the veil into the hell dimension. Its darkness was visible with a storm rolling in the background.

Cornelius ran over to Georgette grabbing her quickly before she passes through, hugging her tight he then kisses her lips saying, "Please be careful, Georgie. I'll be waiting here on your return, no matter how long it takes."

She answer's him, "I promise you, I will return."

Cornelius whispers under his breath, "I love you."

Leading Georgette towards the veil, Toby puts his big arm around her shoulder. He nods to Cornelius giving him a reassuring smile.

They both step through the veil as it starts to close slowly behind them. Everyone stands silent in the field. Turning towards her friends Georgette takes one last look at their faces, filled with so many different emotions, some with fear, some with sadness, but all of them with hope.

Chapter Twenty-Six

Georgette's heart sank seeing such a horrible place. Her thoughts turned to Amelia right away. Georgette prays to the stars, hoping her sister is still alive and safe. She thought of how frightened she must have felt when she got trapped here. She knew it must have been horrendous for her. And it was.

Amelia did feel frightened on that terrible day when she entered this hell hole. Thinking back, she remembers, she was confused at first. Drowsy and disorientated. She lands on a cold, wet surface. Opening her eyes, she realizes what has happened. She was taken. It had been a large Johnagock that threw her, with force onto the wet, cold, muddy ground. She thinks she hit her head.

Her hands were bound behind her back with enchanted iron cuffs, preventing her from using her magic. Looking up she watches red sparks fade into ash as the entrance to the veil closes shut, sealing her on the other side. She was in shock. She couldn't hear or see properly, her vision was still blurred, her hearing muffled, side effects from the potion that Gregor's hench men gave her no doubt. Squeezing her eyes shut she shakes her head, trying to gain focus. Hoping this is a nightmare but instead she feels the cold sludge of mucky soil beneath her hands. This is real. Suddenly the cold air hit her body. Trembling with fear, the enormous echoes of thunder began to pierce her ears as her hearing starts to return. Looking through blurry eyes she can see Johnagock surrounding her, roaring with growls and laughter, triumphant in their victory. She lifts her head and tries to stand up. She is still weak, and the soggy ground is holding her in place like glue.

Amelia is shocked when she suddenly realises Henry Hawthorn was kneeling a few feet away from her. At first, she thought she was hallucinating. The Johnagock Augustus stood beside him with a spear pointed at his throat. Henry's hands were tied behind his back, his Tara brooch ripped from his chest and thrown on to the mud. Amelia screams, "Don't! Please don't hurt him!"

Henry looks at Amelia, relieved she was awake, alive. He had thought the worst when he saw her hit her head with such force. Augustus grabs Henry's head with his long skinny boneyard fingers. Gripping his hair, he pulls Henry to his feet and drags him over to Amelia, "I see you care for this one, Witch," he snarls viscously. "I will use this to my advantage." he grins with his small mouth, showing his razor-sharp teeth. Amelia's heart was pounding. She couldn't catch her breath. She was overcome with fear as she watched Augustus drag Henry away.

Amelia then felt large bony hands grip her shoulders. Nails piercing her skin like cold needles. Two Johnagock pull her from the ground. Her clothes

Chapter Twenty-Six

stuck to her body, the wet thick, dirty mud weighing her tiny frame down. Standing up she felt beating rain hit her as it lashed from the sky. She looks up searching for the moon only to find a small spot far off in the distance. Only a dark black sky was above, no stars. Lightning strikes with unbelievable force and deafening bangs. She felt a push from behind as they yelled, "Move Witch. Walk."

Amelia was finding it difficult to move, the thick, muddy marshland was dragging her down. Augustus shouts, "Lift the witch and the Warlock. They're holding us back. Put the prisoners on a beast, the storm is worsening."

The Johnagock lift Amelia like a twig throwing her over the saddle. She pulls her leg over with all her strength then sits,. She feels the Johnagock mount the beast behind her. The smell was disgusting. She can see Henry in front of her, mounted on another beast. These creatures were not like anything she has ever seen before. They are terrifying. Henry turns to look at her. She could tell he was frightened too.

Augustus shouts out loudly while raising his spear high in the air, "To the castle, and stop for no one." They take off at great speed.

After some hours of travelling Amelia notices the sun beginning to rise. But this wasn't like the beautiful sun rises in Belfast. This sun was hot, very hot. So much so, it began to burn her skin. She looks at the land, as day light breaks and thinks to herself, "Everything here is dry, dead and scorched". She knew in that moment she was truly in hell.

Looking at Henry, she could see he was injured and weak. His head was hanging low. The Johnagock riding the beast found his amusement on their journey by punching him with force in his ribs and head. Amelia felt useless and frightened as she was overwhelmed with concern for Henry. He had to endure so much pain and humiliation.

Augustus suddenly shouts out with a roar, "Open the gates." Then a loud horn was sounded.

Amelia lifts her head, the sun was so bright she could barely see. She could just about make out the outline of a castle.

Moments later they enter a courtyard where hundreds of Johnagock are gathered. In the middle of the courtyard the King and Queen of the Johnagock realm sat on two large wooden thrones, with brown canvas canopies covering them. The King stands up. He looks at Amelia and Henry, then speaks, "Where is the other Witch? Where are the Fisherweed?" Augustus nervously explains, "This was all Gregor's fault." The King is enraged. Storming across the Courtyard he drags Henry from the beast, pulling him along the ground. He snarls, "Is this one a Wizard or is he human?"

Amelia screams, "Please stop. Please. I beg you. Stop."

Augustus replies, "He is a Wizard." The King lifts his foot and kicks Henry in the head knocking him unconscious. Amelia screams. The King orders they be put below in the dungeon with the other mongrel slaves. Amelia was then pulled from the beast and

Chapter Twenty-Six

dragged by two Johnagock. With her arms still tied behind her back she was pushed into a doorway where a female Johnagock stood waiting. Amelia was pushed to walk forward.

Amelia notices her Tara is gone, the deep sorrow she previously felt had now turned to despair. She thinks to herself, "I'll never get to go home. I'll be stuck here in this nightmare forever."

Back on the other side of the veil on the Cavehill, Lord Anthony addresses the crowd. "We must remain here until they have returned. There is nothing more to be done here tonight. Get the tents set up and fires lit. Let's pray to the stars they return soon, safe and sound."

Isadora takes her sons hand in hers. "She's strong, Cornelius. If anyone can get through this it will be Georgette Crescent."

Turning towards his mother, he puts his arm around her in a warm embrace. Without taking his eyes away from the cave entrance. "I love her so much. I hate this, not being there with her. It's killing me. I feel so useless."

Isadora puts her arms around her son, hugging him tight. "I feel the same way son. All we can do is wait here darling, just pray she finds Amelia.

Toby and Georgette watch the last flicker of light fade from the veil as it seals shut. They stand alone on the other side. It was a cold, chilling wilderness. The moon could barely be seen it was so small, far off in the distance. The dark empty sky made it hard to see what the land really looked like. Only glimpses of scenery could be seen each time the lightening exploded, filling the sky with sharpen sparks of violent light. The sound of thunder pounding with such force was an explosive loudness they had never seen or heard before. Flashing colours from the storm filled this strange place. Purple, blue and white light filled the land and skies above with every crash and bang, throwing out sparks of brightness, then turning it black and dark once more.

The thunderstorm was getting closer. Bolts of fork-lightning strike the ground with a force that shakes the very ground they stand on. Toby tries to get a good look around him, but there's nothing to see. Just the outline of the hills, and the odd skeleton shaped tree.

"Well, we're here young miss. What now?" he asks.

Georgette answers, "I don't know Toby. But I've got this strange feeling, like a pulling sensation. I can't explain it or put it into words, but I know it's telling me, Mia is here.

Toby cups her tiny hands in both of his, saying, "Then why don't you try and contact her through the power of your Tara brooch?"

Georgette nods, then takes hold of her brooch saying, "Amelia, can you hear me? Let me know where you are."

Georgette looks at Toby. "I can't connect with her, Toby. I don't know why." Georgette frowns. Suddenly Toby can see a little green glow, sparkling under the darkness of the mud Reaching his hands down into the sludge, he is stunned to find Amelias Tara brooch, still intact. Henry's too lay right beside hers. He holds them

Chapter Twenty-Six

both up to show Georgette. His heart sinks as he fears the worst has happened.

But Georgette lets out a sigh of relief as soon as she held Amelia's tara. She felt her essence still within the brooch, and Henry's as well. Relieved, she smiles, "They're alive Toby, they're both still alive."

Toby lets out a big breath then hugs Georgette. He takes a look around once more then tells Georgette, "We need to find shelter. I've never seen a storm like this in my life. Those lightning bolts are piercing the very soil open, and they are drawing closer. We should probably head towards that mountain. There are bound to be caves there where we can bed down for the night."

Georgette pulls her hood up as rain starts pouring heavily, making their walk across the fields more difficult. She follows Toby as they both make their way towards the dark mountain.

It takes almost an hour to reach, struggling through open fields of wet, soggy muck. Georgette wished she could use her broom, but she knew she couldn't. It wasn't worth the risk, exposing her magic.

Toby smiles. Looking ahead he can see the entrance to one of the many caves. Wiping the rain from his face. "Yes, just as I thought. There seems to be a few caves there at the bottom. Let's get you out of this storm."

Cautiously they enter the cave. It was very dark, deep, and damp. It was hard to see beyond its end. The blackness seemed to go on and on forever, deep into its depths. Toby looks at Georgette. "We won't venture any further than here, young miss. Nope. We will stay here just at the entrance, I think. At least here there's a little bit of light from that unbelievable, ugly small moon."

Georgette reaches into her small bag pulling out two tiny blankets only the size of her hand. She commands, "Returnus Backis." They return to their full size, thick and warm. "We can't light a fire or use too much magic. It will draw attention to us. I'll only use small spells when needed." She then commands, "Dryis Backis." Within seconds they both felt their wet clothing become dry again.

Toby smiles putting his hand into his bag, he takes a flask out with two tin cups. "Here you go, young lady, this will warm you up. You're not the only one with a helpful little bag," he jokes.

Georgette smiles, taking the mug from Toby. He pours hot coffee into her tumbler. Taking a seat on the ground, the heat from the cup warming her hands. Toby wraps the blanket around her shoulders, then taking the other blanket he joins her sitting on the ground. They both watch as this angry storm takes hold of this foreign land. She rests her head on his shoulder as they sit quietly, waiting and hoping the storm will soon pass. They don't know what the morning will bring but they were both glad Amelia and Henry are still alive. They are grateful to have each other and not be there alone. It is a cold, empty, lonely place.

Toby looks at Georgette, then with a half-smile says, "This really is a hell hole, and Gregor being sent here is the only thing giving me satisfaction right now."

Chapter Twenty-Six

Georgette lifts her head. "Yes Toby, I agree. I've no sympathy for that man being sent here. He's the reason we've lost so much. He shattered so many lives, let him live his days out here. He deserves it."

It was a long night, with neither of them having had much sleep. They take turns to rest their eyes.

As the storm subsides, dawn finally arrives, bringing light to this desolate land. They could both see the carnage the storm left behind.

Toby speaks, "I thought it might look a little better in daylight, but it's worse. What a place. It's like no-mans-land."

Georgette stands, looking in front of her. She says, "There's nothing here, Toby. It's just dead, burnt trees and dried out mud for miles. Which direction do we go?"

After a few moments Toby answers, "Look, I think I can work out a path. Black, burnt patches sprayed throughout the land from last night's lightning bolts seems to lead to some kind of a remnant from a previous pathway. Look can you see what I am seeing?" he asks.

Georgette looks again. "Yes, I see it. The trees must have lined the pathway before the storm. I think we can follow it, even though the storm has done a lot of damage. This heat is unusually hot for a morning sunrise. Be sure to cover your skin, Toby."

They pack up their belongings and begin their journey heading south. After some time walking, they start feeling tired. The heat of the morning sun is slowing them down. The land is scorched and dry, filled with pale, decaying skeleton trees.

Toby thinks aloud, "I don't understand why this land isn't flourishing. There was enough rain last night to fill an Ocean. Look at this soil, its dead. Where are the birds? I've not seen one animal. We truly are in hell."

Georgette looks at Toby and asks, "How long have we been walking?"

He answers, "Oh, I'd say two hours or so."

Georgette tells Toby, "I am going to climb that tall tree, I need to see what lies ahead of us."

She walks over to the tree. Its branches look brittle and weak. Toby asks her not to, but she is determined to climb it.

"Just stay underneath me in case I take a fall. We need to see beyond this dry woodland. Give me a heave up."

Toby holds his hands together in a cup. Georgette put her foot into his hands grabbing onto a branch. "Please be careful, go slowly," Toby asks concerned.

Georgette takes her time taking each step lightly, eventually reaching the top, she can see a good distance ahead.

Toby asks, "Well, what do you see Georgie?"

She answers with a surprised voice, "I see a castle. Its lower down the valley. My goodness, its big, Toby. Really big. It's surrounded by a moat, I think. It's too far to tell but there's definitely something surrounding it"

"How far is it from here?" he asks.

"By broom I'd say a half hour at most," she replies.

Chapter Twenty-Six

"Is there any sign of life, houses or farms perhaps? Are there no villages near by, Georgie?" Toby wonders aloud.

"No Toby, but I can see smoke coming from small dwellings close to the castle."

Toby holds up his arms. "Come on now, down you get. And please take your time, this tree is ready to fall apart."

Georgette climbs back down carefully. Once on the ground, she looks at Toby. "I think we can use our brooms with two invisibility potions. There's no sign of life for miles. I don't think we will be spotted."

Toby rubs his chin saying, "Are you sure?"

Georgette nods saying, "Yes, we're wasting time walking. We can get there quickly if we fly."

Toby takes a look around then takes Georgette's hand saying, "Okay then, we fly low. Just a few feet of the ground. And quietly."

Georgette agrees. "Definitely low, Toby."

She hands him a small potion bottle and they both drink at the same time turning themselves invisible. They fly at a low, steady pace. Only tumbleweeds rolling past them on the dusty desolate path. Time passes with them traveling on their broomsticks, silent not speaking a word to each other, watchful and cautious as they get closer to the castle. Toby notices the dense woodland with its dead trees starting to flourish a little. He knew seeing this change in the land could only mean one thing, the Johnagock had to be settled nearby. The small patches of green grass are now starting to grow as they draw closer to the outskirts of the castle. The smell of firewood comes in waves of wind being carried across their path.

Suddenly the silence breaks. They hear the sound of cattle bells coming from the next bend. Cautiously they get off the path, hiding behind fallen tree stumps, still invisible and out of sight. As the cattle came closer, Toby and Georgette look at them with astonishment. They are not cows at all. They have bodies that look like cattle, but each one of them has three heads! They are grey in colour and twice the size of a normal cow. Toby keeps shaking his head bewildered at the mere sight of them.

Toby and Georgette stay quiet and still. Suddenly they hear a voice. It is a woman's voice. Slightly high pitched, they couldn't make out what she was saying exactly, but she sounded angry. She was shouting at the strange cow like creatures. Georgette and Toby wait patiently staying deadly silent. Georgette thinks for a mere second it could be a slave herding the cattle, hoping it was and she would be alone. She desperately wanted to talk to her. But reality hit her all at once. There weren't any slaves left here. They were all long dead. She felt stupid and angry for thinking such a thing, but then felt sad remembering the dead were once her own people. Witches and Wizards lost in this hell hole. She forced her thoughts to stop she needed to concentrate on the matter in hand.

The voice wasn't a slave of course, they soon realised it was that of a Johnagock. She was alone with her cattle and seemed upset having tripped over and landed in some cow dung, covering her clothes in the

Chapter Twenty-Six

faeces and muck. Toby found this hilarious, but stayed quiet, holding both his hands to cover his mouth and stifle his laughter, He hid his amusement.

Georgette whispers to Toby, "I think we should capture her. I'll cast a truth spell on her. Get what information we can, then shove several bottles of sleep potion down her throat after we're done. Enough to knock her out for days."

Toby whispers, "I can't believe I am agreeing to this." He shakes his head. "Let me pin her down. She's a big woman. You get the potions. I'll get her."

Toby tries his best to tiptoe toward the Johnagock. He stands on an old branch, cracking it in half. The sound draws the Johnagock's attention in his direction. A low growl escapes her. "Who's there? Come out. Show yourself," she shouts.

Toby stands deathly still. She speaks again, "Who's there?" she shouts with an angry voice. She slowly reaches for her sword, pulling it from its pouch behind her back.

Toby leaps toward her grabbing her from behind. The Johnagock was strong, but struggling with the size and strength of Toby. She wasn't going down without a fight. Toby was finding it hard to pin her down, but he manages to shuffle her off the path. Holding tight, he pushes her to the ground, behind the fallen tree.

Georgette, raising her hands, shouts, "Frozel!" The Johnagock woman freezes to the spot, unable to speak or move. Georgette then empties the first potion down her throat. It is a truth potion.

"We are going to ask you some questions and you will answer us truthfully." The Johnagock shocked to see Georgette and Toby's faces appear as their invisibility potions begin to wear off.

Georgette starts her interrogation. "Do you know where the prisoners are being held?" she asks.

"Yes!" the Johnagock snarls.

"Tell me where they are," Georgette demands.

The Johnagock, fighting with all her might against the potions affects, grits her sharp teeth.

"The more you fight the potion, the more painful this will be. So just answer my question." Georgette warns.

The Johnagock cries out in pain, "The castle!" she screams. "All the prisoners have always been kept in the castle dungeons."

Georgette looks at the Johnagock suspiciously. "What do you mean by all the prisoners? How many prisoners are there exactly" The Johnagock screams out in agony. Georgette grips her by the hair, forcing her mouth open she pours another truth potion down her throat. "How many?" Georgette screams with a fierceness in her eyes.

"Five!" cries the Johnagock. "Just Five. The Witch, the Wizard… and the children."

Georgette stumbles backwards. "Children?" she whispers, shocked.

Toby steadies Georgette. "Are you alright, Georgie?" he asks her.

Looking into Toby's eyes Georgette snaps out of her shock. "Toby, they're alive. She says children! It must

Chapter Twenty-Six

be them. It's got to be Christine and the Winchester twins!"

Georgettes heart leaps. "Mia and Henry must be with them."

Toby's brows shoot up. "Oh Georgie, do you really think so?"

Georgette nods. "Only one way to find out. Let's get to that castle."

Georgette orders Toby to force the sleeping potions into the Johnagock's mouth. She was out cold, sleeping within moments. Toby takes hold of her feet, dragging her away from the path.

"My goodness this woman weighs more than I do. I'm surprised the stench of her own feet didn't knock her out. We could have saved ourselves the sleep potions," he jokes. He places the Johnagock behind a bunch of old tree stumps, covering her with fallen bark. "There now. No one will see her for days. I doubt even the ugly cows will miss her, now."

Georgette rummages through her bag. "I've eight bottles of invisibility potion left. I'll take one to enter the castle, then another when I leave. I'll pass out five potions to the others before we escape. That leaves one for you. I have a plan and I know you won't be happy with me, but I need you to stay here and guard this wretched Johnagock woman. We simply can't take any chances of her waking up. If she does, then she will alert the castle of our being here. You need to make sure that doesn't happen. Hold on to your potion in case anyone should come looking for her."

Toby is adamant. "No, nope! That's not the plan! That's not going to happen. You're not going in there alone without me."

Georgette smiles, "Toby I'm more powerful than you. I need to do this, Nothing will get in the way of me rescuing my sisters. I love you Toby, like a father. I could never forgive myself if I let you go in there and something happened to you. I am stronger now. I know I can do this. Trust me."

Toby knew that once Georgette had set her mind to something, there was no changing it. He takes a deep breath. "Tell me what I need to do."

Georgette gives him a reassuring smile. "I need you here at this very spot. Keep your broom close and be ready to fly immediately. Please keep your potion in your pocket, you might need to use it quickly. I'll take my invisible potion just before I leave for the castle. It should give me enough time to get in and out unnoticed."

Reaching into her bag once more, she hands Toby a few magickal items. "This white flower is for protection, keep it on you at all times."

Toby tuts, "But I am a protector you silly girl. I have no need for this."

Georgette sighs then explains. "Your magick doesn't work here, Toby. That's why protector folk were never used or captured by the Johnagock. They were of no use to them. Please listen to me. The flower will protect you, so don't let it leave your person.". She then hands him the gold coin. "This will shine a light as bright as the sun if we need it. Keep it in your pocket. I am

Chapter Twenty-Six

taking the ball of twine, it confuses the enemies, I am also taking the ring Queen Opala gave me. When we leave this hell hole, I'll use the ring. Its stone will seal this place shut forever. Gregor must think I am stupid not knowing of its powers. The man is a fool. I am giving you one last thing, the fairy dust. It needs to be emptied over Gregor just before he is pushed into the veil. It will strip him of all his magic. The fairies used the power gifted by the seven realms to create a stronger dust. Gregor will be completely stripped of his powers, he won't be able to use magick again, which means he can never escape this realm."

Toby takes hold of Georgette, hugging her. A tear falls down his cheek. "I understand. I know now why you chose to take me with you through the veil. It was because my magick wouldn't work here. And these gifts were needed to see this plan through properly. You planned this entire journey. I'm so very proud of you Georgette".

Georgette smiles. "That's not the only reason I chose you to accompany me here. I also chose you because I trust you the most." Georgette hugs Toby one last time. "Now enough of this, let's stop our whinging and go get our family back."

Toby wipes the tears from his face and stands up straight. "Yes, young miss let's do just that."

Chapter Twenty-Seven

Toby and Georgette wait quietly as the sun goes down. Nightfall comes quickly.

Georgette drinks her potion, then mounts her broom, flying upwards to the sky and staying quiet as she goes.

The low light coming from the small moon made it hard to see. Georgette starts to descend, flying lower. She wasn't happy. She couldn't quite see the grounds or the layout of the castle properly. But then as if by a stroke of luck, the Johnagock begin lighting torches around the castle below, giving her a better view than before. Looking down from above, Georgette could see the moat contained very little water, and most of it was muck and mud. The drawbridge was closed, with guards standing at each side. Music could be heard, scratching fiddles and dull sounding drums. Large barrels of wine were being rolled out into the courtyard.

"They're celebrating," she thought to herself, with a look of disgust on her face.

Georgette hovers just above the castle grounds, observing the Johnagock and their movements. Many of them now started to gather in groups. There is a large wooden platform in the centre of the courtyard,

Chapter Twenty-Seven

with wide steps leading to its top, and torches burning on each of its corners. Looking around the courtyard again she was trying to figure out which entrance would be safest to use to enter the castle. There were three large doors, but before she can decide on which door, she is distracted by a Johnagock's roars. Their cheers and laughter growing louder, filling the castle. She knew something bad was about to happen.

Below the castle, deep down in its dungeons. Amelia is being held in a cell. With her little sister, Christine, cradled in her arms. Amelia is holding her, hugging her tight. Both sisters are trying to comfort each other. Henry Hawthorn had just taken another bad beating from the guard.

Amelia and Henry had gotten very close over the last week since being captured. She now knows he is no longer under the power of his father. He is a good man, the man she first met and fell for in Causeway City. That trip felt like a long time ago.

Most of poor Henry's beatings are due to him trying to protect the younger children. Each time the Johnagock guards wanted to amuse themselves, they tended to use violence. The guards didn't care which person their abuse was aimed toward, so Henry took the brunt of it, in order to stop Amelia and the children from getting hurt. He didn't want them to suffer any more than they already had.

Amelia felt lost without her magic. The guards had kept Henry and herself shackled in magickal handcuffs since their arrival.

Young Christine and the Winchester twins, Owen and Charles, were used to the Johnagock. They had grown up here, and had become accustomed to the abuse, having had to adapt to it from a young age. The Johnagock only remove their cuffs when they needed them to enchant things, like growing crops and seeds for food, or occasionally healing the sick Johnagock. No sooner were their cuffs off and they would quickly bind them again.

Christine, Charles, and Owen are very close. They don't know about their past, or their real home. They don't even know of the other side of the veil. They don't know there are others just like them. When Amelia and Henry were caught and thrown into their cell, the children were shocked, mesmerised and even a little frightened to see them. Amelia was distraught that night when she saw Henry lying on the dirty ground in the cell next to hers.

"Please wake up, Henry. Please don't leave me here alone," she cried. Then a little girls voice could be heard on the other side of the cell. "You are not alone, please don't cry." Startled, thinking they were alone, Amelia stands to see a young child, with long black hair, and large brown eyes looking at her. She remembers thinking how familiar those eyes were staring back at her. The child wore dirty rags as clothing. Amelia noticed two young boys cowering behind the girl at the back of the cell, looking just as dishevelled as her. All three children were bare foot.

Chapter Twenty-Seven

Amelia grabs the bars on the cold iron cell door. Staring at the little girl, one word escapes her mouth. "Christine?"

The little girl steps back, confused. "That's not my name," her soft voice replies. "We don't have names here."

Amelia's heart breaks. To think something so innocent could be treated so horribly. It brings a tear to her eye, swallowing back a sob. Amelia explains to the girl, "You do have a name, your name is Christine Crescent." Amelia could see it so clearly now. She understands why the girl's big brown eyes were so familiar to her. They were her mother's eyes staring back at her. Filled with emotion. Amelia smiles softly and says, "You are my sister."

The girl looks at Mia with confusion on her face. "I don't have a family, the Johnagock told me everyone who knew me are dead."

Anger wells up in Amelia. "The Johnagock lied. We are going to get out of here," Amelia shouts. "I promise, I am going to take you all home."

Amelia begins frantically trying to open the door, kicking at the bars. The three children wave at her and whisper, "Stop! Please stop. They will come back in if you keep making noise."

Amelia stops, then falls to her knees, staring in the direction of the children. The three children sit on the floor facing her, all cross legged and intrigued to see her. The twins are fascinated, inching closer to the bars they whisper, "Where are you from? How is it you look like us?"

Amelia gives a half-hearted smile saying, "You, young sirs, must be Charles and Owen Winchester."

Both boys eyes widen with excitement. "We have names too!" they shout quietly.

Amelia begins to tell them who she is and who they are. She tells them of their families. Explaining to them what happened to her and Henry and how they came to be here. Amelia tells Christine about their older sister Georgette. She tells her of Georgette's strength and how she knows in her heart that Georgette would not rest until she rescued them and brought them all home.

Over the next week Amelia would tell the children stories about their families and what life is like back home, across the veil. Christine would listen with such joy in her heart as Amelia spoke of their home. Giving in-depth descriptions of the clock tower, Belfast docks and big Toby. Their eyes would light up when Amelia told them about their mystic shadow cats. Christine deeply wished she had a shadow cat too. Amelia told them about the ancient ceremony where a young Witch or Wizard would be presented with their shadow on their first birthday. The shadow would be in the form of a tiny kitten. Amelia describes the secret incantation that would be spoken, completing the spell and joining both Witch and Wizard with their shadows as eternal soul mates. All the family would be there with close friends, she tells them. Once the small kitten was placed into your hands and the Tara brooch draped around your neck, both souls were connected forever.

Chapter Twenty-Seven

Amelia tells Christine her magick is still deep inside her. Christine never received a shadow cat or even a Tara brooch, she was kidnapped at such a young age. Amelia reassures her that her magickal powers will be restored as soon as they get back to Ireland. She also tells her that when a Witch or Wizard dies, their shadow cats die as well. They would just fade and dissolve away like dust.

"I know my Bijou is sad and missing me. I can feel him. I get a little comfort knowing that Georgette knows I'm still alive because he's still alive too. I just know she will find a way to rescue us. She's an amazing Witch, and the best sister. You will love her, I promise you."

Christine smiles, hugging Amelia. She was so glad she found her, but sad and angry knowing her life could have been so much better had the Johnagock not taken her as a baby. Christine told Amelia she had always had an emptiness inside her, a sadness she could never understand. She always felt a piece of her was missing, but couldn't understand why.

It was her family of course, and the shadow cat she never got to meet. Everything made sense to her now, even though she was still a child.

Henry told Owen and Charles about their family. Their estate, parents, and their famous grandfather. How he was well-known throughout Ireland as the best swordsman in the realms, and the most generous, kind landlord to his many tenants. He told them about Morning Star, and how fast his ship could sail. He tells the boys he would take them fishing when they returned to Belfast.

The boys would listen with excitement in their eyes. They had never seen an ocean before, so the thought of sailing on ships and swimming in the sea excited them. Henry promises them he would get them all home one day. They all had hope that Georgette, Toby, Cornelius, Isadora, Hickory and Despina would find a way to cross over the veil and get them all back home to Ireland. But days had passed and, with each passing day, poor Henry grew weaker. He wasn't going to last much longer if he kept taking such violent attacks from the Johnagock.

The day Toby and Georgette entered the Johnagock's realm, Henry received his worst beating yet. Owen and Charles could hear Henry being dragged along the hallway. They heard Amelia screaming, "Where are you taking him? Can't you see how weak he is? Haven't you hurt him enough already? Let him go."

But the guards just laugh saying, "Its best you all say your goodbyes now, because this mongrel isn't coming back. He's been chosen for tonight's entertainment."

Amelia starts sobbing. Clawing at her cuffs, she tries to pull them off. They don't budge. She keeps trying until her fingernails start to bleed, and her wrists bruise. But she can't get them off. Falling to her knees crying, she feels her heart is breaking in two. Christine holds her in her arms. Owen and Charles' cries could be heard echoing throughout the dungeon.

Meanwhile upstairs, Georgette was still flying overhead, watching the courtyard from above. She notices the Johnagock dragging a person to the platform. She gasps when she suddenly realizes it is

Chapter Twenty-Seven

Henry. Badly beaten, she could see how weak he looks, his hands and feet bound in cuffs and chains. She watches on as the Johnagock guards pull him up the steps to the middle of the platform, spitting on him as he passes. The largest Johnagock stands waiting on Henry. He pushes him to his knees.

Addressing the crowd, "Look," he shouts. "This pathetic Wizard is what our people have feared for too many years. Look at him now! He can no longer use his magick for we the mighty Johnagock have perfected these cuffs and chains, stripping him of his powers."

Grabbing Henry by the hair, he shouts into his face. "Look at you. You're nothing. We will enter your realm and all the other realms thereafter. We are going to take all of them for our own. We the Johnagock will rule once more."

The Johnagock grow louder, cheering with growls and roars as they celebrate. Georgette knows now more than ever she needs to find her people and get everyone as soon as possible. Flying in low, undetected, Georgette hovers in front of Henry. On his knees with his head slumped down. She isn't sure he is even conscious.

She speaks quietly in his ear, "Henry, please don't be alarmed. Stay quiet. It's me Georgette."

Henry tries to open his eyes. They are so badly bruised they have shut with all the swelling. Shocked, he thought he was hallucinating. "Are you real," he whispers, overwhelmed to hear her voice.

"Yes, I'm real, I am here. My god, what have they done to you?" Georgette can feel the anger welling up inside her. "Henry, we don't have much time. I am getting you all out of here. I need to know where everyone is being held. Is Mia safe?"

Henry makes a small movement nodding his head. Georgette sighs with relief. She can feel her throat tighten with emotion with her next question.

"Henry, is Christine alive? Is she with Mia?" Henry again gives a small nod, undetected by his guards. Emotional Georgette needs to keep quiet. She won't allow herself to cry.

"Henry, I need to rescue them first, then I'll come back for you." Tears start running down his face. He whispers one word. "Dungeons." He is so weak, he can hardly manage to speak.

Very gently placing her hands on Henrys face she whispers, "I promise, I will come back for you." The mere touch of Georgette's hands, just that small warm embrace, overwhelms him. He feels her hand slowly leave his face. Then he hangs his head again. Except, this time it was to hide his smile.

Chapter Twenty-Eight

Georgette pops her broomstick into her bag, then quietly walks towards the dungeon. She sneaks through without being noticed. The corridor leading to the dungeons is dimly lit, the smell so strong and foul she can taste it in her mouth. At the end of the hallway is a steep, stone staircase. She takes the steps as quickly as possible. As she reaches the last step, she almost trips at the sound of hearing Amelias voice. She couldn't believe it.

Georgette sprints to the cells where Amelia is being held. Still cloaked with her invisibility potion, Georgette comes to an abrupt halt as she notices one Johnagock guard stationed outside the cell door. She tiptoes past the guard undetected and looks through the bars. The sight brings her to tears. In the corner of the cell, Amelia is lying on a dirty floor with only straw as a bed. She looks so sad, cuddling a little girl in her arms.

Georgette whispers softly, "Mia."

Amelia jumps to her feet. "Georgie!" she shouts, grabbing the bars. Her voice alerts the guard. He walks over to the cell and whacks her hands hard with his baton. He snaps at her, "What are you saying mongrel?"

Chapter Twenty-Eight

Jumping back from the bars she answers, "Nothing. I fell over, that's all."

He growls, "Then shut up! Before I make you shut up!" He bangs the bars with his baton once more. That was enough for Georgette to lose her temper.

Georgette's nostrils flare. A heat comes over her entire body from head to toe. She feels an immediate rage boiling over inside her. She snatches the baton from the Johnagock's hand and whacks him across the head with full force, knocking him unconscious. He falls hard to the floor.

"Now that's enough off that, you, overgrown pig." She then opens his mouth, pouring sleep potion down his throat.

Amelia can't believe what's just happened. Looking around in astonishment she calls, "Where are you, Georgie? I can't see you." A small gasp can be heard coming from behind Amelia. Georgette looks over her shoulder. Turning around and walking to the cell door she can see the girl more clearly now, along with two other children huddled in the back of the cell. The girl can't believe her eyes.

"Did you really just do that?" she asks Georgette in awe.

The two boys walk forward. "That was brilliant!" says one of the twins. "Is it dead?" asks the other.

Georgette smiles. "No, it's not dead, just knocked out." Moving forward, Georgette takes a close look at the little girl standing next to her sister. "Christine?" she asks with a shaky voice.

"Yes," Christine answers. "That's my name," she announces proudly.

One of the twins shouts, "I have a name too! I'm Charles."

The other boy shouts, "I'm Owen!"

Georgette and Amelia both let out a tiny laugh. "Well, it is very nice to meet you both," Georgette states. Her potion has worn off.

Stepping closer to the cell she looks into Christine's eyes and asks, "Do you know who I am?"

Christine nods, "You're my oldest sister. You're Georgie. Are you here to take us all home? Mia said you would come."

Georgette's heart feels like it could burst. Christine looks to Amelia, then back to Georgette.

"Yes, we are all going home. Everyone stand back, I need to open the lock," Georgette states.

Mia tells them, "I told you she would come!" Then she continues, "I can't believe you're here, you're finally here!"

Georgette fills with emotion looking at her sister. "I'm here, sister. Give me a moment I need to find the keys to open the cell."

Georgette looks about the room for the keys. Young Owen says, "I think they're around the Johnagock's belt."

Moving toward the foul lump of a creature at her feet, Georgette lifts her foot and taps the Johnagock with the tip of her boot. She needs to find a way to turn him over.

"Just push him over," Amelia suggests.

Chapter Twenty-Eight

Georgette raises her eyebrow. "Under no circumstances am I putting my hands anywhere near that filthy creature. It stinks."

The children laugh.

Once more, placing her pointy boot on the Johnagock's back, she kicks with more force until its oversized body slumps on his side. "There now!" she can see the keys. Unhooking the belt, she grabs the keys and opens the cell.

Amelia runs to her sister throwing her arms around her. "I knew you would come Georgie. I just knew it," she cries.

Christine walks toward Georgette, completely throwing Georgette off guard she wraps both her arms around her waist. Georgette drops to her knees and pulls Christine in tight.

"I am so sorry; I didn't come sooner. I thought you were dead" Georgette apologises.

Christine cries, burying her head into Georgette's chest. "It's okay Georgie, you're here now."

Releasing her sister from her arms, Georgette tells the group they need to leave quickly. "I need you all to drink these potions now, and remember with this potion, you can't be seen, but you can still be heard. So it's very important that you stay quiet. Do you understand?"

They all nod.

"When we get outside the dungeon doors I need you to all jump on my broomstick. When you do, make sure you hold on for dear life and don't let go. Is that understood?"

Amelia interrupts, "We can't. Look Georgie, they put these magickal cuffs on us. We can't remove them. They drain our magick completely."

Georgette looks at Amelia's wrists, noticing the cuts and bruises. Her temper boils over. Pointing to each of their wrists, one by one she commands, "Dhighlasàil," causing the individual cuffs to unlock and each drop to the floor with a loud thump.

Amelia grabs Georgette saying, "Henry! Georgie, they took him upstairs."

Georgette answers. "I know Mia, I spoke to him already. We're going to get him too."

She tells everyone to follow her and to stay quiet. Then she leads the way, bringing them back up the steps.

Once they reach the exit to the dungeons and everyone is on the broom, Georgette asks if everyone is ready. Three young nervous voices reply, "Yes, Georgette."

Georgette riding upfront and Amelia at the end, make sure the children are safely secured in the middle. It is Amelias job to grab Henry once they fly past him.

As they approach the platform they can see Henry is still on his knees. Georgette flies in closer and the broom comes to a stop. Hovering just above Henry, Amelia takes hold of him with every bit of strength in her body. She tries to swoop him onto the broom, but she wasn't strong enough to pick him up. He rises in the air, then falls again.

Chapter Twenty-Eight

The Johnagock, stunned to see this, begin to shout, "Witchcraft! There's another witch here! Spread out, find her."

Lifting sawdust from the ground and throwing it high into the air. The dust lands on the broom, then on each of them, shows the outline of their bodies. The Johnagock knew then where they each are.

Georgette races at speed heading towards the path where she left Toby. Amelia was crying uncontrollably.

"We can't leave him, Georgie. It's my fault I let him fall. I didn't have the strength to hold him. We need to go back."

Georgette lands abruptly, rushing to Toby. She hands him her broom and instructs him, "Take them back to the veil. Give me your broom, I need to go back for Henry."

Toby did as he was told. He knew he had more than one person now to protect. Toby takes off at great speed, carrying Amelia, Christine, and the twins with him.

Returning to the castle, Georgette pulls the ball of twine from her bag as she approaches the courtyard. The guards were on high alert, knowing the prisoners had escaped. The Johnagock take up positions pointing their arrows to the sky. Georgette, flying directly toward them throws the ball of twine in their direction. It opens up, unravelling itself like thousands of snakes, clinging and wrapping around the guards in a deadly grip, confusing and catching the Johnagock by surprise. They began to shoot their arrows sporadically, killing and injuring one another instantly.

Georgette approaches fast, She spots Henry being dragged off by two Johnagock. She screams, momentarily distracting the two Johnagock, long enough to kick the largest one on his head with the heel of her boot, knocking one into the other and leaving them both unconscious. Georgette flies to Henry, pulls him from the platform, swinging him with such force high into the air. She holds him tight. Once she has him securely on the broom she leaves at high speed.

The Johnagock, are hot on her heels, following quickly behind. Riding their mounted beasts, they were just as fast as her broom. Black bodies, built like horses but with heads like vultures. Razor sharp teeth and huge wings they were a terrifying sight to behold and were dangerously closing in on Georgette and Henry. Georgette can see Toby and the others far ahead in front of them. Amelia looks behind. She shouts to Toby, "Turn around! We need to get Georgette and Henry. Look they're behind us!"

Toby turns to see the Johnagock gaining on Georgette, the beasts snapping and snarling as they quickly catch up to her.

Georgette screams out loud, "Ionsai!!" Sparks of blue light fly from her hand directly hitting the mount and the Johnagock riding it. Watching them fall to the ground, Toby speeds up, flying as fast as the broom will allow him, trying to get her. Georgette is glad to see Toby heading in her direction. She knew the broom she was on couldn't outrun the Johnagock with their flying beasts.

Chapter Twenty-Eight

When Toby reaches Georgette, he hovers beside her. "Get on quickly," he shouts. Henry manages to pull himself onto the broom, but Georgette knew they couldn't outrun them all.

"We split up," she instructs. "Divide and conquer." Toby nods, knowing there is no time to argue. They fly off in opposite directions, but still within sight. Georgettes old broom flies much faster without the added weight of Henry on the back. She circles back to the castle, raising her hand as she yells the word, "Sruthan!" Bright flashing red lights shoot from Georgettes palm, engulfing the castle in fiery flames below.

The flames of the fire frighten the mounted beasts, causing them to flee. Georgette takes off and races toward the others. She notices Toby batting off the one remaining, straggling mount still chasing them. He kicks it with his large boot, tumbling it to the ground. Now none of the terrifying beasts remain behind them.

Georgette catches up with Toby and the others. They reach the field where the veil is.

Georgette jumps off her broom and hugs her sisters tight. Mia is amazed at the power her sister just unleashed back at the castle.

Once everyone else has dismounted the broom safely, Toby grabs the sisters in a tight embrace. "That was absolutely amazing, Georgie! Who knew restoring your powers would give you abilities like that? Honestly if it wasn't for you, I don't think we have stood a chance against those bloody, oversized devil chickens! Look what one done to my boot!"

Toby proceeded to show Georgette the bite size hole in his shoe sticking his foot out and wiggling his big toe through the hole. "Lucky I didn't lose my leg!" he shouts. Everyone bursts out laughing.

"Open the veil, Toby. Get these chains of Henry and keep the children close behind you. I don't think we've seen the last of the Johnagock just yet. The sooner we cross the veil and get home the better."

Georgette holds Henrys cuffs saying, "dhìghasàil!" His cuffs clink open, falling to the ground.

Toby gathers the children first while Georgette stands at the veil. She then casts the spell:

> *open this world far from here*
> *drop the veil for me to steer*
> *its fabric veil torn in two*
> *permit me now*
> *the passage through*

Handing everyone a bottle of Gregor's potions, she instructs them to drink quickly and get ready to run. The veil begins to slowly slice open.

Toby cautiously looks behind them scanning the field. He can see torches in the distance. He shouts, "We need to go! More Johnagock are coming!" The gap in the veil gets wider, enough to pass the younger ones through first.

Meanwhile, back across the veil on the Cavehill mountain, Cornelius lay on his back looking up at the night sky, trying not to worry himself into an early grave. Telling himself repeatedly, everything will be

Chapter Twenty-Eight

fine, Georgette will be fine, and she will be back safe and sound any second with the others. He had been telling himself that same sentence every minute since Georgette and Toby crossed into the veil.

Suddenly a bright light appears, alongside a deafening crash of thunder, revealing the veil. Shouting could be heard coming from the other side of the portal.

"Georgette! She's back!" Cornelius shouts. "Get up everyone, quickly. The veil is starting to open."

Running to take his place, he knows what's expected of him. He shouts so loud everyone pours out of their tents, running to the veil.

Gregor's face was like thunder. He thought Georgette and Toby wouldn't finish their rescue mission, or even return.

Cornelius calls him, "Get over here Gregor, you're needed to close this veil as soon as they all pass through."

Gregor stands beside Cornelius, angry that he had to comply.

Georgette shouts, telling the children to run. Christine first, then the twins, followed by Amelia who is helping Henry, holding him tight saying, "I won't let you go."

He smiles, relieved to be going home. Limping, he holds onto her as they slip through the veil.

"Now you, Toby," Georgette says.

Toby shakes his head. "No Georgette, I'll go last," he insisted.

With a surge of magickal power, Georgette pushes Toby through the veil. He falls through onto his knees. He turns to see the Johnagock right behind Georgette, the veil starting to shrink.

Cornelius frantically shouts to Georgette, "Come through Georgie! Hurry!" as he holds out his hand.

Georgette screams to Toby, "Toss me the coin." Toby takes the gold coin from his pocket tossing it through the gap. It flies towards Georgette, spinning a rainbow of colours in motion as it travels. Georgette catches the coin, then yells the incantation engraved on the coin:

Beam of light shine bright
Dark of day take away

The coin lights up, as bright as the sun, sending out blasts of dazzling light with such force it throws the Johnagock backwards. Georgettes powers were immense. She raises both hands saying, "Scrois!" The sky turns purple, with the very ground starting to open up beneath their feet, swallowing the Johnagock whole. Thunder and lightning roars, bringing a storm like no other.

Georgette then runs into the veil, taking hold of Cornelius' hand. He throws her straight into Toby's arms.

Toby holds her tight saying, "We did it, Georgie. We did it!" he smiles. Big tears falling from his face.

Georgette looks at Cornelius and nods. She can see the expression of relief on his face.

Chapter Twenty-Eight

Gregor shouts, "My contract first! Then I lock the veil."

Toby takes the contract from his pocket. "Here!" he shouts. "Give the dog this." He throws the contract to Cornelius. Cornelius catches it. Hidden behind the scroll was Queen Opala's ring. Cornelius knew in that moment what he had to do. Georgette needed him to seal the veil shut and he was the closest to Gregor and the veil. Cornelius slams the contract into Gregor's hand. Gregor is overjoyed to finally see it. He joins both parts of the parchment and they magically seal together. Its distraction gives Cornelius the opportunity he needs to grab Gregor with all his might, throwing him into the hell dimension. Georgette had taken the magick fairy dust from her bag and emptied it into her hand while waiting on Cornelius to take hold of Gregor. Now she blows the dust in Gregor's direction, quickly saying these words.:

Take these powers
strip them clean
an empty soul dwells between
dark and light take them here
no more power lays here

The dust lands on Gregor rendering him defenceless as Cornelius picks him up and forcefully throws him through the veil into the hell dimension. Gregor's face begins to age, his body starts to hunch over and shrink. His three hundred years of life are now apparent as his magick leaves his body, leaving him powerless and frail.

Cornelius looks at Gregor and smiles saying, "Enjoy your new home old man," he watches the last thin threads dissolve in the opening of the veil. Bending down to use Queen Opala's ring he seals it shut.

As Cornelius was sealing the last of the veil shut, suddenly a long, thin, pointed kestrel feather flew through, just before the veil disappeared. It was heading straight towards Georgette's back. Toby spots it quickly. Turning Georgette in the opposite direction, he presses the little white protection flower into her hand. Georgettes eyes grow wide in shock as she looks at Toby's face. Turning pale, he lets out a painful groan.

Georgette screams, "What's happened? What's wrong?"

Toby falls to his knees. Gregor had thrown his tam cap feather. It had a sharp tip blade bound into its base. He was hoping to pierce Georgette, but it struck Toby instead piercing his back. The blade ripped through Toby's clothes and skin, stabbing him in his heart.

Georgette screamed, "Help me!" as Toby lay dying in her arms. Toby looks at Georgette then slowly closes his eyes, taking his last breath.

Georgette screams, "No! Toby stays with me."

Amelia runs to her sister, hearing her painful screams. "What's happened Georgie?" She falls to her knees, grabbing Toby's hand sobbing, "This can't be happening, someone help him."

Cornelius has finished sealing the veil. He quickly runs to help Toby. He pulls a small black box from his

Chapter Twenty-Eight

saddle bag, no bigger than a box of matches. Cornelius then tells everyone to please move back as he needs space.

Isadora helps Georgette to stand, and Henry helps Amelia. Cornelius kneels beside Toby, opening the small box. There are two small bottles of potion inside, wrapped in white parchment. One bottle was labelled "Life", the other "Death."

Georgette knew instantly they were the same two potions from her father's collection. A glimmer of hope fills her breaking heart. She knows if the spell is done correctly, it will bring life back from death.

Everyone gasped seeing the potions. They were rarely seen, and almost never used. Cornelius carefully takes one bottle from the small box, then hands the other one to Hickory. Hickory was well versed in the teachings of black magic. He carefully puts the potion away in his pocket. Cornelius then proceeds to pour the remaining potion into Toby's mouth. Placing his hand over Toby's heart. He begins the spell:

Darkest nights
Stars of love
Bring this spirit
Back from above
Glide his soul
To his body once more
Reunited from deaths black door

Cornelius chants the words to the spell repeatedly. The magick is draining him. He is finding it hard to keep going. The spell is so strong.

Suddenly Cornelius feels a hand on his shoulder. It is Hickory. He smiles and chants alongside Cornelius, sharing his powers to help. Then one by one all the elders that were there in the field place their hands on each other's shoulders, kneeling in a circle around Toby's body, they join Cornelius in chanting the spell.

A trickle of tiny, white sparkling lights appear, floating just above Toby's body. Everyone watches in amazement as the lights slowly grow bigger, then softly widen out. Settling like a blanket of stars on top of Toby. Covering him from top to bottom.

Then a gasp of air fills Toby's lungs. He takes a deep breath and opens his eyes. Cornelius takes his hand away from Toby's chest to find the tip of the blade nestled in his palm.

"You had us worried there for a minute, big man. We thought we lost you. I've never been happier to see life in those eyes of yours."

Cornelius tries to stand up, but stumbles. Lord Anthony and Lord Riverdale grab hold of him, helping him to a nearby tent. Hickory joins them saying, "That was a big spell, young man. It took a lot out of you. You'll need to rest for a day or two to recover.".

Amelia and Georgette both relieved to see Toby alive, help him to his feet. Hugging him, not wanting to let him go.

Chapter Twenty-Eight

Toby cries, with big teardrop's falling fast from his eyes. He hugs the sisters tighter. "I can't believe you brought me back." He kisses their foreheads in turn.

Georgette explains that it was Cornelius that brought Toby back to life.

Toby asks where Cornelius is, he wants to thank him personally.

Cornelius was laying down on a camp bed in Hickory's tent when Toby enters. Opening the flap of the entrance, he smiles seeing Cornelius, taking a seat beside him. They just look at each other and start to laugh. Both are delighted to see each other again.

Cornelius tries to sit up. Toby lifts his hands, gesturing him to stop. "Stay as you are master Cornelius, don't get up. I know a big spell like that will take a day or more to get over. Better to let everyone make a fuss and give you some pampering," he smiles.

Cornelius looks and feels exhausted, but is so relieved to see Toby well again. "Gosh, it's good to see you big man, I thought you were a goner."

Toby puts his hand out to shake Cornelius's, but Cornelius manages to sit up and give him a manly hug instead. Toby holds back his tears saying, "Now that's enough of that. You get some rest and let time do its healing, young sir. I'll be taking the girls to my house to pick up their shadows and big Tucker. Then we will all head to the clock tower. Your mother and Despina will have you brought back to Albert Clock soon. I think it best you rest up there and, take advantage my boy. There will be many women running circles round you while you're there. And young Henry will be staying too. That poor lad is in a bad way, but your mother will soon put him right. I'll come see you later this evening."

Toby gets up to leave the tent as Georgette enters.

Georgette kneels on the ground beside Cornelius, holding his hand she kisses it softly. "What you did for Toby I'll never forget. I know there are no words to describe how difficult that spell must have been for you, Cornelius. You were amazing."

He grins. "I know, I am amazing. A spectacular one man show," he jokes. "But I suppose I can't take all the credit. I might have had a little bit of help from a few of the elders."

Cornelius lifts his hand gently touching Georgette's face. That one small gesture filled with such warmth and affection filled Georgette with emotion. She takes his hand in hers and gives it a gentle squeeze. Taking a deep breath, she then stands up, dusting down her dress. She puts on her hat, tilting it to one side.

"There now, will I do, Mr Delaney?" she asks him, with a wink.

He grins saying, "Yes Miss Crescent. But you forgot one thing." He beckons her with his finger to come toward him. She smiles bending down, knowing exactly what he wants but she plays along anyway.

"What did I forget exactly?" she asks.

Cornelius whispers, "You forgot my kiss."

Leaning down, Georgette softly kisses his lips. She then says, "I never break a promise, I told you I'd be back."

Cornelius looks at her amused as she walks out of the tent.

Chapter Twenty-Nine

Lord Anthony and Lord Riverdale offered to accompany the Winchester twins home to their family. Their faces light up with excitement when they see the large carriage with six giant, white horses. As the children climb into the carriage with Lord Anthony, he explains to them that their grandfather lives in Bangor, but their parents currently live in New York, in America. Lord Anthony thought it would be best not to tell Lord Winchester about his grandson's rescue in case they weren't successful.

Charles asks, "Will we get to see our parents? Is New York far away?"

Lord Riverdale assures the boys that their parents would arrive very soon, by passage through the clock towers.

Owen smiles, "Yes, I remember Amelia telling us about her clock tower. Will our mother and father pass through the Albert Clock?"

Lord Riverdale shakes his head. "No, my boy. Albert Clock hasn't taken any travellers this last week or so. But I am pretty sure it will be up and running again very soon now that all three Crescent Sisters are home. Your mother and father will most likely pass through McKee's Clock Tower. It's closer to your family home than Belfast. Now, let's get you both something nice to eat."

Chapter Thirty

Meanwhile, back at Albert Clock Isadora had put Cornelius and Henry into the third-floor guest rooms. These rooms had magickal doors which were only seen when the rooms were put into use. They were both comfortable and cosy. Henry and Cornelius were tucked up, relaxed and glad to be in warm beds in the tower. Despina had made some potions to help them with healing and to get their strength back. She put two large steaks on the grill.

She tells Isadora, "Supper will be ready in an hour. In the meantime, there's hot tea and sandwiches made for the lads. Give them their potions with a warm drink. It will speed up the healing."

Isadora smiles, "Yes, that will do perfectly until their supper is ready. I'll take these up to them now."

Pointing towards the tray Isadora commands "Teacht!" A small spark of purple light shoots from her finger and the tray begins to float towards her, following her out of the door.

Isadora heads upstairs, stopping outside Henry's room first. Knocking on the door she asks if she can come in.

"Yes," Henry replies in a quiet weak voice, sitting up in bed, and still aching with pain all over his body. He smiles at Isadora.

Isadora stands beside the bed. The tray following closely behind gently rests itself on the bedside table. Isadora begins fluffing up Henrys pillows behind his back. She helps him up in the bed saying, "Now young man, you need to drink this potion. It's to help ease your pain and speed up your healing. Eat this sandwich and drink the tea while its hot. Your supper will be ready in an hour."

He smiles awkwardly. He isn't used to people making a fuss of him, but he's grateful all the same. Taking her hand he says, "Thank you, Mrs Delaney. You're very kind."

"Oh, shush and no more Mrs Delaney! Call me Izzy. Now just you get plenty of rest. These potions will have you up and about tomorrow."

He sips his tea and thanks her again. Isadora wants to tell him about his mother's soul being trapped in the painting back at Belfast Castle, but she changes her mind, thinking he's been through enough for one night. Letting out a breath, she decides to change the subject

"Darling, I just thought you might like to know that Morning Star is fully restored. She's sitting in the harbour waiting for her captain. She is a beautiful ship."

Henry loved Morning Star all of his life, but knowing the evil deeds that had taken place aboard that ship due to the decisions of his father, filled him

Chapter Thirty

with sadness. Even more so knowing his mother was killed on her decks."

"Thank you Izzy, but I can't be her captain. Morning Star is not the ship I loved growing up as a lad."

Izzy frowns, "Now you listen to me, young man. Your father was a monster, a vile man, cruel and corrupt. That ship was never his. To begin with, most of her crew were devoted to you, not him. Did you know the ship first belonged to your mother? It was her grandfather that built the vessel, not here in Ireland but across the pond in America. Your great grandfather built it to sail his family to Ireland because this was his childhood home. He originally named her 'Rising Sun'. Your mother adored your grandfather, and that ship too. Your father changed the ship's name to Morning Star when he married your mother. So now you see darling, Rising Sun belongs to you, and may I also add, Belfast castle as well, with the entire estate, and all the money! Your father's family had no wealth left. They only had their Aristocratic Family Name. That old, nasty step-grandmother of yours, Lady Celine, with her daughter, your stepmother, only married into your family for the money. Speaking of which, Lady Celine, along with everyone involved have been arrested. They are all in Portmarnock jail. Oh, and one of your ship crew as well."

This didn't surprise Henry. "Let me guess. Was it Harlow?"

Isadora replies, "Yes, how did you know?"

Henry scoffs, "I knew it had to be him because he was my father's right-hand man, and I know Gregor would have taken him under his wing when my father died. What news of my stepmother? Has she been found yet, Isadora?"

Isadora shakes her head. "No, Henry. I'm afraid not."

Henry shrugs, "I am sure they will get her eventually, or if she's smart, she should take herself far away and never return."

Isadora lifts the blanket tucking Henry in. "I won't tire you out tonight with all of this. There will be plenty to tell, but that can wait until tomorrow. You will be feeling much better by then. That tonic should have you fit as a fiddle. Get some rest. I'm going to check on Cornelius."

As Isadora gently shuts the bedroom door, Henry looks at her with a caring smile. Isadora reminds him not to forget supper which will be ready in an hour.

Back at Toby's house, Amelia could hear Bijou from behind the door. He was fully formed, scratching up Toby's door, yelping and crying with excitement. He knew his beloved Amelia had returned. Big Tucker and Tailsa, seeing Bijou so overwhelmed, started to join in on the joyfulness, barking, groaning, jumping and stumping, waiting for the door to open.

Toby pushes the handle down, the door swings open as Bijou jumps up into Amelia's arms. Still fully formed, he knocks her over onto the floor. She presses her head into his as they both begin to cry happy tears. She wraps her arms tight around his body, overjoyed with so much love at seeing him again.

Chapter Thirty

Amelia calls Christine, "Please come meet the famous Bijou, the one I've told you so much about."

Little Christine is introduced to Bijou first, then Tailsa and big Tucker. They make such a fuss playing with her on the floor. Toby, Amelia, and Georgette sit quietly watching them, relieved and happy and just living in the moment.

Suddenly, three white feathers float down in front of Christine, landing on her lap. Christine picks them up then places the little feathers into Toby's hand. She smiles then says, "I think you should keep these, Toby."

He puts them in his pocket. "Thank you, young miss. I'll treasure them always I promise."

Toby whispers to Georgette and Amelia, "Where did she get the feathers?"

Georgette shrugs saying, "I don't know."

Amelia adds, "I have no idea."

Letting it go for now, Toby then asks if we are ready to take this young girl back to her family home.

Little Christine leaps to her feet. "Yes Toby! I'm ready. I can't wait to see the clock tower," she shouts.

Georgette and Amelia giggle.

Toby says "let's get your cloaks on, its nippy out there."

As Toby stands up, he suddenly hears a faint little cry. "What's that?" Christine asks.

Amelia puts her finger up to her lips saying softly, "Shush little sister."

Everyone stands still and silent. They look around the room. They hear it again, two small cries this time, a little louder than before.

Bijou, Tailsa and big Tucker each take a seat at Toby's feet. He looks down at them thinking, "That's strange. What is it? Are you hungry?" All three animals sat still, staring up at Toby.

Amelia then calls Bijou, but he doesn't move. Georgette tries calling Tailsa, but she won't move either.

Then the little cries began again. Suddenly Toby feels a twitch in his pocket where he'd put the little feathers. He looks at Georgette, Amelia then Christine. He whispers, "Girls, there's something moving in my pocket."

Georgette tells him, "Then get your hand in and see what it is."

Toby answers, "No, what if it bites me?"

Amelia busts out laughing, "I'll pull your pocket out then, and you can have a look."

She puts the tips of her fingers in the slip of Toby's big coat pocket, and she gently pulls it open. They all look in anticipation to see what it was inside. Out pop two tiny little black fluffy pointed ears, followed slowly by two bright orange amber eyes, a perfect pink nose and long white whiskers.

"Meow! Meow! Meow," cries this tiny, adorable kitten. Christine knew right away it was her shadow cat! She giggles with excitement.

Toby gently lifts the kitten out from his pocket, then hands it over to Christine. Overjoyed she holds it in her arms. She couldn't believe it. The love she felt was instant and unconditional, their souls connected at once.

Chapter Thirty

Toby then reaches into his pocket again. This time he found a small silver Tara brooch. It was attached to a brown velvet ribbon, and it had an orange stone in its centre, with a crescent moon engraved into its border.

Toby smiles holding the little piece of jewellery in his hand. "I think this belongs to you, little miss Christine." He opens his hand showing everyone the brooch.

Georgette says, "I know this isn't the big celebration you normally get on your first birthday, or the large gathering of family members and friends. Not even a party little sister, but please may I have the honour of presenting you with your Tara?"

Excited Christine yelps, "Yes please!" as she beams with delight.

Georgette and Amelia both sit on the floor in front of the fireplace beside Christine. Their shadow cats huddled around them. Everyone is making such a fuss of the new baby kitten.

Amelia asks Christine, "Well, little sister, have you thought of a name yet?"

Toby interrupts, "Well now, before you do young miss, I think we should perhaps see if it's a boy or a girl. May I do the honours?"

Christine gently hands Toby the little ball of fluff. Toby very gently turns the kitten over in the palm of his hand and smiles with a great big grin.

Georgette and Amelia both enquire, "Well, come on, were dying to know."

Toby places the kitten back into Christine's hands. Then he announces in a proud voice, "It's a girl, ladies."

They are all overjoyed with the latest addition to the family.

Bijou, Tailsa and big Tucker introduced themselves one by one. It is adorable. Big Tucker, trying hard not to be his usual clumsy self, tips his big snotty nose to the baby kitten. Bijou, then Tailsa lick it clean again, being overprotective. Everyone is fixated on this adorable little kitten.

Amelia then asks, "So now we all know she's a little girl, what name will you give her?"

Christine looks at her kitten for a few moments, just gazing at her with such affection. "I think I've decided." Holding her up to her face, she gently kisses her head, then looks into her eyes. "I wish to call you, Layla."

Georgette strokes Layla's head softly saying, "Little Layla. This name suits her perfectly. It's meaning is beauty of darkness and divine."

Amelia agrees, "You couldn't have chosen a better name for her. She's just too cute." She strokes Layla who gives out a little purr.

Georgette then takes the brooch from Toby. She drapes it round Christine's neck, tying the velvet ribbon in a bow. "Are you ready little sister? Its time."

Christine nods, "Yes, Georgie I am ready."

Georgette begins to speak the sacred words:

Shadow and brooch found their host.
Forever as one the days that come.
Love life star and light
crescent moon shining bright,

Chapter Thirty

two souls now joined forever more
with love now bound
until deaths black door

The little Tara brooch begins to luminate, its light connected with Amelia's and Georgette's brooches. Sparkling trails of dust flow towards each sister, blue, green, and orange. Twinkling strands of glitter connect in each sister's Tara brooch. All three sisters are now united.

Christine holds her little black kitten close, tucking her up under her chin and kissing her tiny face. She had fallen so deeply in love with her. Toby was the first to congratulate her, then Georgette and Amelia.

Toby then says, "I think when we get things settled, this celebration will definitely need a party. A proper big shindig to welcome miss Christine and little Layla back home where they belong. Speaking of which, lets get you all home to the Albert Clock."

Christine hands Layla to Toby. "Can you please hold her for me. I'll only be a moment, just until I put my cloak and hat on."

Georgette giggles watching Christine, as she struggles to wrap the cloak around her shoulders. It is dragging on the floor, way too big and far too long. She pops the tall, thin, pointed black hat on next. It falls down, covering her entire head and face.

Amelia starts to laugh, "Georgette please do something."

Georgette answers, "Oh for goodness sake, this will never do. Stand still young lady while I adjust your hat and cloak." She presses her Tara brooch with her hand saying these words:

> *Large to small*
> *snug not tight*
> *make this fit*
> *and place them right*

The cloak and hat adjust themselves, fitting Christine perfectly. Georgette takes Christine's hand and spins her round in a circle. "There now," she says. "Much better. And tomorrow we will have you sorted with a full chest of lovely new, black dresses and boots to match."

Amelia laughs as she interrupts, "Not all black, Georgie! Izzy will be better at choosing some nice clothes for you Christine. Please don't ask Georgie."

Christine smiles saying, "I'm happy with anything I am offered." She then asks Toby to pass little Layla to her, but to her amazement little Layla decided she wanted to be fully formed just like the other shadows.

"Aw look at her," Toby says. She's a beautiful baby panther cub. I must say she's a wee dazzler, she's so adorable"

Christine looks at Layla and giggles out loud, "I didn't know she could do this so quickly, I thought she had to be all grown up. You're so smart my gorgeous girl."

Georgette and Amelia look at her with pride.

Big Tucker opens the door with his paw. Toby pets his head. "That's our cue to leave ladies.".

Chapter Thirty

As they cross Albert bridge, Christine is in awe of everything she could see. Belfast is just beautiful, and the Albert Clock has her fixated as they drew closer. She stops outside the door, looking up at its tremendous height.

"Is this real? Am I dreaming?"

They all look at her little face. She cuddles her shadow saying, "We are home, Layla. Isn't it unbelievable?"

Amelia opens the front door and Georgette holds out her hand to take Christine's.

Toby speaks, "Yes, you're home little miss Christine Crescent, and a happy ever after home it will always be young lady."

Meanwhile inside, Isadora and Despina are sitting quietly in the parlour room, waiting on the girls to return with Toby. Cornelius and Henry are both fast asleep. The potion they took did the job. Not only did it numb their pain, but it helped relax them both. They were out for the count within minutes of taking the elixir.

Isadora hears the front door open. "That must be Toby with the girls," she says. Sure enough, they all walk into the parlour together. Isadora takes a deep breath, seeing Christine again, made her feel tremendous amounts of joy. "Look at you! You look so smart in your witches cape and hat. And who's this little cub?" she asks.

Christine smiles excitedly. "This is Layla, my shadow!" her voice full of pride.

Toby nods saying, "I'll tell you later Izzy."

Isadora then asks if anyone is hungry. Christine nods, "Yes me, I am hungry."

Izzy replies, "Then come into the kitchen with me. Let me fill your little belly. And bring your shadow cat Layla, I'll get her some milk."

Christine picks Layla up in her arms, then takes Isadora's hand. She looks around every part of the hallway and into the next room, not wanting to miss anything. It is just as Amelia described it would be. This is her home, and she loves it here.

Toby stays in the parlour with the girls. Despina is still sitting in the rocking chair by the fireplace. "Well, how did everything go? Is the child okay, Georgette?"

"Yes Despina, she's more than okay. It almost feels like she's been with us a lifetime. We presented her with her Tara brooch and shadow tonight, don't ask me how. But they both came to us at the same time. I did the sacred spell at once of course, just as it would be on a first-year birth ceremony. We were amazed to see our three Tara brooches connect as one, even though both Mia and Christine's powers remain bound in the bottle. It is strange. Anyway, we said we will give her a proper, big party to celebrate soon."

Despina thinks this is wonderful. "Wow, that's amazing Georgette. I'm so happy for all three of you."

Amelia asks, "Have you heard from Lord Anthony about the twins yet?"

Despina nods. "Yes, I have. He sent a cinder note not twenty minutes ago saying their grandfather was in shock when the boys arrived. It was at least ten minutes before the man could speak a word. He thought he was

Chapter Thirty

dreaming, the poor man. The twin's parents were sent for right away. They should be arriving at the family estate round about now. They asked to meet with you, Toby, and your sisters tomorrow. Either here, or at their estate in Bangor, whichever you prefer. They want to thank you all personally themselves."

Georgette says, "I'll send Lord Anthony a cinder note telling him to come here tomorrow afternoon. Henry still hasn't been told about his mother. We need to handle that first. Hickory will come here in the morning. He will perform the spell to release her soul. We will give Henry time to say his goodbyes to her. Amelia will explain everything to him in the morning. The poor lad has gone through a lot."

Despina agrees, "Well it's been a long day and my old bones need a drop of that tonic Izzy made. I'll take some home with me to Carrick castle. Can you see me to the passer door please, Georgette?"

Georgette walks Despina out. "Yes of course. Let me get the key."

Downstairs in the kitchen Isadora has made a full plate of supper for Christine. It was Toby's favourite, champ and fish, with big blueberry scones.

Toby enters the room. "What's that I smell cooking?"

Isadora smiles and tells him to sit down. "I've already put a plate out for you, and kept you some blueberry scones too."

Toby takes a seat at the table holding his knife and fork up straight, happy and content, waiting on his supper. Christine thanks Isadora for her food. She said it was the best meal she had ever tasted.

Isadora looks at her wee face and tries not to show her emotions. "We have a lovely bedroom prepared for you, with lots of gifts inside. Would you like to come see it? I am sure you must be getting sleepy little one."

Christine answers, "I have my own room? I'd love to see it." Her eyes sparkle with excitement.

Isadora, Georgette, Amelia, and Christine walk up the spiral stairwell. Christine knows about its twisting turns and creaks, she knows about the coloured glass in the lanterns which light up the walls with their many different colours. She knows because Amelia told her the same stories every night and every day while they were stuck in the prison world. They stop on the first landing. A magickal door appears in front of them.

Isadora announces, "This was the room Mary your mother and I prepared for you as a baby, but we closed it shut after you were taken. Mary asked me to be your godmother. I was thrilled, and said yes, of course. I helped her pick out your blankets and pillows. We both made a large pink crocheted bed throw," she laughs. "It was far from perfect, but every stitch was made with love. I hope you find this room as lovely as Mary wanted it to be."

Georgette puts her arm around Isadora, rubbing her arm gently with care.

Christine walks in first. It is a beautiful room, sweet and cosy. A white single bed, with the pink woollen throw lying perfectly on top. There are two gorgeous, embroidered cushions. One read 'Crescent Family', the other 'Baby Christine'. A white rocking chair with a large, white chest sits in the corner. In the centre of

Chapter Thirty

the room is a white wooden dresser with a dainty white mirror on top. Pictures of the family hang on the walls and there is a shelf on the far end of the room lined with lots of dolls and story books. On the floor beneath it was a beautiful doll's house and a miniature Albert Clock. There were so many things capturing Christine's eye, but to her surprise, Layla had followed them upstairs, with Tailsa and Bijou not far behind. All three cats jump up onto the bed.

Christine sat on the edge, picking up the cushion that said, 'Baby Christine'. Holding it to her nose she inhales deeply. "I smell berries."

Georgette, Amelia, and Isadora smile. They know it was Mary's scent still lingering on the pillow, even after all these years.

Christine looked at Isadora and asks, "Izzy, does this mean you're still going to be my godmother?"

Isadora draws a breath. She takes Christine in her arms. "My darling girl, I've always been your godmother. I don't need a piece of parchment to tell me that. I am Amelia and Georgette's godmother too. You're all like daughters to me. I love you all so much." Isadora then smiles and lifts her head. "Now what's this I hear about black dresses?"

Georgette rolls her eyes, looking at Amelia. Amelia starts laughing, "What? Don't look at me like that. I did say she should ask Izzy. Georgie you might like dreary old long black dresses, but some of us like a bit of colour," she mocks.

Isadora says, "Now darling, I've filled this trunk with many clothes in many different colours, all of them just for you. And I've left a cute, wee nightgown under your pillow. You get yourself changed and into bed. I am sure you're tired."

Christine smiles saying, "This will be the first time I've ever slept in a bed. I only ever went to sleep on a floor with straw."

Isadora holds back the tears saying, "Then you're in for a treat, my darling. And it's the best nights rest you'll ever have."

Amelia tells Christine, "I'll come back up in a little while to tell you a bedtime story, just as we always do. Yes?"

Christine says, "I can't wait."

As everyone leaves the room, Christine asks, "Please don't lock the door though. I'd like it left open if you don't mind."

Georgette answers, "That's no problem." She lifts a large book from the shelf and lays it in front of the door. "There now, see. That should hold it open for you."

A happy Christine says, "Thank you, Georgie."

Once out on the landing, Isadora whispers quietly, "Girls, I'm exhausted. I think I'm going to call it a night and get some rest. I will see you both in the morning. Tell Toby I said goodnight. Oh, and there's sandwiches made up for you both in the kitchen."

Georgette says, "I'm going down to lock up. I'll let him know."

Isadora gives a little wave as she heads toward her bedroom. "Thank you, darling. I'll see you all in the morning, but not too early. I don't do stupid o'clock."

Amelia laughs, "We know!"

Chapter Thirty

Amelia then goes back into Christine's room to tuck her in and tell her a story.

Georgette walks downstairs. Toby has finished his supper and is now sitting in the parlour. He had his big coat and hat on. Georgette asks, "Did you enjoy your grub, Toby?"

Patting his belly he replies, "I did indeed. I am ready for my rounds, and then my own cosy bed. That's a cold night out there. How's miss Christine liking her room?"

"She loves it," Georgette replies.

"Bless her," says Toby. "It's so beautiful watching her take all of this in. It's going to take time for her to adjust fully, but everything from here onwards will only get better, I say. And on that note, I'll be off. Come lock up behind me and get yourself to bed, young miss. Sleep easy tonight Georgette and dream gentle dreams." He then hugs her and kisses her head as he heads out the door.

Georgette locks the clock tower up for the night. She takes the sandwiches from the kitchen with two glasses of milk. Blowing out the last candle in the hall, she takes the stairs and heads up to Christine's room. Stopping at the doorway, she sits on the steps outside and listens to Amelia telling her little sister a story. Amelia hadn't long begun the story when Christine drifted into a deep sleep. Amelia quietly lifted the pink woollen blanket and covered Christine. Layla was curled in a ball, tucked close to her chest, purring softly.

Amelia tiptoes out of the bedroom. She leaves a little pink flame magically burning in the oil lamp in case Christine wakes up in the night. She leaves the door wedged open as well. Leaving the bedroom, she notices Georgette sitting on the stairwell. She holds both hands out to help her up.

"Are those the sandwiches Izzy made?" Amelia asks.

Georgette answers, "Yip."

Amelia giggled quietly, "Oh dear, this means they're more like doorsteps. I am frightened to look inside. Heaven only knows what she packed into them."

Georgette smiles, amused. "Isadora is known for being a feeder. Cheese, ham, beef, tomatoes, celery, and honey. Oh, and butter. The woman must think she's feeding two dockers. Do we eat these or climb them?" Georgette jokes.

Amelia giggles quietly again, not wanting to wake anyone up. Georgette tells her take the plate with her and a glass of milk. "Bijou and Tailsa will finish off whatever food we leave."

Amelia takes her plate and glass. Both sisters walk towards Amelia's bedroom. They enter together and set the plates and glasses on the dresser. Amelia then walks over to Georgette, hugs her tight, taking her a little by surprise. Amelia softly says, "I knew you would come and get us. I knew you would somehow find a way, Georgie."

Georgette holds her sister tighter. "We're home now and we're all together."

Chapter Thirty

Both sisters sit on the end of Amelia's bed drinking their milk and trying their best to eat Isadora's very large sandwiches.

Chapter Thirty-One

Next morning Georgette was first to rise. She did the usual thing, making breakfast and feeding the cat. Soon, footsteps can be heard coming down the stairs. It is Cornelius. He enters the kitchen, white shirt half open, hanging loose and half tucked in his trousers, bare foot, and with messy morning hair. Georgette notices he needs a shave. She bites her lip, staring at him. "He looks good. Really good," she thinks to herself. He stops in the doorway of the kitchen, leaning his big shoulder against the door frame, crossing his arms, just watching Georgette.

"Good morning, Georgie," he smirks. "I came down to see if you need any help. I could smell your delicious coffee from the top of the tower."

She suspiciously raises one eyebrow saying, "I thought you detested my coffee. Too strong, too bitter, as I recall," she mocks him.

Cornelius walks over to her, taking her hand in his, he spins her round allowing her to do a tiny twirl, then wraps his arms around her waist, pulling her in tightly. Leaning down he whispers in her ear, "Me? Say that about your coffee? Never! That doesn't sound like me at all. You must be mistaken."

Chapter Thirty-One

His sarcastic tone causes her to grin cheekily. Leaning in further, he places a kiss on the nape of her neck, his stubble gently tickling her as he moves, sending tingles throughout her body. Kissing her again, then again, he makes his way up her neck, over the point of her jaw until his mouth meets hers. She still gets butterflies when he kisses her. His kiss deepens. Georgette pulls away, slightly breathless. Looking into his eyes, she thinks this man couldn't be any more perfect.

A cough, from the corner of the room pulls her attention away from him. It is Henry, trying to politely let them know he is there. "Sorry should I come back? Do you two need a moment?" Henry asks jokingly.

Cornelius grins, "Yes, that would be perfect. Thanks."

Georgette playfully slaps Cornelius with her kitchen towel. "Good morning, Henry! Please ignore Cornelius. Come in and I'll get you something to eat," she laughs.

Cornelius tries to hide his amusement. "Did you sleep well, Henry? I know I did. Whatever my mother put in that potion worked wonders. I feel great."

Henry says, "I slept really well too. Whatever it was she put into the potion most definitely worked."

Georgette puts a pot of coffee on the table. "Breakfast will be ready soon. How are you feeling, Henry? You look so much better."

He pours himself a cup of coffee. "I feel so much better. I am still a little sore, but my goodness, compared to yesterday, I feel like a new man. I must thank your mother, Cornelius. She's obviously amazing with potions."

Cornelius nods, proud as punch. "Yes she certainly is my friend," he replies.

Henry asks if Amelia is awake yet. Georgette tells him she isn't, but she should rise soon.

Henry looks a little anxious. "Can I ask you both a question?" he asks.

Cornelius and Georgette look at Henry, a little concerned. "Of course. What is it Henry? Are you all right?" Georgette asks.

Henry nods, "Sorry, I don't want to worry anyone. It's just I still feel my shadows presence, but I don't know where they put him. I don't feel he's hurt or injured, but I feel like he's trapped in some way. Can you possibly help me later with a spell to locate him. I am starting to really worry about him. He normally shows up when I arrive home from a long journey. More so because I've been missing this last week. Am I being stupid? Could he possibly be in the prison world?"

Georgette answers, "No, he most definitely isn't. Try not to worry too much. We will find him by the end of the day, I promise you."

Cornelius slaps his hand on Henry's shoulder saying, "If anyone can find him it will definitely be this Witch. Trust me, she knows the best spells my friend."

Henry looks at them both hoping they are right.

Amelia walks into the kitchen. She smiles saying good morning to everyone, then takes a seat beside Henry. He pours her a cup of coffee, then takes hold of her hand under the table. Henry quietly speaks to

Chapter Thirty-One

Amelia, "This time yesterday morning you and I were in a very different place. How blessed are we on this lovely morning?" He gives her hand a little squeeze.

Mia takes a sip and sets her cup on the table, then throws her arms around Henry saying, "Very blessed, Henry."

Georgette sets two plates in front of them saying, "Two large breakfast plates at the ready. And in the words of our loveable, big Toby, get that down ye." Everyone laughs.

The laughter in the kitchen wakes Christine and Isadora. Christine wakes with a smile on her face realising where she was. She jumps from her bed lifting little Layla as she runs into Isadora's room. Isadora is still in bed. She sits up upon hearing Christine entering the room. Isadora had white silk pyjamas with a matching silk eye mask on.

Christine asks, "What's that over your eyes, Izzy?"

Isadora lifts the mask up from one eye saying, "This darling? It's just a little mask that helps me sleep. Blocks out all the lights."

Christine jumps on the bed, Isadora puts her arm around her. She asks Christine, "So tell me then, how was your first night in your very own bedroom?"

Christine, swinging her legs off the side of the bed, excitedly tells Isadora, "Oh! It was lovely Izzy! The best sleep I've ever had!"

Isadora, relieved to hear this says, "And tell me young lady, did you wake up hungry? Because your big sister is cooking breakfast. I smell bacon and eggs coming up from the kitchen. Doesn't it smell good?"

Christine replies, "I'll wait for you. Then we can both go down together. How's that sound Izzy?"

Isadora smiles then says, "I never get to lay in in the morning when I visit this tower. Why do they all rise at stupid o'clock?" She pulls her eye mask back down and throws her head back on her pillow letting out a loud groan.

Christine finds this hilarious. "You're funny, Izzy".

Sitting back up Isadora kisses Christine on the head, then gets out of bed. She slips her white silk dressing gown on and puts her feet into her pink fair slippers. "Okay, I am up. And there better be coffee. Let's go darling."

Christine holds Layla in one hand, then takes Isadora's hand in the other.

Downstairs in the kitchen Toby has called in and the noise around the table has got even louder. Everyone is laughing, talking and eating breakfast.

Isadora stands in the doorway. She looks at everyone with so much contentment. It reminds her of happier times when Mary and Sean were alive.

Amelia says, "Well hello little sister. Come sit beside me. Let's get you something to eat."

Cornelius offers his mother coffee. "Yes please. And make it a strong cup darling. How can all of you be so dapper this early in the morning?"

Everyone laughs. Cornelius hands Isadora a large mug of coffee. "I am taking this coffee up to bed. I need to send some cinder notes so please shout a little louder. I don't think they can hear you all at the docks,"

Chapter Thirty-One

she says jokingly as she leaves to go fetch parchment and ink.

After breakfast Amelia asks Henry if he would like to see the view from the bell tower.

"Yes," he says. "I'd be delighted. Then perhaps you might like to join me on a stroll to the harbour. Apparently repairs on Morning Star are finished." Henry pauses, realising his mistake. "Nope wait, the ships name isn't Morning Star anymore. Its Rising Sun," he announces with a boyish grin on his face.

Amelia smiles at his expression. "He really is very handsome," she thinks to herself. Aloud she asks, "I am confused, have you suddenly changed her name?"

Henry answers, "It's a long story, but I'd be glad to explain. Let's go up to the bell tower. I've so much to tell you Mia."

Amelia looks at Henry. She was dreading having to tell him the news about his mother. She smiles. "Come on then, let's get you up to the top of our home. Bring our coffee with us. It's cold up there at this time of morning. The hot drinks will warm us up."

As they reach the top of the tower Amelia asks Henry in a caring voice, "You go first, what is your news? Then I'll tell you mine."

Henry tells Amelia about the conversation he'd had with Isadora. "I wanted to sink Morning Star to the bottom of the ocean at one point. I couldn't captain that ship knowing what horrible things had taken place on it. But then hearing the full story and learning the truth of what really happened from Isadora, knowing about the ship's history, I've changed my mind. I want to keep her and the castle as well. It's what my mother and grandfather would have wanted. My stepmother is still in hiding. She has no claim to my estate. She will be caught eventually I am sure of it. I plan to put the castle back to its original state, take out all that stupid pageantry Celine packed into it."

Looking at Amelia, Henry notices she looks sad. Confused he asks, "What's wrong, Mia? Are you feeling unwell. You look pale."

Amelia takes both Henry's hands in hers. "Listen Henry, I brought you up here to tell you something very important. I have news about your mother's death."

Henry is taken aback.

"We didn't want to tell you yesterday because you were so ill, and still in recovery. It was decided by everyone to tell you this morning." She starts to explain everything she'd been told about his mother's soul being trapped in the painting, and the heart-breaking news of Celine and how she murdered her.

Henry is initially shocked to hear the news. He takes a moment to let it all sink in, his shock turning to sadness, and then anger. "I must go right away to the castle. I need this put right. I have to see my mother. If I speak to her, will she hear me?"

Amelia answers, "Yes, you will both hear each other. But you will only have moments while Hickory casts his spell. He will be here soon to take you to the castle, and he will perform the spell to free her soul using the black candle. Would you like me to go with you?" she asks in a caring soft voice.

Chapter Thirty-One

Henry puts his arms around her, pulling her in tight. "Yes, please Mia. Please come with me. I can't do this without you. I'd like Georgette and Toby to come too."

Amelia and Henry spend a few more minutes up in the bell tower just holding each other, looking out to sea, wrapped in each other's arms for comfort.

Chapter Thirty-Two

Downstairs waiting in the hallway is Georgette. In her hands, she holds a single pink rose. She hands it to Henry. He knew it is for his mother. It is a pink, pony rose, his mother's favourite.

Henry struggles to hold back his tears as he takes the rose from Georgette's hand. He looks at her with kindness. "Thank you, Georgie." Then he asks, "Can you please come with me to the castle? Toby and Amelia are both going."

"Yes, of course. I'll go get my hat and cloak."

Once outside, Toby opens the door to the carriage as they enter one by one. Hickory is already inside.

The journey to the castle is quiet. Everyone feels sorry for Henry. The carriage stops at the castle gates. They are locked. Henry steps out of the carriage. He walks toward the large gates. Then lifting his hands, he places them on the cold iron bars and pushes the gates open. Suddenly they begin illuminating. He quickly takes his hands off the bars and moves back. The lights disappear.

Toby opens the carriage door. Looking toward Henry, he asks, "What's wrong?"

Henry puts his hands on the gates once more. They illuminate even brighter than before, then start to vibrate. Everyone in the carriage climbs out as they watch the scene unfolding before them. A strong wind begins to pick up, rushing past everyone, clearing fallen leaves and foliage from the path. All around them flowers begin to bloom, and trees began to flourish. An array of beautiful colours now fills the once dark, gloomy forest. The group watch in bewilderment at the magick unfolding around them.

Hickory on the other hand isn't surprised at all. He knows the reason this is happening. The estate is greeting its new owner. It is welcoming Henry back. Gregor's nasty enchantments that once poisoned this estate are gone.

Suddenly a large key appears on the ground in front of Henry. Bending down, Henry tilts his head to one side, curiously looking at the key. He picks the key up. The moment he places the key in his hands he knows instantly it belongs to him.

The key is made from heavy iron. Its design is beautiful. It had swirling edges cut perfectly into every groove. He places the key into the keyhole, turning it once. There is a loud clank. The enormous, decadent gates slowly start to open.

Henry places one foot over the threshold and onto the castle grounds. At that moment a large ring of multiple old iron keys present themselves to him, floating in midair and waiting for Henry to accept ownership of the estate. They are the keys to his castle. The castle is welcoming him back home. A small gust of wind intensifies the fresh smelling grass with an

Chapter Thirty-Two

array of wildflowers, which fills the air around him. Henry is astonished. He turns to the others.

"Welcome home my boy. And may I say what a beautiful welcome" says Hickory.

"It feels like home. For the first time in my life. It's strange. I can't understand why. But I just feel like I belong here now," says Henry.

Hickory walks over to Henry and places his hand on his shoulder. "I can tell you why, young man. Gregor, Celine and your stepmother clearly had the castle enchanted. They must have bound your presence from being its rightful lord and master. The spell is broken now. Everything you're seeing now is how it should have been for you as a child."

Henry looks around his estate, taking in its beauty. "I remember when my mother was alive, how beautiful these woods used to be. It's all coming back to me."

Amelia steps forward taking Henrys hand. She leads him back to the carriage. "Let's go finish this, Henry. Let's put everything right". She smiles.

The ride along the path of the castle grounds was spectacular. The estate seemed to be given a new lease of life. The horses stop at the front entrance. The castle itself looks bright and polished, everything clean and fresh once more.

Henry walks over to the large entrance door. He can see it is still locked. Taking the ring of keys out, he instantly knew which key to use. He turns the lock and opens the door.

Georgette and Toby are amazed, captivated in the castle's glorious presence. It wasn't like this when they were last here. It was dark, damp and gloomy. Almost depressing.

They all stand behind Henry at the foot of the grand staircase. He places his hand on the wide wooden handrail. With a thick luxurious carpet beneath his feet, he takes his first step. They follow him up to the Ben Madigan room. He stops at the door. Hesitant, anxious to enter.

Amelia stands next to him and takes his hand, entwining her fingers with his. She looks up at him, "You can do this. Have courage. Be brave."

Toby puts his hand on Henry's shoulder staying close behind him. Taking a deep breath, Henry steps inside.

Once inside, Henry looks towards the fireplace. The portrait is still covered with a large white sheet. The room is quiet, only the sound of creaks coming from the wooden floorboards under their feet can be heard.

Hickory steps forward. Holding the black candle in his hands he commands, "Solos." The flame flickers the candle to life. "You can talk to your mother Henry, but it will only be moments my boy. Once I start this spell to release her soul, she will leave the portrait quickly. Are you ready?" he asks.

Amelia still clutching Henrys hands, gives him a gentle squeeze for reassurance. Georgette points to the picture saying, "Notch". The sheet slowly begins to drift away from the frame. It falls gracefully to the floor. Henry looks at his mother with such sadness on his face. She smiles. Looking back at him with so much warmth in her eyes.

Chapter Thirty-Two

"Mother, I am so sorry I didn't know! If I'd known you were trapped here all these years, I would have helped you!" he sobs.

The sound of his mother's soft voice can be heard echoing through the canvas. "I love you, Henry. You are my only son. You have nothing to be sorry for. Please don't cry or be sad for me Henry. My family wait for me beyond the black door of passage. This castle was once a very much-loved family home. It's yours now Henry. Make your life long and happy my son. We will see each other again one day. I promise you this". A tear falls from her eye, as her image begins to slowly fade away. Glittering speckles of dust can be seen floating from the portrait, rising up into the air, until nothing remains but an empty canvas.

Henry's mother's last words whisper throughout the halls. "I love you, Henry."

Henry looks up into the swirling pools of glitter surrounding him and smiles saying, "I promise. I'll make you proud mother. I love you too".

Hickory quietly continues with the spell.

Whispering words and a purple flame
I reverse this Curse and release their claim
From this picture you must depart
Freeing your spirit with a mended heart

The black candle sparks with purple flashes. Then slowly disappears, with only a single grey strand of smoke. The room is silent as the black candle dissolves into dust. The atmosphere in the room feels lighter.

Taking the rose from Henry, Georgette places it on top of the mantle. She smiles knowing this lovely lady is finally at rest. Henry hugs Amelia saying, "I don't feel guilty anymore. I feel a weight has been lifted, Mia. I will make my mother proud. I know she is at peace now. I'll make this castle my home once more and make lots of happy memories here."

"I'm so happy for you, Henry" says Georgette.

Hickory interrupts, "Sorry to push in on this lovely moment you're all having, but we are needed back at the clock tower. We have visitors waiting."

Georgette asks, "Who?"

"Young Charles and Owen are there with their entire family," answers Hickory.

Amelia bursts in, "But they're too early! We weren't expecting them until this afternoon."

"Well, they're here now ladies. Shall we go see them?"

"Yes, of course," Georgette says. "That is, if Henry doesn't mind?"

Henry answers, "I'd love to come too. I am dying to see the lads again. I can come back later to check on the castle and grounds. I've plenty of time to sort things out here," he chuckles. "I've the rest of my life, as it happens."

They close the door to the Ben Madigan room, then walk towards the staircase.

Henry abruptly stops halfway down the steps. "Stop everyone!" he shouts. They all halt, frozen to the spot.

"What's wrong? What is it?" Toby asks.

"Can't you hear that?" replies Henry.

Chapter Thirty-Two

They all listen intently, but no one can hear anything unusual.

Henry continues to walk the last few steps. "I hear a cry," he explains. He walks over to a large, old, gothic wooden door. He takes his keys and opens the lock. A narrow, wooden, spiral staircase stands in front of him. Henry begins to walk down first, with everyone following close behind him. Once he reaches the bottom step, he realises this room is an old wine cellar. As he walks further into the cellar, he can hear the weak little cry again. "There! Can you hear it now?" This time everyone else hears it too.

"That's my shadow!" he yells. "Where are you, my boy?"

The little cries are low, but constant. The cellar is dimly lit. It is full of large, wooden wine barrels, with racks of dusty wine bottles stacked on top of shelves. It is hard to see.

He commands, "Solos!" The wall torches begin to burn brightly. Henry can't believe his eyes. Poor Shane is trapped in a small cage at the far end of the room. He is still small, not fully formed. Henry quickly runs to free him. Suddenly, out of nowhere, a large fully formed white lion leaps towards him, sharp claws fixed, with piercing white teeth, mouth full wide open and ready to attack him. Henry raises his hands to cast a protection spell.

Amelia, Georgette, and Hickory do so as well. Then suddenly, just as the huge shadow cat descends on Henry, it mysteriously starts to evaporate and disappear into a plume of dust. Everyone stands stunned and shocked.

Toby shouts, "What in the name of the stars was that about?"

Hickory walks over to Henry. "Are you okay? Did the cat harm you?"

"No, I am fine," Henry replies a little shaken. He bends down to unlock the cage. His poor shadow, too weak to even stand is so relieved to see him. Henry picks him up. "Georgette please tell me you have something, anything on your person to help him."

Georgette kneels beside him. "Yes Henry, I have. Now hold him and stay still." She takes a small potion from her bag and pours it into Shane's mouth.

Henry holds him close, then stands up. "It's not working, Georgette."

Hickory interrupts, "give it a moment Henry. Its Nettle Weed and Energisum seeds. Shane will be fine my lad. Just wait." Moments later Shane opens his eyes. His strength returns and he takes full form again, letting out a large roar.

Henry beams with delight holding him tight. "Who did this to you? I don't understand."

Hickory speaks, "That shadow cat that just attacked you has just passed away. Which means its soul mate has died as well. What's more important, that shadow cat belonged to Gregor, which I'm afraid means he's dead. No doubt by the hand of his Johnagock friends. I can't say I am sorry, but I can't say I feel joy either."

Henry speaks, "Why did he attack me?"

Chapter Thirty-Two

Hickory answers, "The poor shadow was only doing as he was commanded to. Your shadow cat had clearly been held here all this time, captured by Gregor. He knew that if Shane disappeared in that cage, then you were dead, and this castle would become his. He wanted the deeds, crafty old man. He knew every trick in the book."

Toby snaps, "Not every trick! Long runs the fox as they say."

Hickory nods saying, "Quite right, Toby. Quite right. Now everyone. Let's get back upstairs. What a morning this has turned out to be."

They take the windings steps back up to the front hallway. Henry looks around. "Such a difference from one day to the next, I can't believe how lucky I feel right now. I am Truly blessed, I really am."

Toby pats him on the shoulder, "Thank the stars, my lad. Now come on, lets go see Owen and Charles."

Thirty minutes later the carriage pulls up outside Albert clock. Smiling happy faces come outside to greet them.

Chapter Thirty Three

Isadora, Despina, Cornelius, and Christine stand outside the door. Waiting in the hallway, proud as punch, stand Swift Winchester, the twin's grandfather, with Owen and Charles behind him and Seamus and Molly the twin's parents.

Isadora speaks, "You have visitors, girls."

Georgette and Amelia smile. "So we hear."

Cornelius opens the door wide. The twin's parents step forward. Seamus speaks, "I know we're early, but we simply couldn't wait any longer to see you! I hope you don't mind."

Molly takes a deep breath then instantly throws her arms around Amelia. "You gave me my life back. There are not enough words to say thank you."

Seamus reaches out his hand to Henry, "My boys told me about the sacrifices you made to protect my sons. I'll be forever in your debt."

Henry shakes Seamus' hand. Seamus then pulls him close, giving him a heartfelt, manly hug.

Swift then walks towards Georgette. He holds both his hands out to take hers. "You wonderful young lady. You my dear have brought such joy to my family. Your bravery and love know no bounds. You, Toby, Henry and Amelia. Thank you."

Chapter Thirty Three

Big Toby enters the hallway. Swift, Seamus, and Molly circle around him. Molly hugs him tenderly. Then Seamus and Swift shake his hand. Seamus speaks, "Toby, my friend, you gave up your very own life to save another. Your caring nature and loyalty are beyond anything I've ever known. We will be forever grateful and thankful to you."

Molly looks around the hallway. "Everyone here that played their part in this, and everyone we haven't yet met, we will never be able to thank you all enough."

Lord Anthony steps out of the parlour. Swift turns to look at his friend. "Yes, Anthony. You as well! We know how much you helped. You're all amazing, kind people. We will never be able to repay you."

Molly then walked over to Georgette and says, "You have given me a reason to live again. Thank you, Miss Crescent. There not enough words to say how grateful we are." She then kisses Georgette's cheek, "Thank you."

The hall goes quiet. The sound of little cries are heard coming from Toby's pocket. "Oh no not this again," he chuckles.

Georgette, Amelia, and Christine knew instantly what he meant. "Look!" Christine said, "Your pockets are moving." She started to giggle and jump with excitement.

Toby speaks, "Shush now everyone. I need you all to be very quiet." He then calls Owen and Charles. "Stand here, my lads. Big Toby has something that belongs to you. Hold out your hands."

Cornelius and Isadora tried hard to hold in their laughter. Toby reaches into each pocket. Then he slowly lifts out two little kittens, white as snow, with silver-grey long whiskers, powder pink noses, and ice blue coloured eyes.

Everyone in the hallway gasps. Voices are heard saying, "Oh my stars. Oh my goodness."

Toby kneels on the floor. The twins stand near him, just gazing at the kittens. Toby tells the boys "Now lads, be gentle, they're only babies." He places the two little kittens into the twin boys hands and then speaks further. "Wait a wee second, I forgot to see if they're little girls or boys." He laughs, then holds the kittens up and smiles. "Well now, let me have a quick look. Oh yep, they're both girls," he chuckles. He sets the little kittens into each of the twin's palms.

Owen and Charles can't believe it. They have their very own shadows. The boys loved them instantly.

Swift, Seamus, and Molly stand watching with tears running down their faces. They can't believe what they are seeing. Toby then reaches back into his pocket. He takes two Tara Brooches out. Both are silver, with a blue topaz stone in the centre. They had long silver chains attached. He hands one to Molly and one to Seamus. "No time like the present to do this ceremony. Who will do the honours?"

Molly and Seamus look at Swift. Seamus asks him, "Father, will you please do the honours?"

Swift smiles with pride and nods. He clears his throat. "Nothing would give me greater pleasure my son."

Chapter Thirty Three

Molly and Seamus drape the chains around each of the boys necks, hanging their little Taras on them. Everyone stands still and quiet while Swift put his hands on each one of his grandson's shoulders. Then he begins to say the sacred words.

> *Shadow and Brooch found their hosts*
> *forever as one the days that come.*
> *Love life star and light*
> *Sacred moon shining bright.*
> *These souls joined for evermore.*
> *Bound together until deaths black door*

Molly, Seamus, and Swift held their Taras tight. As bright blue shards of light began to flow from the twin's Taras into theirs. The magickal connection is complete. Everyone starts to clap and congratulate the boys.

Toby speaks, "Well now. I think this calls for a wee drop of Salt Sea rum. I happen to have a bottle tucked away in the kitchen. Let's go get some glasses and toast this properly". Moments later he returns with a tray of glasses and the big bottle of rum. He puts three glasses of milk on the tray as well, for the children. "Okay everyone, please take a glass and let's have a toast. I would like to congratulate young Master Owen and Master Charles on this blessed day. A big welcome to your beautiful cubs and your loving family." He winks at Christine with a big smile, "Not forgetting little Miss Crescent and Miss Layla, of course! Health and happiness to all of you! Slainte!"

Toby then laughs out loud. "Oh my stars! I almost forgot. What names will you pick for these little ones?"

Owen speaks first. "I am calling my shadow Henrietta in honour of you, Master Henry."

Henry beams with delight. "Thank you, Master Owen, I am overjoyed. That's very thoughtful of you."

Toby speaks, "Now you, young Charles. What name for your cub?"

Charles lifts his kitten up. He looks at her. Then a moment later he says, "I've got one." Everyone laughs. He continues saying, "I am going to call you Mary Grace, in honour of Christine's mother."

Toby looks at him and takes a big deep breath. "Well now, that I wasn't expecting. And I must say I am thrilled. As I am sure the girls are too."

Amelia, Georgette, and Christine, all smile, then nod saying, "Yes, that's just perfect Charles. Thank you."

Swift, beaming with pride, announces to everyone, "I think these three young ones deserve a proper, big party, with lots of gifts and plenty of cakes."

Owen, Charles, and Christine scream with delight, filling the clock tower with laughter.

Henry interrupts tapping his glass. "I have a suggestion. How would you all feel if I could host the party on Rising Sun? My ship is docked in the harbour with a full crew ready to help."

Cornelius says, "Yes! a brilliant idea. And why don't we do this on Monday. There is a blood red moon on that day. The girls will be taking their powers back. Let's make it a big, massive occasion to celebrate

Chapter Thirty Three

everything. What do you all say? A proper big shindig on board my ship. With lots of friends and family, good food, old friends, plenty of rum and great music. I'll even let Izzy sort the guest list. And we can get some fireworks in too! How's that sound Toby?"

"Yes, a brilliant idea, young Henry. And a chance to get everyone together again. I'll even let the Dockers know. They all love a good knees up."

Swift, Molly, and Seamus look at Henry and smile, "We agree. That's very generous Henry. Thank you."

A few days pass and Christine can't wait until the party. She is standing at the kitchen table with Amelia. It is her very first baking lesson. Back in the prison world the Johnagock women didn't bake or cook anything, not like her sisters did. The daily diet consisted of any kinds of meat, pork, fish, chicken, and any kind of vegetable grown from the ground. If they were lucky. Mostly they just got potatoes. Everything was boiled in pots of water or cooked over a spit. The only fruit to flourish was wild berries and they only came once a year, in summer, and only when the Johnagock used the children's magick to grow them.

Amelia and Christine are covered in flour. They are making such a mess. Georgette walks into the kitchen and raises one eyebrow. Pointing to the table and floor she says, "You two better clean this up when you're finished." She then half smiles at Christine as she leaves the kitchen.

Amelia and Christine burst out laughing. Amelia speaks, saying, "That's me getting us into trouble. But she won't be so cross when she tastes our delicious apple pies later, will she Christine?"

Christine smiles asking Amelia, "Are you happy, Mia? Its only one more day until we take our powers and we have the big party on Henry's ship. I can't wait I feel so happy."

"Yes, Christine. I am happy too. I can't wait to see everyone again. Isadora has sent out so many invitations. It's going to be fantastic. I am going to see Henry now. Would you like to come? He's decorating the ship for the party tomorrow and wants to know if I approve," she smiles.

Christine giggles, "I'll go get our hats and cloaks." She skips from the parlour into the spell room, quickly grabbing the cloaks from the back of the door. The hats fall from their hooks along with them. Christine catches everything in her arms, then skips back into the parlour. Little Layla is sleeping on the rug beside Bijou and Tailsa. "Shall we bring our shadows, Mia?" she asks.

"No," Amelia replies. "I don't think so. Let's leave them sleeping. They look so cosy and relaxed."

They pop their hats and cloaks on. Amelia calls to Georgette who is upstairs, "I am just taking Christine for a walk to see Henry. We will pop in on Toby too. We should be back home in an hour."

Georgette shouts in reply, "That's okay! Have fun you two. Oh and let Toby know I've plenty of food made if he wants to join us for supper. And let him know we need him here by 6 o'clock tomorrow. We

Chapter Thirty Three

can't have you two taking your powers back without him."

Amelia smiles, "Yes, I agree Georgie. I'll be sure to let him know."

Just as Amelia is ready to leave with Christine, Georgette shouts, "Oh, Mia. Tell Toby that Flanna is coming in the morning. She asked if she could do some baking in Toby's house as its closer to the ship. She's making pies. Let him know."

Amelia answered, "Okay, will do." She closes the front door, then takes Christine's hand. It is raining, but Amelia didn't mind. She loved walking in the rain. She hands Christine an umbrella.

Christine looks up to the sky seeming a little confused. She takes a firm hold of Amelia's hand then speaks, "Will there be a storm, Mia? With lightning?"

"No Christine. It's just rain. Why?"

Christine answers, "Because it's dangerous to walk in a storm. Lightening strike's the ground with force every half mile or less."

Amelia looks at Christine. "Listen my dear little sister. Our weather here isn't like that in the hell dimension. We get thunder and sometimes lightning, but nothing to be afraid of. And nowhere near as bad. But we do have a thing here called fireworks. They kind of resemble a storm. They are really loud and flash the most amazing colours. But they're not dangerous when used correctly. People use them for celebrations. In fact, there will be some after the party. They're great fun. I promise. Do you not like the rain?"

Christine answers, "No, not really. I mean I didn't before. Perhaps here I might."

Amelia speaks, "I love walking in the rain. It relaxes me."

Christine giggles, "Really? Surely not?"

Amelia smiles, "Have you never been for a walk in the rain?"

"No never. We were always kept inside when there was a storm."

"Then let's make this your first time. I promise no harm will come to us. Do you trust me?"

"Yes, I do very much."

"Then come on, lets go for our walk."

Christine looks up again, trusting Amelia's word, but still watching the skies above. Big, wide, mirrored puddles started to form on the ground reflecting the street lanterns. Christine thought they looked so magical.

Amelia smiles looking at her little face. She speaks, "I remember when I was your age. Toby would take me for walks in the rain too. It was so much fun jumping in puddles. Toby always helped me find the very biggest ones. My feet and boots would be soaked right through, but we always ended up in the station house with hot drinks and warm buttered toast. Socks, boots and cloaks drying by the fire. Georgie never knew," she giggled. "It was our silly little secret."

Christine laughs, then walks forward. She then says, "Like this, Mia?" She took a little jump into the nearest puddle, the water splashing upwards and outwards.

Chapter Thirty Three

Amelia laughs, then takes a look around her. She answers saying, "No, more like this!" She runs to the biggest puddle she can find and jumped into it as hard as she could. The water splashes up into the air. Christine thought this was hilarious, so she took a big jump in too. Both sisters playing in puddles, creating memories and having such innocent fun.

They walk hand in hand the rest of their way to Toby's house, finding puddles to jump into.

Toby sees them coming, he was looking out his port window. Laughing, he enjoys the lovely happy memories flooding his mind. He opens his door.

Amelia and Christine are soaked. "Come in," he said. "I'll put the tea and toast on. Sit down there next to the fire and warm up. No need for me to dry them shoes and clothes, you can easily cast a spell now to sort them out yourself, Miss Amelia. You're certainly old enough now," he chuckled.

Christine laughs. "Can you dry just our socks in front of the fire though, Toby. I'd like to create a memory just as my sister did. She told me all about her puddle jumping days with you, when she was my age."

Toby smiles. He looks at Amelia. "That, young lady, was meant to be a secret."

Amelia shrugs her shoulders and looks at Christine. "Shush you. Stop getting me in trouble."

Christine giggles. Amelia casts her spell to dry them off:

Dry these clothes.
from cold wet form
to wear on skin soft and warm

Suddenly thousands of tiny little drops of water start to lift upwards from their clothing, rising gently above them. They disappear as they reach the ceiling. Christine watches with excitement. She loves watching her sisters do spells. She can't wait to get her magic. She was looking forward to starting school next fall. Charles and Owen were going to be attending Carrick Castle too, and Georgette was a teacher there. She felt so happy, so many delightful thoughts whizzing round in her head.

Their clothes dried in moments and their hair, too, was now soft, glossy and dry.

Toby speaks, "So why are you two out this evening? Apart from playing in the rain?"

Amelia answers, "I was told by Georgie to call in to see you first. She said to ask if you want supper. She has plenty. And to let you know to be at the tower by 6 o'clock tomorrow. Georgette wants you front and centre in the bell tower. There will be you, us of course, Cornelius and Isadora. We will take our powers back."

Toby smiles, "That's not a problem. Tell her I'll be there by 5.45pm sharp."

Christine smiles, "Toby, Georgie said to also let you know Flanna is calling to your house tomorrow morning."

Toby turns bright red. "What? Why? Why is she calling? I mean what time? And why is she calling to my house?" he asked again, scratching his head.

Amelia tries not to laugh but it was so transparent. Toby clearly liked Flanna a lot! She answers, "Well, the tower is going to be quite busy tomorrow, including

Chapter Thirty Three

our kitchen. Flanna asked if she could make her pies here for the party. That is, if you didn't mind."

Toby smiles with a great big grin, then tries to act unconcerned. "That's fine of course. She can use my wee kitchen." He rubs his belly with both hands saying, "I might even get a few pies out of it."

Amelia sips her tea, looking at Toby, then Christine and half smiles. They eat their lovely, warm buttered toast and drink the nice, sweet tea. It was so cosy watching the fire glow listening to the rain tapping on the windows. Time passes, and Amelia notices Toby seemed distant, like his mind is elsewhere. She smirks knowing this was Flanna's doing. Toby stops daydreaming. "Girls, I don't want to rush you, but I've a spot of tiding up to do. These floors need a sweep. I might give that oven a rub as well."

Amelia puts her hand to her lips trying hard not to giggle. Toby is working himself up into a state. She speaks, "Well, to be honest, we were just about ready to pop our socks and boots back on."

Toby takes the mugs and plates over to the sink. He scratches his head again then asks, "Amelia do you think a red tablecloth or blue would look better? I have both."

Amelia giggles then answers, "For this wee table under the window, Toby?"

"Yes, he says.

"Then I'd say blue."

He rubs his chin then asks, "And if, say there was a vase of flowers on that table what flowers would suit it best?"

"Probably some yellow daffodils. There's wild ones growing at the end of the dock."

He answers, "Oh is there. Can't say I've noticed before." He rubs his chin again. "Okay, now off you both go." He hands them a large umbrella, practically rushing them out the door. He tells them, "Now off you both go, and don't be getting wet again. And tell Georgette thank you for the offer of supper, but I am too busy tonight. What's she cooking by the way?"

Amelia answers, "Lamb stew."

"Oh!" Toby says. "Then tell her to keep me a wee drop. I'll get it tomorrow."

Amelia finished tying Christine's shoelaces on her little black boots. They both hug Toby then leave.

Chapter Thirty Four

They arrive at Henry's ship. "Wow," Christine says. "I've never seen a ship as big as this one before. It's enormous!"

Amelia takes a breath, "Rising Sun looks fantastic," she replies. The gangplank is down as they take their first step to board. Amelia looks at Christine. Her face so happy. The ships lanterns are all lit reflecting her image on the sea surface below her. The rain is starting to fall again, heavily.

Amelia tells Christine to be careful walking up the gangplank as it is getting a little slippery. They reach the deck. It is empty. Everyone must be down below. She shouts, "Ahoy! Is there anyone home?"

Henry is in his cabin. He runs upstairs on hearing her voice. "Well, hello there you two! Come, come, let's get you both out of this rain." He takes them down the steps to his cabin. "Can I offer you anything to eat or drink ladies."

Christine answers, "We just had tea and toast at Toby's thank you."

Amelia smiles. "No thank you, Henry. Georgie has supper on. I said we would be back soon. You're welcome to join us in the tower if you like."

Henry smiles, "Yes please. That's sounds great." Then he asks, "Christine, are you excited for your party tomorrow?"

"Yes, I am Henry. And I can't wait to see Charles and Owen again and the kittens."

"How do you like the ship? Isn't she looking great for your party?" asks Henry.

"Yes, I think she's amazing Henry. She's a lot bigger than you told us, and a lot nicer too."

He smiles, then tells her, "I've got lovely bunting made by the fairies. They will hang it in the morning. They also made us beautiful firefly lanterns."

Christine feels overjoyed. She runs over to hug Henry. "Thank you, Henry! For having our party here. I can't wait."

"Neither can I," Amelia says. "Now let's be making tracks, or Georgette will be very unhappy."

Henry grabs his coat and hat.

Little Christine takes the steps first. Just as Amelia moves towards the steps. She catches a glance of the door on the left. She knows this is the door to the room where the Fisherweed were held by Henry's father. She got chills just thinking about the cruelty that went on in there.

Henry takes her hand saying, "Let me show you inside. I promise it's not as it was before." He then shouts to skipper, one of his crew, "Can you keep an eye on Miss Christine please. We won't be long."

The skipper shouts, "Aye, aye captain!"

Henry then opens the door. "Trust me Mia. No locks, no keys."

Chapter Thirty Four

Amelia is shocked looking at what stands in front of her. The room has been painted white, with bright lanterns placed on the walls. Beautiful paintings of Salt Sea City hang on each side, flames illuminating each canvas. There are shelves and shelves of books stacked high. She notices a tall glass cabinet holding dozens and dozens of tiny bottles of potion. Twenty hammocks hang, brand new, with soft white pillows and warm woollen blankets. Amelia walks in, she is happy now, and relieved.

She asks, "What's all this?"

Henry takes both her hands. "I was going to show you tomorrow, but when I saw your face just now, I didn't want you having any bad feelings about Rising Sun. I've turned this once abysmal, dark room, with all its dark memories, into something light and useful. This room is for safe passage, mainly for Fisherweed. No more paying those old crones high coin for passage. If any Fisherweed folk need to come on land and can't afford the ridiculous charges, they can have potions free. And free boarding on board my ship. Cuttlefish was here these last two days helping me prepare the room. He asked the royal Salt Sea city guards if it was okay for my ship to enter their waters again. You'll never guess the reply. Queen Opala personally sent word saying 'Yes' and she would be delighted to someday come and see my ship in person. Cuttle has been amazing. I couldn't have done or thought of all this without him. He told me what books to buy, what canvases to hang. He even told me to paint the walls white."

Amelia feels a warm, loving sensation flow over her body. She wraps her arms around Henry, holding him close, giving him a massive hug.

He releases her. "Do you really like it, Mia?"

Amelia looks at him, then glances around the room once more. She smiles pacing the floors, then says, "I love it, Henry. It's just perfect. And such a brilliant thoughtful idea. So many Fisherweed folk can now visit our lands, many of whom never could before."

Henry catches Amelia's gaze while she is admiring the room. He walks over to her, nervous, not knowing if she felt the way he did. He stops, not inches from her body. Frozen to the spot they look into each other's eyes. The room is quiet. Just the sound of wood creaking, the ship, gently swaying from side to side. He puts both his hands on Amelia's face, then speaks in a low voice, "Mia. I've fallen in love with you."

Amelia' feels her tummy somersault. She blushes, taking a deep breath. Nervously she says in a soft voice, "I feel the same way too Henry."

He smiles leaning down to kiss her lips. Amelia slips her hands around his waist, his warm lips touch hers, sending chills down her spine. She pulls him in closer. Henry runs his hands down her cheeks onto her neck. Amelia feels warm inside. She wants to stay in his arms forever. They slowly part lips, then Henry holds her tight, pressing her head gently into his chest.

He sighs, then says, "You don't know how long I've thought about this moment. I never dreamed it would come true. I've been in love with you from the first time

Chapter Thirty Four

I saw you and that fiery red hair of yours in Causeway Clock Tower."

Amelia giggles.

A voice shouts from above. It is Christine. "Come on you two! Hurry up! Georgette just sent me a cinder note. She said to tell you get home now or the cats are eating our supper. Oops, I accidentally broke the parchment so I can't read the last part. And I can't reply. I have no magick remember," she shouts. "But I'll be getting it back tomorrow," she giggles. Christine was spinning round in circles up on deck still enjoying the rain.

Amelia and Henry bust out laughing. They walk to the steps. He puts his hands on each side of her waist, lifting her like a feather onto the first step. Once they were both up on deck Christine says, "What's took you so long?"

Henry answers, "It's a surprise for tomorrow. And you, little nosy miss, are not being told."

Christine looks at Amelia. She raises one eyebrow, looking exactly like her eldest sister, and says, "It's okay. I'll get it out of Amelia later."

Henry looks at Amelia, "Oh my stars! She's turned into a mini Georgette."

They all laugh, then walk down the gangplank heading home to the Albert clock.

After supper, Amelia walks Henry to the front door. He puts both his hands on her little waist, then tenderly pulls her close to kiss her goodbye. Georgette walks into the hallway. She smiles, then turns back into the parlour room. Amelia and Henry quietly giggle.

Henry hugs Amelia. "Goodnight Miss Crescent. Until tomorrow."

"Goodnight, Henry." She watches him walk away as she slowly locks the door and the magickal gates inside.

Georgette stands in the parlour doorway with her arms crossed and one eyebrow curiously arched. Amelia starts to laugh then says, "What?"

Georgette speaks, "Don't what me! Tell me everything. I saw that kiss."

Amelia puts her nose in the air. "What kiss?"

Georgette rolls her eyes. "I am not blind. Tell me Mia, come on. Was that your first kiss or has there been more. Well?"

Amelia laughs.

Georgette speaks again. "When did this happen and why haven't you told me?"

Amelia walks over to Georgette. She smiles then hugs her sister saying, "Mind your own business. I'm off to bed."

Georgette laughs too. "No I won't. I want details and lots of them." She then takes Amelia's hand. "Sit with me. I am not letting you up those stairs until you tell me everything," she grins.

Amelia rolls her eyes smiling. "Oh, okay then. I'll tell you but I want details about you and Mr. tall, blond and handsome. I've got eyes too you know!"

The two sisters sit at the bottom of the spiral staircase laughing sharing their romantic news with each other.

Chapter Thirty-Five

Monday morning finally arrived. It is a lovely morning. Amelia, Georgette, and Christine are up at the crack of dawn, washed, dressed and ready to soak in the magickal day ahead of them. Cinder notes are coming in fast all morning, for Amelia and Georgette, wishing them well and congratulating them. Christine jumps for joy when she gets her morning cinder note congratulating her on the coming day ahead. She is overjoyed when it happens. Amelia and Georgette are so proud of her.

"Look," she shouts. "It didn't burn this time, and I didn't snap the paper." The note was from Charles telling her he couldn't wait to see her this evening at their party. The note falls through her fingers like dust. Then another spark. "Oh look, sisters, it's another one," she shouts. This time it was from Owen. He told her he was very excited and was looking forward to seeing Layla again.

Christine was also happy. "Can you show me how to write a reply please."

Amelia smiles, "Of course we will, but I am afraid it will be me or Georgie sending it. You haven't had your powers returned yet. The twins can send their own cinder notes because Owen and Charles got their powers on the same night they got their shadows and Tara's. Your powers, little lady, are under lock and key. But not for much longer. We get them back as soon as the moon is full in the sky this evening. Now let's get you into the spell room. I'll show you how it's done, and then tomorrow evening you can send as many cinder notes as you please. How's that?"

Christine smiles. "Yes, that sounds brilliant Mia. Thank you."

Amelia takes Christine into the spell room. There is a knock on the door. Georgette speaks, "I'll get it. You go ahead and teach Christine a few magickal beginner's spells. I'll join you as soon as I see who this is."

She opens the door to find that it's big Toby. "Good morning, young miss. How's everyone feeling this lovely day? Where are the girls?"

"Good morning to you as well, Toby. They are both in the spell room. Have you eaten yet?"

"Oh yes," he says, patting his belly. "I've eaten for sure. Flanna put a breakfast out for me and it was fit for a king. My goodness that woman must think I am the size of an elephant."

Georgette raised one eyebrow. "Knowing you as I do, I am sure there was nothing left for the crows."

Toby rubs both hands in a circle on his large belly, then slaps it twice. "Well, it would be rude not to clear a plate now, wouldn't it? Anyways, the reason I am here is just to see if you need any help with anything for tonight?"

Chapter Thirty-Five

"No thank you, Toby. Everything seems to be sorted."

"Let me say a quick hello to the girls, then I am back home to help Flanna."

Georgette walks into the spell room. She stops and smiles. Toby is right behind her.

Amelia had opened a pillow. She is showing Christine beginner's spells. Hundreds of tiny little duck feathers are floating above their heads. Christine is spinning in circles in the middle of the room with her arms held out wide.

Toby suddenly catches hold of a memory. It is Georgette doing the exact same thing with her father, in the very same spot. He smiles. He can see by Georgette's face that she, too, was remembering the same thing. He then recalls a conversation Sean had with him on that very same morning. Sean told him that if Mary and him were ever blessed with a third daughter they would unbind all their powers as one. He joked saying, "Did you know the power of three Crescent sisters could allow veil people to pass into our realm? Imagine how fantastic that would be for Izzy and so many other cast out magickal folk. Izzy could come home again with young Cornelius and Francis. There's even a spell in the family Grimoire to do such a thing, but its useless to any of us. Only the power of three can cast it."

Toby remembers them both laughing, then Sean saying, "Let's hope one day we are blessed with another child."

They never spoke of it again.

Toby started to feel excited. He calls Georgette into the parlour and he tells her about his memory. She is excited and overjoyed.

"Oh Toby, if this is possible, then Cornelius can come home with Izzy and Francis. My goodness, Francis crossing the veil. How amazing that would be." She calls Amelia and Christine into the parlour and tells them both everything.

Amelia speaks, "So, who wants to do the honours? Who wants to look in the book?"

Toby answers, "I think all three of you should."

Georgette agrees, "I think Toby's right. The spell never presented itself to any of us before. Perhaps it needs all three of us here together in order for it to show itself."

Toby lifts the book carefully from its stand. He then sets it gently on top of the table. The book opens and the pages start to whizz past in a flash. Finally, it stops at a blank page.

Amelia' speaks, "I don't understand. There's nothing written here."

Georgette flicks through the other pages, making sure the many other spells are still there. Everything is as it should be, but for this middle page. Why is it blank if we're meant to see it?"

Christine speaks, "I think I know why." They all look at her with caring expressions.

"Tell us, little one."

"It's because I don't have my powers yet, silly."

Toby burst out laughing. "She's 100 percent right I am afraid. We are silly, Miss Christine. You're the

Chapter Thirty-Five

cleverest little witch here. Roll on seven o'clock, I say. Let's get you back your powers. And top yours up, Mia, of course. This is going to be be one huge party. We can surprise Izzy with a visit from her darling husband, Francis Delaney," he laughs. "I can't wait to see the look on her face when Francis boards that ship. Hehe, it's going to be priceless' I'll cross the veil and let Francis know. But I can't go until Izzy is here. What time is she due back?"

Georgette answers, "She said she will be here by lunch time, I think. Twelve o'clock. We have loads of food to prepare still."

Good then, I'll pop across the veil at One o'clock then. Is Cornelius coming with her?"

Georgette answers, "Yes, he is. The girls take their powers back at seven. Then it will be straight down to the party. Izzy, Cornelius, and you will be here for the occasion. How can we do the spell if Cornelius and Izzy are here?"

"Don't you worry. I'll get them both downstairs, then bring the book up to the bell tower. You three can do the spell while we're downstairs. I'll arrange for Francis to wait on Albert bridge on his side of the veil, agreed?"

"Yes!" The girls agree one by one.

Toby speaks, "Then I'll be on my way. Lots of things to do. I'll see you three later." He leaves happy and singing a bonny tune as he goes.

The girls go into the kitchen to start preparing food for the party. The day starts to go quite fast.

Cornelius and Isadora call in as well. Georgette sets Cornelius to work right away, sending him back and forth to the ship with trays of food. Isadora, on the other hand, makes her way upstairs. She tells the girls not to peep in their bedrooms because she'd left a surprise for each of them. She helps them clean the kitchen after the food has finally been prepared.

She then calls the girls into the parlour. Georgette rolls her eyes. "Let's go see what Izzy wants."

Christine, Amelia, and Georgette hang up their aprons, then walk into the parlour. Georgette stands in shock when she opens the door. Amelia giggles and Christine smiles, not knowing why there are four Frazzle Fairies floating beside Isadora, each of them holding a red carpet bag.

Georgette speaks, "What's going on, Izzy?"

"Well, firstly let me introduce you to Aoife, Erin, Emmer, and Mona. They are here to help us look our very best for tonight's party. We're having our hair done, our nails painted, and a little bit of makeup added too. Some of us need it more than others, but the less we say about that the better. Anyway, listen darling, it's my treat."

Amelia throws her arms around Christine saying, "Oh wow, this is going to be amazing." She then asks Isadora, "Did you bring clothes too?"

Isadora smirks saying, "Yes darling, you know me too well. I just couldn't trust Georgette with dressing herself, so I am afraid I had to take things in hand myself. Now then, I've left a choice of three outfits in each of your bedrooms, with a lovely little surprise

Chapter Thirty-Five

from my darling husband. He chose the gifts personally himself and said to tell you how sorry he is because he can't be here. But hopefully, you will all visit him this week. He can't wait to meet Miss Christine. He said to have a fantastic evening at your party."

Georgette speaks, "I think I can manage to dress myself, Izzy."

Isadora rolls her eyes. "Georgie, my dear. I love you and I say this with kindness. But no, you can't. Not for this occasion. A black velvet dress with long brushed hair just isn't going to do it I am afraid. Now don't worry. I've left you three beautiful dresses in your room. And I promise they are all very much to your liking. But there's no black!"

Amelia speaks, "Oh, just go try them on Georgie. Let's have some fun with it."

Georgette smiles, "Okay, just this once. Let's go up and see what she's put out for us."

Christine and Amelia run up the stairwell first with Georgette following behind them. Amelia screams with delight from her bedroom, then Christine joined in with laughter.

Georgette smiles walking into her bedroom. Three gorgeous gowns hang waiting on her approval. A red velvet dress, long sleeved, with crystal buttons on the cuffs and, down the length of its back. A green silk, plain dress was next with white lace trim on the collar and cuffs. Finally, a blue taffeta. It is slim line with long, sparkling, transparent sleeves and a dip in its back. It had a sweetheart neckline with white lace trim. Georgette holds the dress up against her body. She thinks the gown is beautiful.

Amelia enters the room. "Oh wow, Georgie. The blue gown is stunning. You must wear that one."

Amelia had chosen her gown too. It was a long, red velvet off the shoulder trumpet style dress. She held hers up saying, "Well? What do you think?"

Georgette answers, "Amelia, that dress is just perfect for you. I love it."

Christine runs into the room with her dress too. It is white as snow, covered in crystals and silver trims. She starts spinning in circles, giggling, petticoats bouncing on each of her turns.

Amelia and Georgette smile as they look at Christine with so much love and affection.

Then there is a knock on the door. It is Isadora. "Well ladies, have we decided on which gown yet?"

Amelia speaks, "I've chosen this red one. I love it thank you Izzy."

Georgette then speaks' "I love this blue one, Izzy. You took a chance on the shapes and colours, but I must say, even I was surprised how beautiful the gowns are. I was undecided between the blue and green, but it's definitely going to be blue for me, thank you. It's stunning."

Christine giggles, "I had three white dresses to choose from, but I want this one. Its' like a big fluffy cloud. I love my dress too, Izzy. It's so pretty. Thank you so much. What dress are you going to wear?"

Isadora answers, "I am wearing a gorgeous black velvet gown. I'll show you shortly."

Chapter Thirty-Five

Georgette looks at Isadora then says, "Black velvet, Izzy? Really?"

Isadora smiles saying, "Yes. I am older and wiser than you. And besides, you wear black every single day, I did you a favour" she laughs.

Amelia and Christine giggle, while Georgette can't keep a straight face as she speaks, "Oh well, I suppose. When you put it like that, I'll let you wear the black then."

Isadora laughs saying, "Oh, you'll let me? Will you now?" The girls all laugh loudly.

Isadora speaks again, "Did anyone open their gifts from my darling husband yet?"

Christine runs out of the bedroom saying, "No, but I'll go get them for you."

Moments later she comes back into the room with three small red paper bags. Isadora reads the tags, then hands them to each of the girls. "Go ahead, open them up my lovelies."

Christine takes hers out first. It is a black satin box. She opens it to find a small silver tiara inside, lined with white diamonds, pearls, and moonstone. She holds it up. "It's so pretty. What's it for, Isadora?"

The girls all smile. Isadora takes it from her hands, then says, "Let me show you." She places it on Christine's head. "There now," she says. "That's what it's for. You wear it on top of your pretty head. But not just yet. You can wear it after we get your hair done. You are wearing it up tonight, with lots and lots of curls. Darling you'll be the bell of the ball."

Christine giggles, "I don't know what that means, but it sounds like fun."

They all laugh. "Okay, me next," Amelia says taking a small red silk box from the bag. Nervously she opens it with excitement. Then she gasps, "Oh Izzy, oh wow. It's beautiful." Francis had chosen a hair clip for her. It was in the shape of a butterfly, made with rubies and diamonds.

Georgette speaks, "Oh my goodness, Mia. That's gorgeous. It will be perfect with your dress tonight."

Christine interrupts, "Your turn, Georgie."

Georgette smiles, taking her box out of the bag. It is a navy velvet box. She slowly opens it. Then she puts her hand up to her mouth and draws a sharp breath. It is a set of small, elegant earrings. Deep blue Sapphire, with diamonds and topaz. She speaks, "I am lost for words. Thank you, Iizzy, and Francis of course. The gifts are all beautiful."

Amelia interrupts, "Those earrings will match your gown perfectly. It's as if they were chosen to match the dresses."

Isadora smiles. "Gosh, what a coincidence," she laughs. Then she says, "There are shoes to match each dress as well. I knew you would pick blue, Miss Georgette. I knew you would toy with your decision, Miss Mia, but I was confident you'd go with the red. And the party princess could have chosen any one of them dresses and she would still be the bell of the ball."

They all join in laughing. Isadora then opens the bedroom door and shouts to the four Frazzle Fairies, "Come on up girls. It's time to work your magic." The

Chapter Thirty-Five

fairies fly into the room one by one, then quickly set to work preparing everyone for the party.

Across the veil in Belfast, Toby is on route to call on Francis. He has hired a small horse and carriage to take him to the Delaney estate. He can't wait to see Francis again and is looking forward to telling him the fantastic news. He smiles with delight thinking about Isadora's face when she sees Francis finally crossing the veil. It's only ever been a dream for her and Cornelius. They both never thought it could be possible. Toby was full of happiness and joy. He smiles throughout the entire journey.

The driver speaks, "The Delaney estate is coming up on the next turn, sir."

Toby answers, "Very good thank you."

Moments later the carriage pulls up outside the gates. The driver speaks, "I am sorry sir, but I can't take you any further. The gate is locked."

Toby smiles, then hands the driver two silver coins. The driver looks at the money then says, "That's far too much sir. You paid me too much!"

Toby answers, "That's okay my man. Go enjoy it. Buy the wife a new hat, or a roast chicken, or something. I don't know what veil people like," he laughs.

The driver looks at him confused.

Toby speaks, "Oh, never mind. On you go sir. I'll just pop in through the side gate. Just grab my bag please if you don't mind."

The driver thanks Toby, handing him his bag from which the sound of clinking bottles is heard. "Oh,"

Toby says. "Careful with that. It's Salt Sea City rum. Hard to come by."

The driver, still confused, had never heard of this rum before. But he takes the coins, then thanks Toby. He hops back up into his carriage and, with a crack of his whip, the horses move on.

Toby walks quickly along the gravel path up to the house. He can't help but chuckle to himself just thinking of Francis finding out such fantastic news, and the shock on Izzy's face when she sees her husband across the veil. "Yes," Toby says out loud, "It's a happy day, a very happy day indeed." He knocks on the door.

Moments later, young Maggie the maid answers.

"Why hello there, young lady. Is the master of the house home?" he asks.

Maggie remembering Toby from his last visit answers, "Yes Toby. Please come in. He's in the morning room. I am afraid Miss Delaney isn't home. Neither is Master Cornelius."

Toby smiles. "Oh, that's okay young lady. It's Francis I need to see anyway, thank you."

Maggie wraps on the morning room door then waits. Francis shouts, "Come in."

Maggie enters first. "You have a visitor, sir."

Francis asks, "Who?"

Toby walks in. "Why it's me, big Toby, my dear friend."

Francis leapt from his chair. Laughing he hugs Toby. "Oh my gosh, it's good to see you, Toby. What brings you here? Oh wait, is there anything wrong?"

Chapter Thirty-Five

"No nothing is wrong," replies Toby. " In fact it's good news I bring. You might need to sit down though," he laughs.

Francis speaks, "Maggie, can you get cook to put a pot of tea on. And a plate of grub to feed this big lad. Give him plenty."

Maggie smiles, "Right away, sir."

He then tells Toby, "Sit down put, your feet up and tell me what news it is you bring." Toby begins to explain everything that's happened and the plans to cross Francis over the veil.

Francis looks shocked. He can't speak for a few moments.

Big Toby sits, twiddling his thumbs for a few moments saying, "Just you talk to me when you've had time to absorb everything."

Francis stands up. He rests his hands on the fireplace, rubs his chin, looks at Toby then speaks, "So you're telling me I can cross the veil. Me?" he said holding his chest. "Me? I'll see your world. And my wife and my son will be able to see me too?"

"Yes," Toby answers with a great big grin. "You will see everyone, and everyone will see you as well."

Francis burst out laughing, slapping Toby on one shoulder. He says with excitement, "I can't believe this. It's like a dream come true. And neither Izzy nor Cornelius know a thing about this?"

Toby chuckles. "Nope, not a dickybird. Only me, you, Amelia, Christine, and Georgette know."

Francis laughs again. "Oh wow, this is amazing. I can't wait to see my wife's face. And my son's. I really can't believe I'm going to the party now as well. What should I wear? What clothes, Toby?"

Toby laughs, "I think you should choose whatever Izzy would normally choose for you."

Francis smiles, "Wise man, good thinking."

Maggie knocked the door. "Your tea is ready, sir. Will you both eat in the dining room? Or would you like a tray brought in here?"

Francis answers, "Just bring it on in here please, Maggie."

Toby speaks, "I can't stay long, Francis, but I'll have a wee bite to eat. Then perhaps you could take me back to Albert Bridge in your fancy car?"

"Yes, of course I will."

Maggie enters the room with the tray. She sets it on the coffee table. "Will there be anything else, sir?"

"No, no thank you, dear. That's Fine."

Toby and Francis had their tea and food, then sat for an hour talking. The clock struck 5 o'clock. Toby speaks, "It's time to go, my friend."

Francis smiles, "Let me just do a quick change. I will stay in town, then meet you as planned at 7:30 at the veil on Albert Bridge. I'd rather stay in Belfast a few hours than return home alone. I'll pass the time quickly if I am in town."

Francis then runs upstairs to change. He puts on a smart navy suit, a white shirt and matching blue waistcoat and tie. Then he comes downstairs in a rush, forgetting his car keys. He calls to Maggie, "Run up to my bedroom please. I left the car keys. Oh, and fetch my long royal blue overcoat while you are there."

Chapter Thirty-Five

Moments later, Maggie is downstairs in the hall, panting for breath. She hands the keys and overcoat to Francis. "Thank you, Maggie. Tell cook I won't be home this evening." He then looks at Toby asking, "Will I be home this evening, in the morning or the day after?"

Toby smiles, "I don't know. Best ask your wife, Francis." Francis speaks, "Yes, so Maggie tell cook I don't know when I'll return," he laughs. "But we will send word in the next day or two."

Maggie looked at him confused but said politely, "Very good, sir."

Toby then tells Francis, "Let's be making tracks, my friend, or I'll be getting fleck from the women."

Francis opens the door. "Oh wait two minutes. I nearly forgot." He walks into the morning room then comes out holding a very large bottle of Irish whiskey which he hands to Toby. "There you go. Will this go down well at the party?"

Toby chuckles, reaching his hand into his duffel bag. He pulls out two small bottles of Salt Sea City rum, holds both in the air saying, "Good minds think alike." They both smile.

Francis asks, "What is it?"

Toby licks his lips. "This, my friend, is Salt Sea City rum. It's hard to come, by but I managed to get a crate for the party. These two small bottles are for you and Master Cornelius."

Francis and Toby swap bottles. "I'll put them away for a special occasion, thank you Toby. Now let's be on our way."

Maggie opens the door. Francis hands her the two bottles. "Put these away in the wine cellar, Maggie. Make sure they are kept safe," he tells her.

Toby and Francis go to the garage. Once they are both in the car, Francis beeps the horn and starts the engine.

Meanwhile back across the veil, Isadora, Amelia, Georgette, and Christine are dressed and ready for the party. They are waiting on Toby and Cornelius to arrive. The moon is starting to loom. Isadora draws breath standing in the hallway as the three sisters descend down the spiral staircase.

"Oh my goodness, you three look absolutely beautiful. Your mother and father will be so proud. Stunning darling, just stunning."

Then a wrap on the front door interrupts them. "That will be my son, I think. Let him in Christine. I want to see the look on his face when he enters," says Isadora.

Christine opens the door. Cornelius takes a step backwards saying, "Oh my stars. Look at you young lady. You look beautiful. Come on, give me a twirl." He holds his hand out, takes hers and spins her round.

She giggles then says, "Wait until you see my sisters and your mother, Cornelius."

He walks into the hallway. Isadora is standing with Mia at the foot of the stairs. "Wow ladies, you both look amazing. But where's Georgie?"

"She's in the kitchen fetching two bottles of Toby's favourite wine."

"Is Toby not here yet?" asks Cornelius.

Chapter Thirty-Five

Mia answers, "Nope, not yet. But I am sure he won't be long. He's never late. You look very smart my son, very handsome indeed." He was wearing a crisp white shirt with black trousers, his black boots were spotless with a high shine that you could see your face in.

Isadora smiles. "It's such a pity your father couldn't be here."

Cornelius agrees and thanks his mother. "I scrubbed up well, didn't I," he jests. "Georgette doesn't like stubble. She told me to be sure and shave or else."

Then a voice speaks saying, "Or else I'd be telling you off all night."

Cornelius turns to see Georgette walking into the hallway. His jaw drops. He can't take his eyes away from her, standing there speechless. He can't believe how breathtaking she looks in her dress, with her long, white, glossy hair tired up in curls.

Isadora speaks, "Close your mouth, darling, and tell the girl something nice."

Cornelius grins then says, "Georgette Crescent, you look beautiful. You took my breath away. That dress really is stunning on you." He walks over to her, puts both hands on her waist then dips her. He laughs and steals a cheeky kiss.

Georgette can't shout at him. She just starts laughing then says, "Behave yourself."

He answers, "No, not tonight. Tonight we have fun, let the hair down, and perhaps even get a little drunk." The girls all giggled.

Suddenly there are three big bangs on the door. Isadora rolls her eyes. "Oh for goodness sake can that man not learn the word gentle? The door is near off its hinges."

Cornelius opens the door to Toby who walks into the hallway. He too had made an effort to dress up. He was wearing a white shirt, it was a little crinkled, with a red waist coat. He too had even had a clean shave.

Amelia smiles and speaks, "Toby, you look very handsome. I love that waist coat."

Isadora interrupts saying, "Yes, me too. It's very dapper."

Toby smiles from ear to ear with a great big grin. "Thank you, ladies, that's very kind of you." He then complements the ladies in return, "You all look very handsome too, very elegant. You scrubbed up well." Then he asks, "Well now, are we all ready to go upstairs?"

Everyone agrees saying, "Yes Toby."

"Then let's go get your powers back and then we go to your party," Toby cries. They follow him to the bell room. The moon is full, shining bright with a blush strawberry colour illuminating the clock tower.

When they enter the room, Georgette asks her sisters to form a circle. She takes the ship bottle from her pocket, sets it on the floor and asks Amelia and Christine, "Do you both remember the words?"

"Yes," they answered, each in turn.

Georgette places a cloth over the bottle. "Okay then, on the count of three, stamp on the glass, then chant the spell.

Ah hain, a dò, ah trì."

Chapter Thirty-Five

Moonbeams white moonbeams bright
Restore our powers within this night.
For which was mine shall be once more
fully restored forever more,
Sisters three now set in sun.
joined together our powers as one
strong and true forever more
bound with love until deaths black door.

The shattered glass beneath the linen cloth disappears into the floor. Everyone watches as tiny little white twinkling lights start to float up from below the cloth, leaving a misty trail behind. Georgette looked at her sisters. Their skin begins to glow with sparkling shards of glitter. Then suddenly, all three sisters join as one with a beautiful white light filling the bell tower with such brightness.

Isadora, Toby, and Cornelius watch with pride.

Everyone then heads downstairs, but the sisters remain behind.

Toby knew why the sisters were staying in the bell tower. They were going to cast the spell to allow Francis to cross the veil.

The door closed shut, the girls then stand in a circle, holding hands. Then they start to chant these words

Knot of one the spell has begun.
Knot of two our spell is true.
Knot of three magically we will be.
Knot of four together once more
Knot of five this spell is alive.

Knot of six our bond will fix.
Knot of seven events I'll leaven.
Knot of eight this is fate
Knot of nine what's said will entwine.

Suddenly the sound of twinkling bells is heard, then softly fades away. Georgette, Amelia, and Christine knew in that moment that the spell had worked. Georgette says, "Now that this is sorted, let's go get this little girl to her party." They walk back down the stairwell to join the others.

They all reach the hallway ready to go. Then little Christine speaks, "Can you wait for just a few minutes please? There's something I need to do."

They each look at her and smile. Isadora speaks, "Yes of course, darling."

Christine walks into the potion room. Amelia looks at Isadora and Georgette then winks. She knew why Christine went in.

She whispers, "What's she doing?"

Amelia puts her finger up to her lip saying, "Shush. Just wait."

Isadora speaks, "I've left my purse upstairs. I'll be back in a moment."

Cornelius interrupts, "I'll go get it for you, mother."

She tells Cornelius, "No, it's fine darling. I'll go myself, thank you." She walks upstairs to the bedroom. The purse is on the dressing table. She opens the drawer taking a small photograph out. It is her wedding photograph. She kisses it, then whispers, "I can't bring you to the party in person, my darling, but

Chapter Thirty-Five

I can take you in my thoughts." Suddenly she feels a spark in the palm of her hand. She pops her wedding photo into her purse, then opens her cinder note. She burst out laughing. It was from little Christine. It was her first cinder note sent. It said, "I wanted you, Izzy, my god mother, to receive my first ever handwritten cinder note. Yours sincerely, Christine Crescent."

Isadora held her tummy, trying not to be heard laughing. Walking over to the bedroom door she then shouts out loud, "Christine Crescent, I am very proud of you! Well done, you clever little witch."

Isadora hears the girls, all laughing downstairs in the hallway. Everyone was congratulating Christine. Isadora made her way back down the stairwell. Then she walks over to Christine and gives her a great big hug. "That was amazing, darling. Just brilliant. Well done young lady."

Toby then speaks, "I want all of us to create a memory, right here, right now. This will stay with us forever."

He put his hand out with his palm facing down. Then one by one each of them placed their hands on top. Their shadow cats were all there, each by their side, and big Tucker too. Toby then says, "To healthy, happy times ahead." They smile at each other. Toby then hugs Christine. "Now let's get this little lady to her party."

Georgette was the last person to leave the clock tower. She locks the door with her key, then smiles at Cornelius. He was waiting for her while the others walked on slowly. Cornelius holds out his arm then says, "Shall we, Miss Crescent?" She takes his arm to walk with him.

At the bridge the harbour party is alive with music and laughter. Rising Sun looks fantastic, bunting lining her decks and sails, magickal fireflies hanging throughout the ship. Henry had every lantern onboard glowing and every surface spotless. She looked amazing, with every colour of the rainbow shining bright from every lantern on board.

Little Christine spots Owen and Charles. She runs across the bridge with her shadow Layla racing by her side to meet them.

Henry waves to Mia, then shouts, "Come on Amelia, hurry up."

Amelia laughs waving back, then shouts, "I am coming, Henry." She hurries along to catch up with Christine. Toby, Isadora, Cornelius, and Georgette take their time. They want to take in all the beautiful sights and smells. So many magickal folk are now gathered, everyone dressed in their best. They are all happy with so much joy on their faces. So many fair folk are gathered along the harbour wall. Dancing fairies have formed a circle entertaining the children. The leprechaun musicians are playing a merry tune with boron drums, violins, and flutes. It is called 'Dance of the Forest'. The fairies beautiful little pink, green, and lilac dresses spin out wide with every turn of the dance. Their large sparkling wings throw waves of magickal dust into the air, which falls slowly, landing on the little faces and makes the young ones giggle. Fire breathers entertain the crowds, spitting shapes of animal flames

Chapter Thirty-Five

from their mouths with acrobatic displays of danger and delight. Tables and stools line the harbour walls with bottles of wine, whisky, and rum. Large open fire pits are ablaze, cooking roast hog, chicken, and fish. There are large tables with crisp white linen laden with food.

Henry stood on the deck, proud to show off his ship. He glanced at Amelia. "Wow," he thought, "she looks amazing." He was happy to see her. "Come aboard," he shouts to them as they approach. They board one by one. "Welcome everyone. Please make merry, eat your fill, and enjoy. I am so pleased you are all here."

The party is now in full swing. Everyone is having a fantastic time. There is plenty of good food, great music, dancing, and lots of rum.

Meanwhile across the veil Francis is standing on Albert Bridge, nervous, but very excited. Toby whispers into Georgette's ear, "It's time."

She then waves to Amelia and Christine to join her. All four of them sneak off to the bridge. Toby crosses the veil alone, while the sisters stay on the other side.

Francis was pacing back and forth, nervously waiting in hope that the plan would still go ahead. Toby appears out of nowhere. Francis smiles. He is overjoyed to see him. They hug each other and laugh. Toby asks, "Are you ready for this, my friend?"

Francis smiles, "More than ready. Let's do this."

Toby then tells him to stand beside him and wait for the girls to drop the veil. The three sisters join hands, then begin the spell

Drop the veil this once we say.
Allow this human passage to stay.
Bring him here safe and sound.
Into our world spell cast bound.

The veil appears before Toby and Francis, but this time it appears as a green colour. Toby speaks saying, "Oh now, that's new."

Francis looks at him. "What's new?"

"The veil. It's green," laughs Toby. "Can you not see it?"

Francis turns around again. This time he can't believe it. He can see the veil. It is astonishing. Green shards of light which look like frozen rain drops. Francis stands still, taking in its glorious light. Toby then shoves him with a gentle push, saying, "Go on then, get in."

Francis steps towards the veil, then walks through with Toby. The veil drops.

Standing on the other side, Amelia, Georgette, and Christine smile with open arms to greet him. Amelia runs into his arms, hugging him, followed by Georgette. They then introduce Christine. Francis smiles, "Hello little lady. I am so pleased to finally meet you." He kneels to hug her.

Toby, with a glint in his eye, speaks, "Right, come on. Let's go surprise Izzy. I can't wait to see her face."

Amelia pops a hat and cloak on Francis saying, "Let's keep you incognito until we get to the ship."

Francis can't take enough in as his eyes look over this Belfast he never seen before. He said to everyone,

Chapter Thirty-Five

"It's so weird, everything kind of looks the same, but it's not. Although I now understand why Izzy keeps going on about it being so bright here compared to where we live." They all laugh, agreeing with him.

They arrived at the ship where Isadora is dancing with Cornelius and the twins. Georgette waves to Cornelius, then walks on board with everyone behind her. Once on board they each stand in front of Francis. Isadora can see Toby waving for her to join him. He motions to Henry and Cornelius to come over as well. Isadora is flushed from dancing, and she is catching her breath as she walked towards them. She spots the tall man behind them in the cloak and hat. She gasps. "No, it can't be, can it? Is that my husband? Is that my Francis?"

Francis throws the hat into the air, then drops the cloak. She leaps into his arms laughing uncontrollably. "Is this real, darling? Are you really here? How did this happen? How is this possible?"

Cornelius looks in shock from the far end of the ship. He starts running, overwhelmed with joy. "My father is here," he shouts. "Look everyone, my father is here." He stops in front of his parents, looks at them, then hugs them both tight.

Toby speaks, "It is the girls. They did it. Isn't it amazing, clever witches."

Francis, Isadora, and Cornelius stand holding each other. It is all they ever wanted.

Isadora speaks, "I don't know how you three did this, but my goodness what an unbelievable surprise. Girls, thank you so much. You don't know how much this means to us." Georgette Amelia, and Christine were overjoyed to see how happy they are.

Henry walks over and stands beside the girls. He gestures the music to stop. The crowd quietens down. Henry speaks out loud saying, "Can I have everyone's attention, please." Cornelius Albert Delaney would like to say a few words." Henry smiles then shakes Cornelius' hand.

Cornelius then speaks out loud. "I'd like to introduce everyone to my father." The crowd is silent. Cornelius continues, "As you all know, he's a veil man, human. The Crescent sisters made it possible for him to be here tonight. To say we are pleased is an understatement. Can everyone raise their glass in a toast. First to the beautiful Crescent sisters finally united. To my father, Doctor Francis Delaney, Francis to his friends," he laughs. "Welcome. To Owen, Charles, and Christine, welcome home. Congratulations on your celebration tonight. Not forgetting, of course, Toby and Georgette on the rescue of the children. And last, but not least, a great big thank you to Henry for putting on such a fantastic party. This is a blessed day. Happiness and joy. Slainte everyone." Claps and cheers begin, then the music starts again

Henry holds out his hand to shake Francis' hand. "Hello again, Francis. I am so pleased you are here."

Francis then put his arms out to hug him saying, "Thank you, Henry."

Henry speaks, "I hope you're all hungry. There's plenty to eat and lots to drink." He winks at Francis.

Chapter Thirty-Five

Isadora, Amelia, and Toby walk to the end of the ship where the music and dancing is back in full swing. Cornelius puts his arms around Georgette and whispers in her ear, "Will you join me for a stroll?"

Georgette answers, "Yes, but do you not want to spend time with your father?"

He smiles, "My mother will not let him out of her sight for at least another hour or so. She's probably keeping him tight by her side until they go back over the veil."

Georgette laughs, "Yes, you're right. She still thinks she's in a dream."

"Listen Georgie, can I just say thank you."

She looks at Cornelius she could see how blissfully happy he is. He tells her with a great big grin on his face, "You, Amelia, and Christine have given my family such joy, unbelievable joy. I can't believe you pulled this off. It's just fantastic, like a dream come true."

Georgette answers him taking his hand in hers, "It gives us just as much joy as you Cornelius. We were delighted when we found out we could do the spell. Your family are my family too. You know how much they mean to me."

"I know, and we feel the same too," says Cornelius looking ahead. They were near to the middle of the bridge. He started feeling nervous.

After a few minutes of walking in silence, Georgette looks at him. "You've gone very quiet. What's wrong?"

He answers, "Nothing, nothing at all. Let's just stop here for a while. It's a lovely spot."

Georgette smiles saying, "It is. It's me and Amelia's favourite place in the harbour."

He ran his hand along her arm then slipped his hand into hers. He answers, "I know it is, Georgie. That's why I brought you here. There's something I need to ask you."

They stop to stand beside the wall. A cool breeze is flowing, blowing wispy strands of Georgettes hair. Cornelius tenderly tucks them behind her ear, then rubs his thumb along her cheek. His huge hands stroke her neck then slip down her shoulders onto her arms and both her hands. Cornelius looks into Georgette's eyes, bright blue, sparkling and beautiful. He smiles, then gets down on one knee. Georgette felt her body tremble with excitement.

Back at the ship, Isadora was trying out one of the twin's gifts. It was a spy glass. She held it up to her eye, circling the harbour. She says, "Wow boys, this is fascinating. I can see all the way up to the clock. Oh and look, I can even see Cornelius with Georgette on the bridge. Then to her astonishment, she watches Cornelius as he goes down on one knee. Nerves fill her tummy. She shouts out loud, "Oh my goodness, quickly get over here Francis. Your son is about to propose!"

Francis, Toby, Amelia, and Christine burst into happy laughter, each asking with anticipation, "Well, what's happening? Did he ask her yet? What can you see? Tell us, Izzy."

Isadora giggles and answers, "Shush! He's still down on one knee." Isadora then tells Henry, "Get ready to

Chapter Thirty-Five

light them fireworks early, my lad. There's going to be a wedding proposal."

Cornelius looks up at Georgette. He opens the little box. A gold ring with a single white diamond in its centre catches the twinkle in her eye. She knew then he was going to propose. He speaks, "Georgie, I love you so much. You're my world. I've adored you all of my life, even when you drive me nuts."

Georgette gasps, overwhelmed with so many emotions she can't contain her happiness. She says, "Yes, yes, I will."

Cornelius shakes his head, laughing. "Shush woman, let me ask you first."

Georgette giggles, "Yes, sorry please continue."

He smiles, holds the little ring up in front of her with both hands. Then he then clears his throat to speak. "Georgette Crescent, Will you please do me the honour of being my wife? Will you marry me?"

Georgettes eyes fill up with happy tears, her cheeks bright pink. She smiles saying, "Yes again. I'd love to be your wife."

He stands up to face her as she holds out her hand. He slips the ring carefully onto her finger. It was a perfect fit.

Georgette didn't think this day could get any better, but it just did in that moment. Cornelius then lifts her up in the air by the waist and spins her in a circle.

Isadora screams throwing the spyglass into the air. Toby catches it, rolling his eyes.

She shouts, "She said yes, my son is getting married."

Suddenly loud cheers are carried from across the docks. Georgette and Cornelius laugh, looking towards the ship. Georgette giggles, "Did your mother know?"

He laughs, "No, only Toby knew, I swear. But I dare say everyone else on that ship now knows. Imagine if you had said no," they both giggle. Then the fireworks start to explode, thundering, enormous explosions of light, filling the sky with an array of sparkles, reflections of colour from above shower the sea below.

Cornelius looks at Georgette. He feels like the luckiest man in the world. He turns her round to face him, then he kisses her softly on the lips, holding her close with his strong arms wrapped around her. He whispers, "You are my everything, Georgie. I love you."

She smiles then replies, "I love you too, Cornelius." She holds him close, putting her head on his chest. They watch the fireworks display before going back to the ship.

The last enormous flash of fireworks fills the sky, dazzling Belfast docks. Everyone cheers as it's sparks land on top of the dark, smoky, grey sea.

Georgette and Cornelius start to walk back to the harbour. Isadora and Francis rush from the ship to greet them. They wanted to be the first to congratulate them. Isadora, with arms wide open shouts, "Oh my darling, I couldn't be happier. I am over the moon." She throws both arms around Georgette, then Cornelius. Francis hugs Cornelius with a tight manly embrace. He then gently hugs Georgette and tenderly kisses her cheek. Amelia and Christine run towards her

Chapter Thirty-Five

screaming with excitement. Lots of hugs all round filled with joy. Georgette couldn't wait to show her ring to her sisters. Christine says, "Wow, amazing. I love your ring, Georgie."

Amelia then takes her hand. She looks at Georgette and says, "Stunning. It's so elegant, just perfect. I am so happy for you both. Now you know this means it's time for you to enjoy your life, Georgie. You've done an amazing job raising me and taking such good care of us and the clock. I love you so much, Georgie."

Georgette wraps her arms around her little sister. "I love you too, Mia." Tailsa and Bijou grunt wanting attention. Amelia and Georgette hold out their arms so Tailsa and Bijou jump up, brushing their faces.

Isadora stood holding Francis's arm. Toby stood alone, but then felt a hand take his. It was Flanna. "Hello big man. Sorry I am late. I was fixing the station house up."

Toby smiles, "Let me guess. Lots of frilly curtains, cushions, and lots of silly flowers." She shoves him playfully then says, "Well I need to make it nice for you when you get around to proposing to me."

Toby is caught off guard, starting to choke, then cough. Henry pats him on the back and laughs. He asks Toby, "Are you all right big lad?"

Toby speaks, "I am okay. I am okay." He looks at Flanna with big rosy cheeks and bursts out laughing. Then he says, "I'll get around to it, don't you worry woman."

Flanna nudges him with her shoulder and winks. Henry stands with Cornelius, both still laughing at Toby's reaction to Flanna. Hickory and Despina stand with Lord Anthony and Lord Riverdale close by their side. All content and happy with this blessed day. Cuttlefish sits on the harbour wall with his tail splashing the water. Fin Frazzle hovers close beside him.

Chapter Thirty-Six

Amelia, Georgette, and Christine walk to the tip of the bow, looking out at the Irish sea with their three shadow cats, fully formed, sitting by their side.

Georgette speaks, "Look at all our friends and family. We are so blessed." Amelia and Christine smile.

Amelia speaks, "Let's give everyone a blessing with our powers."

Christine looks at her sisters, "Yes, let's do that. Please."

Joining hands tight, they bless the sea and land with a prayer. They hold there Taras saying these words

Peace and light on this blessed night.
Bright moon shine from sky above
Illuminate Ireland with all of your love
Peace and joy to everyone here
live happy and long for many a year

Their Tara Brooches start to loom, throwing a glow of magickal mist up into the sky. It gently falls on everyone below, and into the sea as well. No one noticed, no one knew they had been blessed by the sisters, bringing joy health and happiness to all. The sisters smile content.

The three sisters look out to sea, holding hands, feeling happy and surrounded by their friends and family.

* * *

The old man awakens, groggy and disorientated. There is a foul stench in the air. The smell is so potent he can almost taste it on his tongue. The old man gagged. He braces himself for the oncoming vomit, but nothing comes. His stomach is empty. He hadn't eaten in days.

He looks down at the floor, covered in filth, with only dirty straw for bedding. "How the mighty have fallen," he whispers to no one. Overwhelmed, his eyes begin to sting. But he refuses to cry. Crying is for the weak. The old man pulls himself from the floor, leaning his tired bones against the cool stone wall of his cell. Staring at the ceiling, he slowly fills with rage. He reminds himself who he is and what he must do to survive. "I have no choice," he tells himself. "I need to see this through." He thinks aloud, "Sacrifice is the only way. In death I will live, in death my Magick will be restored."

He grabs hold of the cell bars, pulling his feeble body upright. He takes hold of his Tara brooch which hangs around his neck. He snaps the chain. Holding the Tara up to his face, he takes a moment and looks at the once beautiful blue stone in its centre. It is now faded, cloudy and dark. It is losing its life essence. A tightness forms in his throat and tears finally fall from the old man's eyes, dripping onto the once vibrant stone as he lifts the Tara to his lips. He kisses it softly and whispers, "I'm sorry," through his quiet sobs. He closes his eyes and takes a deep breath then says

"Two souls I rip I break our bond
from this day forth I live as one

I take your power your magick your soul
I take them now and swallow them whole"

The old man presses the stone with all of the strength he can muster, cracking its centre until it snaps into splinters, falling into his hands. He lifts his old frail fingertips and touches the fragments, rubbing them until there is nothing left but dust. Lifting his hands to his face, he breathes in the remains of its Magic. The connection breaks. The sensation overwhelms him. Suddenly, this old man's body being too weak to stand, collapses to the ground, forcing him to his knees. Steadying himself, he places both hands on the wet, disgusting floor. Hanging his head in shame with what he has done. It was unforgivable. To take the life of ones shadow. It was barbaric. A sadness takes over the old man as he kneels sobbing. He is filled with remorse and regret. He feels his heart will break in two.

"What have I done?" he sobs. "My precious boy." In that moment he knows he can't undo what he has just done. He has taken the life of his beloved shadow.

The old man lies in his cell, cradling himself. He can hear chanting and cheering echoing throughout the stone walls of the dungeon. Those disgusting creatures were celebrating. "How dare they?" he thought. They get to live, while he suffers, locked in a cage like a filthy animal. He blames them. "It's their fault," he shouts. They took everything from him. It's their fault his shadow is dead.

An unexpected coldness befalls the old man, a strange, unnatural feeling of calmness. A wicked smile crosses his face as he begins to laugh out loud. The guards hear him and enter the dungeon.

The first guard approaches the cell and bangs on the bars. "Shut up, old man!" he shouts.

The old man laughs harder. A look of unease crosses the guards face. "You won't be laughing in the morning. Your execution has been brought forward by order of the king. You die at dawn." The two guards grin at each other.

With newfound strength the old man stands up straight and walks to the edge of the cell. He places his hands on the cold steel bars and pulls his hood down. He looks directly at the guards with jet black eyes and cold pale skin. His appearance is somewhat changed. Astonished the guards both instinctively step back, fear in their eyes.

With a twisted smirk on his face and an arrogant tone to his voice he replies, "The only one to die at dawn will be your king. And, before I kill him, and your foul queen for that matter, I will kill you both first. But know this, I will be the lord and master of this hellish dimension. All will bow to me."

Both guards, astonished, back up from the cell.

The old man looks at the guards raising both hands. He shouts, "Solos backis!"

The two guards look to each other terrified as they burst into flames, scorching them from their insides out, screaming in agonising pain as the flames consume them whole. The old man watches in delight as their bodies lie dying on the ground. He chants

> *"Open door lock and key let me out for all to see*
> *release me from this prison of steal*
> *rock and stone skin and bone*
> *I sacrifice two lives this night to build my strength and*
> *ground me tight*

The cell door swings open and the old man steps over the fresh corpses. He turns and spits, "Filthy Johnagock!" He makes his way up the old stone steps and exits the dungeon.

The old man walks out into the courtyard. A dark, grey, smouldering smoke leaves a trail behind him. The courtyard is loud, filled with chanting, drunkenness, music and laughter. Upon seeing this a rage fills the old man. Looking towards the crowd of Johnagock, the old man finds a familiar face. Lord Augustus. "Backis Solos," he snarls and the Johnagock bursts into flames.

The celebration comes to an abrupt halt. The courtyard is filled with silence. The old man addresses the courtyard, "Now that I have your attention, I would like to announce there has been a change in leadership. You have two choices, bend the knee to me, or die. But first let me dispose of you two," he points towards the King and Queen. He lifts both hands, looks directly at the Royal couple. Before either even has a chance to speak, the old man commands "Solos backis!" They burst into flames, screaming with pain as the old man stands laughing, not taking his eyes away from them as they slowly disappear into ash.

The old man then confidently walks through the crowded courtyard, steps up to the platform, playfully kicking the Royal remains aside and casually takes his place on the large wooden throne. He smirks, clutching the arms of the chair.

"Yes, this will suit me just fine," he murmurs to himself.

The old man looks out toward the hundreds of Johnagock before him, fear in their eyes, scanning their ugly faces as they bow to him one by one. The old man addresses the court shouting, "You will obey, or you will die. It will take me years to brew the potion to open that Veil again, but I swear, the sacrifices I have made will not be in vain! My name is Gregor Francis MacMahon and I will have my revenge!"

Thanks to Janet Blades and Craig Thompson, owners of Mystique's enchantments